To Ride
a Wylder Horse

by

Renee Canter Johnson

The Wylder West Series

To Ride a Wylder Horse

Cover Art by *Debbie Taylor*

The Wild Rose Press, Inc.
PO Box 708
Adams Basin, NY 14410-0708
Visit us at www.thewildrosepress.com

Publishing History
First Edition, 2022
Trade Paperback ISBN 978-1-5092-4396-9
Digital ISBN 978-1-5092-4397-6

The Wylder West Series
Published in the United States of America

Essie was in no mood to allow such familiar handling despite the shock in the man's tone. With the derringer still in her pocket for reassurance, she snatched the loaded Winchester she kept beneath the counter for just such an occasion. Lifting it, she steadied the barrel against the cottonwood countertop. Its initial fuzziness was polished smooth with plenty of sanding and oil. "Unhand my daughter, sir, while you still got hands."

Before he responded, the front door pushed open again. A man's silhouette filled the held-ajar opening as he swept a glance over the scene. Backlit from the outer sunlit street, the man practically glowed. His top hat shaded his facial features, but his clothing—fine woolen trousers and coat with tails—indicated he was a man of some means. More than that, they reiterated he was the man from the train, the one who'd raced to the street the previous morning when she'd prevented Nancy's fall, and he'd stopped her from falsely accusing her of causing it.

"*Mon Dieu,*" he exclaimed, staring at Essie. "*Monsieur* Douglas, what have you done?"

The man's voice echoed through the opened entryway, across the front room, and through Essie's ears until wedging in her brain where she could make sense of his foreign-sounding accent. He was not from Wylder—that much was certain. Essie fought the effects of his charm, cutting her gaze to the man whose palms still rested on her daughter's shoulders. She cocked the Winchester, readying it to shoot if forced. "Now, sir."

Praise for Renee Canter Johnson

"Renee Johnson is a natural storyteller with a graceful elegance of style."

~*Janet Hulstrand, Author*

~*~

"I want to give thanks for Renee Johnson--her writing raw, sublime, and beautiful, is (there is no other word) a gift."

~*Justen Ahren, Author, Founder and Director of Noepe Center for Literary Arts*

~*~

"With beautifully descriptive language, Renee blends the past with the present and brings it all together in a surprising and satisfying ending."

~*Karen Hunt, a.k.a. K. H. Mezek, Author*

~*~

"*TO RIDE A WYLDER HORSE* is a beautifully written, multi-layered story, set in the 1880s, rich with history and the romance of the old west. A single mother makes a life for herself and her daughter in the town of Wylder, Wyoming. Outspoken and fearless, she battles injustice and con men and rises victorious. She learns how to trust the love of a good and kind man, and the power of friendship. This wonderful book is filled with twists and turns and characters that are as courageous as the state where they live."

~*Pam Binder, author of* WYLDER TIMES

Dedication

For Tony,
the cowboy who gave me my first horse
and traveled through Wyoming's wonders
and Wylder's adventures alongside me

Prologue

1872, Ft. Laramie, Wyoming Territory

The knock startled Essie Baumgardner. *Who would come out here unannounced?* She dropped the half-finished lace, peeked out the small window near the cabin's entrance, and glimpsed the horse—a sturdy gray with a shiny saddle and bridle despite the dust—tethered to the hitching post. Essie's heart fluttered. An official member of the cavalry stationed at Ft. Laramie wouldn't ride out to her tiny abode, regardless of its proximity to the fort, if he didn't have information. She covered the mere few feet in seconds and yanked open the door. Swallowing the growing knot in her throat, she croaked more than spoke. "Captain Puckett? You have news?"

Captain James Puckett pushed his hat lower.

The brim hid his eyes from Essie's stare but it wasn't low enough to hide his crooked nose and pursed lips. His broad shoulders filled the narrow doorframe, and his height of six feet one inch would have made it necessary for him to duck to enter the cabin on the edge of Ft. Laramie's outpost.

Inching forward, Captain Puckett knocked the toes of his boots against the threshold. But he did not advance through the entry, even though his body lurched to the side. He sucked in a long breath and exhaled it. "You can't stay here any longer."

He's not joking, Essie thought. Despite efforts to remain stoic, her lip quivered. "But…"

Captain Puckett pivoted, and the arm he'd kept behind his back swung with the sideways tilt, producing a wiggling eleven-year-old.

"Gus?" Essie squealed as she stretched out her arms for her scrawny offspring that the captain dangled like a kitten.

Squinting, Puckett focused on Essie's face. "Caught at the base again. If you stay here, your child risks getting hurt." He stomped his foot. "I've had my orders."

Gus squirmed free and scrambled to the corner, stopping to glare at the officer.

Essie snapped her attention between the two people who'd just interrupted her tatting. The lace collar should bring a decent price when finished, and lacemaking was her only skill that occasionally brought in a few coins. *If only Augustus would come back…* "But…what if…Augustus…"

Holding open his palms, Puckett sighed. He shifted his weight. "Heck, Miss Essie, it's been more'n ten years. We both know your husband ain't coming back."

She knew the captain meant well. Even now, he tempered his harsh words with a soft tone and a gentle shrug. He often appeared with a skinned rabbit or a few extra potatoes, and on more than one occasion, he had filled her wood bin. Still, the thought of leaving the only home she'd shared—albeit briefly—with Augustus Baumgardner disheartened her. She wrung her hands. "You can't evict us. Where will we go? How will we survive?"

He pulled an envelope from his pocket and smiled. "Being a Pony Express widow, you know the post roads and the code of ethics for handling the US Mail. You need a new residence, and Wylder needs someone to run their post office."

Essie accepted the letter with a trembling hand and carefully peeled open the flap. She extracted the contents and glanced from the envelope to Puckett's face. "Wylder? Never heard of it."

"It's about fifty miles from Laramie." He flattened a palm to the jamb and tilted his chin. "Reckon you know that place well enough."

Essie's resolve replaced her fear. How Captain Puckett knew about her family in Laramie was beyond her, but being disowned for marrying a non-Catholic was none of his business. She pulled up her spine another inch and met his glare with one intended to be equally as sharp. "Reckon I do, and I ain't going back there."

"Nobody's asking you to." He jerked his chin. "But in another year or two, this one won't be a kid anymore. Living on the edge of a fort frequented by men who are far from home is no place for a wandering child."

He was right, of course. Yet, Essie ached at the thought of Augustus wandering back to the fort, oblivious about her whereabouts. "Wylder, you say? A post office? If I decided to take you up on this offer, where would we live?"

Captain Puckett pointed toward the envelope. "May I?"

Shrugging, Essie handed it back. Perhaps she'd misunderstood his intent, and he'd meant the post as a suggestion instead of an offer. She'd happily stay in the humble cabin and opened her mouth to suggest it.

He tugged out a quarter sheet of paper and pointed to a spot marked with a star. "This here is Wylder, a nice little town incorporated about three years ago by the Wylder family who started a mercantile there."

Essie swallowed the retort and peered at the scribblings of a map she hadn't noticed until Captain Puckett retrieved it. Scanning the geometric outlines defining the livery, bank, and saloon, she recognized a hotel and a bakery, but nothing resembling a post office. "So, where is it?"

He drew his finger downward. "The government purchased the two-story bank building and turned the lower level into the post office. Upstairs is a small but serviceable dwelling."

The idea quickly grew on her. "You mean I can live and work in the same place?"

Shoving the map and envelope back into her hands, he pointed toward the corner. "Should make it a wee bit easier to keep an eye on this one."

Wavering, she thought of her husband and how their lives had started in the little dwelling, and every inch held slowly fading memories. Away from it, she feared losing them altogether. "Do I have a choice?"

Crossing his arms, he took a backward step. "Naturally. You can always return to Laramie."

She winced. She'd rather die, and Captain Puckett obviously knew how she felt about such a return. "Wylder, you say?"

He smiled. "We'll escort you through the canyon between here and Wylder. Since the Arapaho consider it sacred, Vedauwoo's rocky outcroppings are tricky to maneuver. Besides, it makes perfect hiding places for angry savages."

Recoiling from the captain, she stared at his withering smile and stony eyes. "Savages?"

He ground his teeth until his jaw twitched. "They're likely the ones as got Augustus. But with enough soldiers to get you through, you should be fine."

Essie weighed the choices. She could face her vindictive mother or the vengeful Arapaho. The answer was easy. "When do we leave?"

Chapter 1

Sunday, June 16, 1878

As it did every Sunday, the train rolled into Wylder, Wyoming Territory, and the buildings near the tracks shuddered from its mighty force. At the first tremor, Postmistress Estelle Baumgardner shoved the pen into its stand. Accustomed to the weekly disruption, Essie spread her arms atop the loose sheets of expensive stationery from the mercantile and tugged back the errant blotter bouncing toward the desk's edge.

The post office walls rattled, swiveling sideways the recent postings where they hung from nails until one jarred loose and fell to the floor with a ping. The stack of pages floated downward as though the criminals they detailed escaped capture. Even the single-pane windows vibrated until she feared one might plop from its frame and land against the sidewalk.

Chuff-chuff-chuff-chuff...chuff-chuff-chuff-chuff
Wait it out.

The Union Pacific's steamy plume magnified the sound of its whistle. Another misty breath belched from the smokestack. The engineer blared the horn, and the brakemen engaged the brakes until they screeched with enough shrillness to set her teeth on edge.

The movement of the ink vial scooting across the

table caught her eye. "Oh, no, you won't." She released the blotter and grabbed the escaping container. Although satisfied nothing would crash to the floor, she didn't release her grip on the objects until the caboose stopped rolling.

As everything except the dust motes settled into place, Essie held her breath. After the final shudder, she exhaled and pushed the unlit oil lamp to the edge of the small desk. June's afternoon sun streamed through the windows and across the half-finished letter. Satisfied the danger of smudging the important note had passed, she lifted the pen. Essie dipped it into the inkwell of watered-down, postal-provided, Prussian blue ink, allowing the excess to drip back into the vial until the last drop plopped from the nib. Angling her wrist against the page, she wrote.

I fear for

Banging noises jolted Essie. *Has the train blown an engine or left the tracks?* She jerked her hand, along with her head, leaving behind an ugly mark and a leaky blob across the letter before she penned the most crucial word in the unfinished sentence.

Augus

Groaning, she held the page and stared at the ink dollop slicing across the parchment. With so much riding on her request, she couldn't send anything less than perfect. She crunched the stationery sheet in her fist and tossed the balled page into the trash bin beside her desk.

The banging recommenced, but this time she knew from where the sound generated. She glanced toward the entry, pushing her spine against the ladderback rungs. The scraping noise of the chair's legs raked equally against the wooden floor and her nerves. Her brows nearly touched with her frown. "Dagnabit. It's Sunday. I'm closed," she yelled.

A softer knock pealed from knuckles tapping wood. "Miss Essie? You there?"

Essie stood with one hand against her lower spine and snatched the scattered *Wanted* flyers. She glimpsed the details of the various criminals robbing stages, stores, and banks across the west—Cheyenne's general store owned by a man named Matheson, Laramie's feed supply, Johnson's horse ranch in Missoula, a bank in Billings, the stagecoach in Kansas City—and sighed. Wylder might not be as big or exciting as these other towns, but they didn't have too many outlaws hanging around.

She stretched as far as she was able at barely five feet tall, but the boot heels beneath her twill skirt added a good three inches to her height, as did her highly-mounded hair. Combined, they tacked on another half-foot. She swiped the sweat from her forehead and stomped to the door. "Who's asking?"

"Your Arapaho sister."

Despite the door's muffling of her voice, when Essie grew close, the intonation was unmistakable. She grabbed the long bolt with both hands and slid the bar from its bracket. "Meadowlark? Is everything okay?" She instantly felt silly for asking such a question. Of course, it wasn't, or she wouldn't be pounding on her door mid-Sunday. "Come on in."

Meadowlark's moccasins slid quietly along the wooden floor. She turned large eyes toward Essie. They instantly softened and welled with tears. "Thank you, Miss Essie. I do not wish to bother you, but..." She bit her lip and winced.

In her mid-to-late thirties, same as Essie, Meadowlark showed no signs of aging. Her skin glowed with the effect of the heat's blush, and her long, lean legs rippled with muscle visible below the tasseled dress that hung to her knees over the laced-up, deerskin leggings. Her dark, parted-down-the-middle hair formed long braids that draped her shoulders. Standing beside her, Essie felt like a tumbleweed beside an aspen. Her heart quickened. "But?"

Meadowlark's gaze drifted and then snapped back as she kneaded her skirt. "It's Tarak."

Essie peered from the still-open door and scanned the area, looking for his tall, willowy frame and long, dark hair. "What is? Where is he?"

"I do not know." Fidgeting, she worried her long fingers from the hem of the deerskin to the corner of her lids. "Tarak...he came to town yesterday and...has not returned."

"Not returned?" Essie snapped. Immediately regretting the alarm in her voice, she swallowed and took a deep breath.

Meadowlark swept a glance around the interior. She nodded toward the desk and its pushed-back chair. "You are busy. I have interrupted."

"Nonsense." Although Essie regretted not finishing the letter to her cousin Blanche in Boston, it could wait. The stagecoach wouldn't arrive for the mail until Tuesday anyway. Tarak and Meadowlark had stood between her and disaster too many times to count, beginning with the incident at Vedauwoo during her ride from Ft. Laramie. She focused on Meadowlark's blank face. "Did he say why he needed to come into town?"

Shrugging, Meadowlark waved her hands. "He came to trade beaver hides."

Essie patted her arm in a manner she hoped was reassuring. "Well, that explains it. The trader probably missed Friday's stagecoach and is now arriving by train. I bet Tarak is waiting by the arrivals platform."

She widened her eyes, and pointed to the exit. "You think? I must go there. I must find him."

Essie considered the steady stream of townsfolk who always crowded the depot to meet loved ones or make a little money by hiring out their carriages and wagons. Soon the passengers would deboard, and Tarak might wander off with the trader. If they hurried, they might get to the depot in time to catch him before he disappeared. "I'll go with you, and we'll search together."

Meadowlark's posture relaxed, but she quickly pulled herself erect. "I cannot allow you to spend your only day off down here. I am sure you must have much that requires your attention."

Pressing a palm into her forearm, Essie nudged her forward. "As I'm sure you did all the times you aided me. Friendship isn't something we give when convenient, but when needed."

Blinking several times, Meadowlark stared through glistening, watery eyes. She held up her index and middle fingers tightly smashed against each other. "You are kind, Miss Essie. We are women; we are mothers; we are sisters."

"Sisters," Essie repeated Meadowlark's description. "Indeed, we are." She meant to say more, but the train's final whistle indicated deboarding would begin.

Essie wasn't above taking advantage of the opportunity either. Although it was Sunday, if she noticed someone with a stack of mail to post, she'd open for their convenience and her commission. The previous quarter she'd raked in more than one hundred dollars in postage fees, but the stingy government cut her percentage from forty percent to thirty-three and a third. The only solution was to sell more if she wanted to save enough for the trip east. Grabbing her vest and cap, Essie slipped them on as she led Meadowlark out the back door and across the rear alley.

Without a stiff breeze, the steam from the engine's last clearing gasp still hovered as though the train had its own rain cloud. "Was Tarak…" Essie paused. She didn't want to offend Meadowlark by asking an insensitive question, but Natives sometimes wore clothing similar to the Western settlers when they came into town for business purposes. However, such attire seemed unlikely for Tarak. "What was he wearing?"

The fringe on Meadowlark's dress swayed as she moved, but her steps were light and soundless. Meadowlark inhaled a long breath. "Tarak is Arapaho. He dressed like Arapaho."

At her near-mistake, Essie winced. Meadowlark's response reiterated the couple's pride in their culture and confirmed she'd been right to ask the question with delicacy. "Good. He won't blend in with the crowd."

"Ha." She exhaled loudly and then giggled. "I would notice Tarak in a battlefield of warriors identically armed. He has…confidence."

As Essie passed the stagecoach office, she allowed her thoughts to scamper backward six years. Tarak perched atop the rocks at Vedauwoo as the troop from Ft. Laramie led her through the pass flashed across her mind alongside the brief skirmish. She would never forget how he lifted the lance and yelled a signal, pausing the attack long enough to determine they were merely travelers headed for Wylder. His intercedence saved many lives that day. "He certainly does."

She led Meadowlark to the right between the train depot and the rail office and continued until the lane ended. The narrow alley turned into a broad swath of prairie with wide train tracks snaking through the sage. The modern steamer cut the sightline, splitting the beige earth and blue sky like a long, black, iron serpent.

Rising steamy bursts continued to burp from the smokestack, generating an exciting buzz from within Essie as it did every time it arrived. Her heart quivered at the thought of joining the travelers headed to a new and curious place. *What would gathering a few belongings into a carpetbag and setting off to a place I've never seen be like?*

As Essie inched closer, the sounds of bouncing wheels and clomping horses accompanied the swarming crowd approaching the arrivals platform. A frenzy of activity commenced. People milled about, and she scanned them and the area, searching for Tarak.

A man waved to someone on the train.

Farther down the tracks, swaying back and forth, a woman repeated the gesture.

Someone extended an arm through an open window inside the train and shook a hat.

Sighing, she ran a hand down her vest front and noticed a blue/black ink smear on the slotted opening in the brushed, beige damask. As she glanced from the stain to the spot on her palm, she groaned. Both were most likely from her thoughtless crumpling of the ruined letter. *What if it's on my cap, too?* "Oh, no."

Casual banter ceased as those around her turned their heads and stared.

Grimacing, she yanked her shoulders upright and strolled closer to the trackside platform. Although she ached to wash the stain, like the letter to Blanche, the cleaning would have to wait.

Meadowlark touched her arm. "What is it, Miss Essie? Is something wrong?"

"I've spilled some ink, that's all," Essie assured her. She pointed to the staging area where the laborers synchronized their movements as they unloaded baggage, heaved the various trunks and cases from the freight car, and stacked them into piles.

A carriage driver pulled near the staging area and loaded a passenger and her trunk.

"You take that side, Meadowlark, and I'll take this one. If Tarak is here, we'll find him faster that way."

She nodded and loped to the opposite end, circumventing the crowd.

Essie scratched her chin as she studied Meadowlark's avoidance of the more straightforward path through the settlers. The indignities to which they had subjected the Natives affected every decision— even one as benign as navigating around them. Minor things she gave little thought to became significant pitfalls for the Arapaho.

A slight breeze swept inward, momentarily swirling the last remaining steamy tendrils from the train's engine across the platform. The smoke obscured the view but slowly dissipated from its white cloud to a gray mist before dividing into puffs no larger than a dandelion seedhead. Something was there—possibly someone.

Essie couldn't pull her gaze from the steam's swiftly changing shapes. Like the magic trick she'd seen at the fair years prior, the smoke turned into a man. He appeared as though manifested from its vapor. She stared until her mouth fell open. It had to be a trick, a sleight-of-hand, a mirage, as this was no ordinary man standing at the portal between the train's interior and the platform's exterior. As the steam evaporated, he developed from a filmy silhouette to flesh and bone, paused in the open doorway, and glanced at the gawking crowd. His clothing defied the weather—top hat, overcoat cropped in the front, hanging behind him to his knees, vest, and a cravat pushing the starched-stiff collar of his white shirt nearly to his ears. A mustache stretched across his upper lip and curled to waxy swirls at the center of his cheeks. He didn't even look real.

The man stepped onto the platform with a tilted chin and straight spine. He glanced across the crowd, then turned and extended his elbow behind him.

A gloved hand poked through the opening and grasped his arm. A figure stooped, the tall hat cleared the exit, and flowers bloomed from its crown until its full garden-covered brim appeared. The graceful figure of the woman whose head the hat adorned popped through behind it.

Essie studied her with the same curiosity. She blinked and stared.

Draped in layers of green silk, lace, and taffeta, the woman pivoted. She eased her bustle from the door

14

frame, and the various materials jointed at her narrow waist formed a cascade of fabric textures. Gripping a parasol, which she did not immediately open, she used it as a cane to aid her descent in tandem with the man's measured gait.

Quiet fell across the gathering throng. The only sounds were the engine's low rumblings, the slap of trunks and luggage pieces as the loaders stacked them against one another, the horses' restless tail-swishing, and the couple's feet hitting the steps as they walked toward the crowd. Few people arrived in Wylder with their elegance and grace, which made Essie even more self-conscious of the stain that was likely permanently drying into her garment. Still, she watched their movements, hoping to spy a cache of unposted letters or postcards.

Another man stepped forward with confidence to match that exhibited by the strange couple. His thick mustache topped his goatee like an oxen yoke. His red hair curled past his neck beneath a large Stetson, and tassels dangled from his suede coat's hem and sleeves. He said something Essie did not overhear and extended a hand.

The man shook the driver's hand before peeling open the left side of his coat. He reached in, pulled a wallet from an inner pocket, and withdrew cash which he handed off to the red-headed man with the goatee.

After accepting the cash, he peeled off a note, shoved the rest into his coat's buttoned breast pocket, and whistled.

A young man with a cart driven by a team of Percherons steered to the staging area. The driver leaped from his seat, pausing to pat his barrel-chested, oversized workhorses whose muscled legs emphasized their ability to pull heavy loads.

The red-haired man tipped his hat. He shoved the money into the driver's palm and pointed.

Essie's gaze followed the gesture to the growing stack of trunks. *They must be moving. That explains the Percherons.* The thought added to the mystery surrounding them. What would be so important to bring along on the passenger train instead of placing it in the one solely for cargo?

The man with the goatee settled the couple into his rig and watched the young cart driver launch each heavy item into the wagon's flatbed. When he loaded the last, he climbed aboard. "Follow my carriage to The Vincent House Hotel."

Leaning out, the woman said something in a strange language.

The red-haired man set the carriage brake and disembarked. He strolled back to the train and motioned for one of the stevedores. After exchanging words and gestures, the employee produced a large, round hatbox he plopped into the redhead's waiting hands. As if it contained a royal crown, he carried it out in front of him, then offered it through the carriage door to the delighted squeal of its apparent owner. Once again in motion, he yanked a hand at the cart driver and released the carriage brake as he fed the reins to the horses.

Doing as directed, the cart driver steered around the perimeter of the depot and into the street behind the couple's carriage. The trunks filled the entire bed, and the horses lowered their heads as they dragged the heavily-laden cart from the commotion.

Watching them disappear, Essie craned her neck.

She'd not receive a reward from them—at least not today. Perhaps they'd send mail once settled. She turned her attention back to the thinning crowd. Her primary mission was finding Tarak, not posting letters on a Sunday. She watched each arrival.

Some individuals deposited belongings into a surrey or wagon.

Others set off on foot with a knapsack or carpetbag.

Essie looked up and down the tracks and across them, but wherever Tarak was, it was not near the train station. She stepped toward Meadowlark, and from behind her, a familiar voice fell across her ears. As she recognized to whom it belonged, her heart sank. *Nancy Finncannon.* She groaned.

Like feathers off a molting bird, arrogance dripped from Nancy Finncannon everywhere she went. Rumored to be the result of a horse-riding incident, her permanent limp did not soften her image or attitude. Essie craned her neck and peered over her shoulder.

The buxom woman motioned for a rail worker. "You there."

As passengers ready for departure approached the staging zone, they threaded through people leaving the area and handed off bags and boxes for loading.

With no sign of Tarak and the next round of passengers boarding, Essie wanted to meet Meadowlark but paused. Her curiosity told her that Nancy was likely up to something. Essie didn't trust her after the threat she'd made against Gus. As though mesmerized by its spreading darkness, she scrubbed the vest's stain but kept her gaze on the rail worker.

The young man eased himself away from the job of

inspecting tracks and pointed at his chest. "Me?"

Nancy walked closer, the thump preceding each step less noticeable against the earth. The cane appeared first, jabbing at the ground with each step as she crossed Essie's sightline in her peripheral vision.

Nancy settled herself near a post and retrieved some coins from a small purse she wore around her neck. She rattled them in her fist. "Yes, you. Come here, boy."

His pace quickened. "What can I do for you?"

She leaned against the post. "I suppose you noticed the esteemed visitors who just disembarked the train."

He shrugged. "The ones with all the trunks?"

"We cannot have them thinking we are all a bunch of savages here in Wylder." She shook her head. "Can we?"

He scratched his chin, but his stare remained on her clenched fist. "Savages?"

Nancy opened her fist and held her palm up to him. "You will take care of this situation right away. Do you understand?" Nancy leaned closer, lifted the cane, and pointed it in Meadowlark's direction.

A carriage rattled past, blocking the sound of Nancy's whispers. *What is she getting him to do?* Knowing Nancy, Essie doubted it was something nice and friendly.

The rail worker nodded. He dropped the tool from his hand, took the money, and shoved it in his pocket. Then he stalked toward Meadowlark.

Glaring at Nancy, Essie turned and closed the gap. "Hello, Nancy," she managed as nicely as possible, although it came out sharper than she'd intended.

Nancy Finncannon smirked and nodded. "Essie,

why are you meeting the train? Not scaring up business on a Sunday, are you?"

Essie lifted her chin. "It would sure be a sight better than directing insults at people. What did you entice that boy to do?"

Fluttering a handkerchief, Nancy faked ignorance. "Why, Estelle Baumgardner, whatever do you mean? I'll have you know…"

As she heard the rail worker screaming at Meadowlark, whatever else Nancy said was lost on Essie. She glanced toward him.

Hacking a mucus plug, the boy spat it on the ground just in front of Meadowlark's moccasins.

Essie's blood boiled. *What nerve*. She ached to slap the sneer off Nancy's face. Her head blazed, and hot fury surged through her veins until her pulse throbbed. She'd deal with Nancy later, but right then, she fixed her gaze on Meadowlark. Essie grabbed handfuls of her skirt and bolted toward Meadowlark.

The boy planted his face inches from hers and shoved.

Meadowlark's shoulders swayed, but she didn't fall.

"Meadowlark," she yelled. Essie waved a hand above her head in hopes of capturing her attention. "I'm coming."

Although Essie's Arapaho friend did not turn toward the sound, a few others who'd remained trackside did.

The youth who'd done the shoving glanced in her direction. He turned and disappeared.

Essie didn't stop running, although her lungs and feet ached from her efforts. When she reached

Meadowlark, she doubled over to catch her breath. "Are you okay?"

She nodded. "I am now."

Essie swiped a handkerchief across her forehead, mopping the sweat from the exertion. "You must be careful." She inhaled. "Not everyone is like the majority of the townspeople. They don't know you as we do." She ached to say more—to tell her to avoid being around Nancy Finncannon at all costs. But Meadowlark's distress was evident, plus she didn't have the breath for a long-winded, cautionary explanation.

The Arapaho focused on the departing train. She didn't speak, turn her head, or move from her crossed-arm position. She remained erect until the final horn signaled its departure. Then she caved inward, slumping to her knees in the dirt.

Essie tugged her elbow, easing her off the ground. "This is just one stop. We'll keep looking."

Meadowlark lifted her teary gaze. "Where? I have searched everywhere."

Patting Meadowlark's shoulder, Essie considered a plan. "We should probably start with the sheriff's office. Earl Hanson might know something. It's a bit of a walk, but I'll go with you."

Meadowlark nodded and fell into step beside Essie. "Thank you."

Essie debated on the route. She could take a shorter course by the Catholic church, but she told herself it wasn't that much closer and retraced her steps from the morning's jaunt to St. Joseph's Episcopal Church near the town's outskirts. She glanced at Meadowlark, but if she knew the path was longer in the way Essie led, she didn't react. "Was the trader someone he knew?"

She shook her head, and her braids danced atop her shoulders. "He said he met a new man who offered a better trade."

Essie winced. She feared he'd stepped into a trap like the ones he set for the beavers and with as much at stake. "You don't know who—didn't catch his name?"

"It was an English name. I do not recall."

She turned left just past the rectory, continued in a straight line beyond the school and the wishing well, and proceeded at a diagonal behind McCabe and McClain Law Office to the sheriff's office. Bursting through the door, she caught Earl Hanson with his head down. Essie cleared her throat. "Sheriff?"

He didn't budge.

Surely he wasn't gone. "Sheriff Hanson, Earl," she yelled. She covered her face with a hand and stared at Meadowlark's shadowy figure in the doorway.

Chapter 2

Meadowlark stopped just inside the door and folded her arms around her midsection. She shrugged. "Is he…dead?"

Despite the heat, a chill settled over her. Essie crept closer and shook his arm. "Earl?"

A snort lifted from Earl's bent head. His shoulders lifted in sync with his chest.

Essie slumped and grabbed the desk. "Oh, thank goodness. He's just napping." Despite his advancing age, Sheriff Hanson was still a handsome man. Even the silver that dusted his hair and mustache did nothing to detract from his chiseled features. But his reactions, including his hearing, were failing. Essie nudged the sheriff's shoulder. "Earl?"

He continued dozing, chin to chest, hat tilted over his eyes and resting on the bridge of his nose, with his ankles crossed and propped on the desk. His chest rose and fell in easy motions, and he whistled with his exhalation.

Essie nudged him. "Wake up, Earl."

His lip curled, but he kept snoring.

Although Essie resisted startling him, she could think of nothing else short of pouring a dipper of cold water over his head. Exasperated, she popped the desk with the palm of a flattened hand. "Sheriff?"

Earl Hanson jolted from his slumber. Blinking

awake, he scraped the desk's edge with his boot heels. As he grabbed his six-shooter, his hat fell to the floor. Reaching for it, he grimaced. "Tarnation, Essie, I nearly shot you."

She pointed a finger. "I could have shot you, and you'd been none the wiser until questioning St. Peter at Heaven's gate."

Remaining seated, he swiped at his face, covering a yawn. "It's Sunday, Essie. What are you doing here?"

"I know what day it is. I missed you at service, but that ain't the reason I'm here." She jerked her head toward Meadowlark. "We're looking for her husband. You seen him?"

Earl Hanson rubbed his neck and winced. He paused and looked beyond her shoulder. "What's it to you if I have?"

Meadowlark stepped closer. "Please." Her lips continued moving, but no sound emitted.

Having gone through something similar, Essie understood how words could form and fail, but she also understood Earl Hanson's pause before speaking—a sure admission of guilt. She folded her arms across her chest and tapped a foot. "Okay. Where is he?"

He puckered his lips inward. "What makes you think I know?"

Essie resisted the urge to tell the sheriff his unbecoming expression made him appear feeble. "Well, you didn't say you didn't know, so that's a right smart clue, ain't it?"

Rising slowly, Sheriff Hanson unfolded his body. He lifted and lowered his shoulders, stretched his back, and steepled his fingertips against the desktop. "Okay. I got him in the jail."

Meadowlark gasped.

As the grip on Essie's arm tightened, she patted her friend's hand. "That's fantastic. You can retrieve him."

The sheriff glanced between her and Meadowlark before focusing his stare on Essie. "Why in tarnation would I do that?"

Essie felt Meadowlark tremble and continued on her behalf. "Why wouldn't you? I'm sure he's done nothing wrong. I'll vouch for him."

Sheriff Hanson pointed at Essie. "Now, listen here. I've got a written complaint that he stole a man's beaver pelts. Until that's resolved, I'm afraid—"

The sheriff's explanation had to be incorrect. Leaning forward, Essie met his glare with one she hoped was equally as forceful despite the difference between his height and hers. "A complaint, you say? By whom?" Without giving Earl a chance to answer, she flailed her arms. "Where are the pelts? What made you believe him over Tarak?"

He lowered his brows. "He seemed sincere, but I did question his soft hands and swirly handwriting. I kept the pelts, though, until it's all figured out." He jerked a thumb. "They're in the storage room across from the holding cell."

Essie considered the options. *Although risky, if he has the pelts, I have one chance to prove ownership.* "That's wonderful. Meadowlark, please describe the pelts—in detail."

She shook her head, and her braids bobbed back and forth. "Detail?"

Motioning for Meadowlark to move closer, Essie nodded. "Tell Sheriff Hanson how Tarak skins beavers."

Meadowlark made the motion of pulling a dress over her head.

Pulling back her shoulders, Essie smiled. "See? You go ask the other fellow how he skinned them, and we'll be done."

Sheriff Hanson's frown deepened. "He's not here, Essie. I can't just go ask him."

Essie slapped both hands to her head, squeezing it like a walnut she intended to crack. "Dagnabit, Earl, didn't you say you had a writ?"

The sheriff rubbed his eyes and stretched a hand beneath the desktop. He tugged on a drawer, and when it gave to his pressure, he pulled out a paper. "Right here."

Telling herself she could catch more flies with honey than vinegar, she forced another smile. "Did he put the location of his whereabouts on it?"

"Well, let me see." He glanced over the paper. "Yep, it says I can return the pelts to him at Wylder Hotel."

While Essie grew impatient with the necessity to direct him, she swallowed her angst and spoke calmly. "Well, there you go. Ride over to the hotel and ask him. We can either wait here or accompany you. But I believe you'll be back soon to release Tarak, so I've got no reason to go far."

He shoved his hat low over his forehead and snatched the keys for the jail from the hook by the dividing door. "Just in case you got any ideas about releasing him in my absence."

Essie gasped, faking shock. "Why, Earl Hanson, are you insinuating I can't be trusted?"

The sheriff ate his lower lip with his upper until it

25

disappeared in the thickness of his mustache. "If I weren't a gentleman…"

"But you are," Essie called, trailing behind him.

Earl Hanson left the door ajar as he untethered his horse and pulled himself onto his back. He mumbled under his breath the entire time but did as she asked.

Meadowlark's breath swept across her ear. "I do not understand. What do you hope to get from the man who accused my husband?"

Essie patted her shoulder. "You said he had an English name, so I'm guessing he's a white man, and most of them skin beavers differently than the Arapaho."

She tugged her brows inward until they nearly met. "Different? How?"

Making the motion of opening her vest, she ran a hand straight down her middle, between her breasts. "They slice like this and then peel apart. He might know this but likely won't if Sheriff Hanson has the pelts."

A shadow crossed her face and clouded her eyes. "And if he does?"

"Well…" Essie chewed her lip. "We'll just have to think of something else, won't we?"

Meadowlark blinked. "I am worried. The Englishman's word is always taken over ours."

Essie draped an arm around Meadowlark. "A man's word is taken over a woman's word." She thought of Nancy and her fine house and large inheritance. "And a rich woman's is taken over that of a poor one. Plenty of injustice to go around, and you don't have to look far to find it. But if you're clever, and I know you are, you can outwit them."

Wrinkling her nose, Meadowlark tilted her head. "What is this outwit?"

Although Meadowlark spoke perfect English, from time to time, a word slipped through that she didn't understand. "Well, it means outsmarting—beating them at their own game." Essie looked at the complaint on Sheriff Hanson's desk. He'd gotten so aggravated he'd not stowed it back in the drawer. She leaned over it and read—*John Smith*. "It says his name is John Smith. What a crock of bull. I'll bet that's not even his real name."

Meadowlark shook her head. "Why would he give the wrong name?"

Her innocence made Essie even angrier. She balled a fist and furrowed her brows until her lids twitched. "Because he's a lazy, lying crook who is stealing furs off the people who worked for them. Don't worry. We'll straighten this out."

The clock in the corner of the sheriff's office ticked. The sun lowered until the sky turned orange. Meadowlark stood tall and regal in the corner like a sculpture. Her only movements were the soft rising and falling of her chest with her breaths. Essie felt each tick of the clock in her chest. *What if I'm wrong?*

Tick-tock.

What if John Smith is his real name? What if he tells the sheriff the right way of skinning the pelts?

Tick-tock.

What will I do then?

Essie paced until she feared the continuous motion might make Meadowlark nervous. Pulling out the chair from Sheriff Hanson's desk, she sat, but her pulse throbbed with urgency. She immediately jumped to her feet and sighed.

Tick-tock.

What will become of Meadowlark? What will they do with Tarak?

Tick-tock.

What if the Natives stage a revolt for the miscarriage of justice?

A crash sounded from just beyond the door. Essie ran forward and slung it open, already thinking of some excuse as to why she and the Arapaho woman were alone in the sheriff's office.

Sheriff Hanson pushed a man forward. "Get in there right now."

The man wobbled from the shove, but he stumbled through the doors. He glanced at her and smiled.

Essie raked a glance across him. His grin appeared turned on from a spigot of them, and he had a greasy look, too. Everything seemed just a bit too slick to grab, from his hair to his hands. His blue eyes sparkled like he knew he was handsome and likely to get anything he wanted because of it.

The man licked his lips. "Well, hello there, pretty lady. What can—"

Sheriff Hanson held up his hand. "Not a word. Don't say one more lying word."

Essie pointed. "Let me guess—John Smith?"

"In the flesh." The stranger shifted his gaze toward the sheriff. "See? This lovely woman knows me. I'll bet she'll vouch for me."

"Ha," Earl shot back. "She's the one sent me after you. Tell me again how you skinned those beavers, and I'll retrieve the pelts."

The man straightened his shirt and tugged on his

sleeve, dislodging something which flew from the cuff. He shoved a foot forward but not in time.

Earl snagged it and held up an ace of hearts. "Well, what do we have here? More proof of your thieving?"

Smith smirked and rolled his eyes. "Of course not. That there card must have landed in my shirt when you dragged me from the saloon."

Hanson thrust out his chin at Smith. "I doubt it. Decks don't normally have more than one ace in each suit."

"I gave back the winnings, didn't I?"

"To save your own hide." Earl tossed the playing card onto the desk. "Let's finish and get you out of town before you rob the wrong gunslinger and get a bullet for your efforts. Show me how you skinned the pelts."

He grinned. "Ain't but one way to skin rabbits, cats, and beavers. You slice them down the center and pull the hide from the body like unswaddling a baby."

Essie's heart fluttered. The man most likely convicted himself by his arrogance and assumptions. If only she could convince Earl to get him behind bars before he realized his mistake. "Didn't you say you took the pelts to the jail?"

Earl snapped toward her. "What?"

"The pelts." She winked. "Didn't you take them to the jail with the feller who claimed them as his?"

His grimace changed to a sneer, and he narrowed his eyes. "I believe I did. Come along, and I'll get them."

The man calling himself John Smith bowed. "Lead the way. I'm anxious to get out of this hick town anyway."

Essie stood at the door dividing the sheriff's office from the holding cell. "I'll lead. Come along, Meadowlark."

Meadowlark stepped from the shadows.

John Smith tilted his head toward the corner and paled. "After you."

Essie inhaled deeply. Meadowlark was about to witness justice work on her side for once, and Essie intended to see to it. She gave her what she hoped was a warm smile as they walked.

Earl unlocked the outer door and threw it open.

A light sliver filtered in from a tiny window set into the upper wall like a single eye. A moment passed as her eyes adjusted to the dimness before she saw him. Tarak sat in the cell, as still and calm as his wife had occupied the corner of the sheriff's office.

He glanced at them without a tremor until he saw Meadowlark.

Essie watched his expression change from blank to worried. She knew the depth of their love for each other and ached for a similar one.

Sheriff Hanson juggled the keys, flipping through until finding the one satisfying him. "We'll just open the door and get them, Mr. Smith."

Smith smiled. "Then I'll be on my way."

Hanson scooped his hand toward him. "Come. I'll need your help as I recall you had too many to carry alone."

"Well, of course." He rubbed together his palms.

Earl stabbed the key into the lock and scooped his hand toward Tarak. "Come on out of there."

"But…" Smith protested.

Hanson patted his back. "Oh, don't worry."

Tarak walked past and through the metal door.

Hanson's pat turned to a full shove as he pushed Smith forward and locked the door once more. "You don't learn, do you?"

Smith's grin turned into a sneer. "What are you doing? Where are my pelts?" His long fingers threaded around the bars, and he used a firm grip to rattle the door.

The sheriff narrowed his eyes and pointed at Smith. "I'm getting a complaint against you from this man. You've filed a false report, made false accusations, and cost Tarak a day's wages by filing the complaint that kept him from his work and his family. I'll notify the marshall as I think we'll discover you've tricked more than one person."

Tarak swept a long stare up and down his wife. Exhaling, he grabbed Meadowlark and hugged her. "How did you…"

She tugged loose and raked a glance over him, inhaled, and patted his cheek. "It was Miss Essie. She freed you."

He took Essie's hands in his. "How?"

Essie slumped and dropped her hand. She hadn't realized how much tension she held in her neck and back until her quick thinking paid off. The situation could have ended badly, but thankfully, it hadn't. She smiled and pointed at John Smith. "There's more than one way to skin beavers, Mr. Smith or whoever you are. You've got to learn before you mess with people in Wylder."

Tarak reached toward Essie with an open palm, fisted his fingers, and tapped his chest. "Miss Essie, you are part of my heart. You have saved my family and me. How can I ever repay you?"

Essie swiped at her sudden tears. "Aw shucks, you two. Since when do we have to repay people we love?" She squeezed two fingers together. "Sisters."

Tarak nodded. "From now on, your Arapaho name is Little Sister."

"I like that."

Earl Hanson scraped his mustache with his lower teeth. "Enough caterwauling already. Let's get them pelts returned to their rightful owner."

Smith shook the bars. "You'll be sorry. Revenge will be mine. I'll get out of here, and when I do—"

Sheriff Hanson closed the inner door. "Hush now. Don't nobody care about your empty threats."

"Empty? I'll show you empty…"

Smith's vows of revenge reverberated in Essie's head. She glanced at the happy couple. They appeared unfazed, but a dark shadow fell across Essie's happiness.

Chapter 3

Monday, June 17, 1878

Essie awoke to the sound of scratching noises in the upstairs room she shared with Gus. She sat up and rubbed her eyes. The nearly full moon shone through the left-ajar window, and the night air had cooled the stuffy dwelling. Shivering, she pulled a shawl around her shoulders. "Gus?"

Her daughter's head popped up from the opposite side of the room. Augusta—named after her father—was on her knees, reaching beneath the iron bed. "Sorry, Ma. I kicked a boot, and it slid against the wall. If I could just reach it…" She stretched farther and grunted.

Sighing, Essie figured she might as well rise and help. Sleep was sure to evade her if Augusta continued flailing around. "Here." She grabbed an umbrella. "Try this."

Gus looked at it and grinned. She dove beneath the bed again and, with one targeted swipe, retrieved the footwear. "That was a good idea."

Essie crossed to the nightstand and lifted her pocket watch. She turned it into the moon's glow and gasped. "Good heavens, Gus, it's barely five o'clock. Why are you gathering clothing at this hour?"

Gus stood and shoved her foot into the boot. She

shuddered and reached for a flannel shirt which she tugged on over the cotton one. "That's a good question, ain't it? I asked Clyde the same thing. Seeing as we're an act, and we've been planning for the Independence Day Show half the year, you'd think that would take precedence over whatever just occurred."

Essie heard the irritation in her daughter's tone and patted her hand. "Maybe his mama needs him. She preserves fruits and vegetables this time of year and always enters a pie or two in the contest."

Gus frowned and plopped on the bed. "I know, and with the moon so bright, we can see well enough. Plus, the temperature is easier on Thunder and Lightning. The afternoon heat was nearly unbearable yesterday. Both horses were in a lather."

Something was still bothering Gus. Uncertainty trembled beneath her daughter's words. She sat beside her daughter. "Those are good reasons to practice earlier in the day, so why are you concerned?"

"I can't explain why. I have this weird feeling." She sighed and leaned against Essie. Moonlight washed across her face and accentuated her furrowed brows.

Essie struggled with what to say. On the one hand, she didn't want her daughter creating problems where they didn't exist and needlessly worrying. On the other, she didn't want to dissuade her from following her heart and listening to her instinct. Remaining silent wasn't the answer either. *Perhaps I'm too lenient with Gus. She would know how to handle these things if I was here instead of working so hard and keeping such long hours to make ends meet.*

Some decisions Gus needed to make herself. "I can't give you an answer. But I can give you some tools, and the first is to listen to your gut. We women ignore our intuition much too often. Pay attention, and if something isn't right, you won't have to guess. Truth always surfaces."

Augusta relaxed against her side and then inhaled and leaped from the bed. "Thanks, Ma. I'll be home before lunch."

Essie watched her leave and then settled back into bed. Sleep didn't come, and she surrendered the effort to force it at six. With the room cooled, the last thing she wanted was to heat it with a fire for coffee and eggs. Rising, she slipped downstairs, out the back door, and strolled along Sidewinder Lane to Wylder Street's bakery. Although closed, she pecked on the door. On occasion, the owner tossed her a few treats and a cup of coffee. "Cissy Arkwright? It's Essie Baumgardner. Got raisin bread or a glazed bun?"

Footsteps commenced, and the door cracked open, allowing the tantalizing aromas of coffee, yeast, and sugar to escape through the sliver. One shadowy eye blinked. "Essie? What are you doing out this time of the morning?"

The bags beneath Cissy's eyes accentuated her surprised stare. "Gus woke me an hour ago. She and that Hartshorn fellow are practicing for the Independence Day show. I swear that girl is driving me crazy."

Cissy widened the opening enough to snatch her arm and pull her inside. "Let me get you a sweet roll and something to drink." She walked behind a divider.

"Thanks. I'd love a coffee," Essie called out.

The owner immediately returned with a steaming cup and bun-filled saucer. "I'm so glad you dropped by.

Rumor has it that swindler attacked you over at the Wylder Hotel."

Essie blinked and pulled a long sip of coffee. Wylder was a small town, and she needed to keep her reputation squeaky clean to remain the postmistress. *Why are people talking about me?* "Rumor? What fellow?"

Cissy frowned. "Mustn't be true. It's just…" She licked her lips and leaned closer. "You were seen coming out of Sheriff Hanson's office yesterday, and he was seen dragging in that card rustler. So naturally…I mean…you would have thought the same."

Essie deposited the mug on the edge of a bread rack and pinched a morsel from the roll. "Oh, that fellow."

Brightening, Cissy held up a forefinger. "Aha. So, the rumor is true."

Chewing the tasty bite for a second, Essie followed it with another sip of the rich, hot coffee. Steam washed over her face, and warmth spread throughout her veins and cleared the fogginess in her mind. "Eh…" She tilted a hand back and forth. "He didn't attack me, but I was there when Sheriff Hanson dragged in the no-account thief for questioning. I even saw a card fall from his sleeve right there in the sheriff's office."

"No." Cissy gasped. She covered her mouth when she chuckled. "That must have been a sight."

Essie took another taste of the roll. "You should have seen his face. But that's not the best part. He even filed a complaint against Tarak after arranging a trade. He thought he'd get those pelts for nothing and accused Tarak of stealing them."

Cissy pulled a stool close and sat. "Did Earl

believe him?"

"Did at first. Sheriff Hanson even locked up Tarak, but at least he was wise enough to keep the beaver pelts until he could discern the rightful owner."

Cissy blinked. "How on earth did he do that?"

The aroma of baked goods nearing their prime filled the air, and Essie feared they would toughen if she kept Cissy from her duties. "I smell the bread, so it's likely ready. Don't let me ruin your morning's work by going on about yesterday. Stop by the post office, and I'll explain it." She stood, drained her cup, and deposited some coins on the counter.

Cissy pushed back the money. "Your money is no good here, Essie, you know that. I'll be by later."

Such gestures always humbled Essie. She nodded and uttered her thanks before slipping out the door. Halting at the corner, she glanced across Wylder Street at the Vincent House Hotel and Restaurant. The image of the couple at the train station instantly flashed across her mind. Given their fancy clothing and confident demeanor, she was more curious about them than the other travelers. She thought of the young woman's directive from the carriage and the driver's persistence with the laborer until he retrieved the large hatbox.

But mainly, one thought occupied her mind—the man appearing through the steamy mist as though its vapor materialized him. *Who is he? What is he doing in Wylder?*

"Essie?"

She jumped. Turning toward the direction of the sound, she resisted frowning, although her lips nearly insisted on the downward bend. "G'morning, Nancy."

Nancy glowered and thrust back her shoulders.

"What in tarnation are you doing skulking around here when you should be opening the post office about now?"

Anger sizzled along Essie's spine. When Nosey Nancy had her cornered in the post office, where she was the customer and Essie was the civil servant, Essie had to mind her manners. But she didn't have the same demands on her own time. Hoping to send a confident message, she pulled back her shoulders in a gesture similar to Nancy's. "When I open the post office is up to me, ain't it? I don't see the title of postmistress following your name."

Nancy slammed the cane's end against the baked-to-a-crust ground. It landed with a thud but didn't have the same clunk as when hit against wood. "Well...I never..." She jerked her chin and pivoted. The cane slipped, and Nancy wobbled.

Despite her irritation at Nancy, Essie couldn't let her fall. She ran toward her, gripping her by the elbows. "Steady now."

Straightening, Nancy pulled at her skirt and pursed her lips. "Get your hands off me, Essie Baumgardner, before I tell Sheriff Hanson you're assaulting me."

Essie released her and stepped back. The threat hit her like a slap across her face, blazing hot with both fear and fury. Flustered, she couldn't even think of a retort.

"*Mais non*," a voice called from the direction of the hotel's porch.

Turning, Essie peered into the face of the man from the train station. She gasped and froze. Shock and irritation fluttered in her stomach until goose bumps pebbled her flesh. Without his coat, the man looked especially elegant in the morning light.

Nancy grimaced and opened her mouth.

As he offered his crooked elbow, the gentleman's sleeves ballooned from his silky vest and matching cravat. "I can assist, *s'il vous plait*. I was about to don my coat but observed your teetering. Naturally, fearing the worst, I raced out the door."

Nancy tossed back her head. "Thank goodness you did, sir. This woman—"

"Saved you from falling. I know. I saw it all. You are most certainly grateful to…" He flourished a palm toward Essie.

The rustling of taffeta and the gargling of strange-sounding words wafted from the hotel porch where the slender woman—in a half-hat as mysterious as her language—paced. She lifted her violet-colored skirts as though bracing to cross a flooded street and pointed the toe of a dyed-to-match shoe, jerking it back to the wooden floorboards at the last second.

She's wearing fabric shoes. Essie lost her patience with the entire situation. "Postmistress," she replied. "I'm Wylder's postmistress." She gestured in the building's direction. "The post office is between the stagecoach depot and the telegraph office. If you want to send mail, stop by." Without waiting for a reply, she hastened down the street and through the back door to the post office.

Although Essie despised doing anything Nancy could claim credit for suggesting, she hustled through the inner chamber, opened the front door, and flipped the sign. Recalling Nancy's accusation made her blood boil. Now she'd gone from threatening Augusta to paying someone to harass Meadowlark to falsely accusing her of pushing her when all she'd done was save her from falling. She pursed her lips. *I'll not repeat that mistake.* Even though she swore it beneath her breath, if the situation warranted intervention, she knew she'd do the same thing again. Her exasperation at Nancy's treachery spawned a surge of energy.

With Augusta at the arena with Clyde, and few people likely to appear early at the post office, Essie needed a focus. Settling into the desk chair, she tugged another sheet of parchment from the stationery package and pulled the pen from its cupped holder. She poised it above the inkwell.

Squeak. Bam. The door burst open. "Essie, are you in here? The sign says you're open."

Scraping back the chair before she got ink on the nib, she approached the entry. She scooped her hand, indicating he should enter. "Fletcher? Come on in."

Fletcher Wylder's boots clacked as he crossed the floor. "Thank you, Miss Essie."

Essie strolled behind the counter. "How're things at the Feed and Seed?"

He reached into his vest and fished out a letter. "They're doing pretty good right now. I just hope this drought won't last, or the credit I extended might come back to haunt me."

Essie clapped a palm to her cheek. "I'm sorry, Fletcher. I didn't think about the repercussions making it down the chain, but I should have."

Fletcher shrugged. "Nobody's fault, I guess. I couldn't refuse good citizens the credit when my parents founded the town, now could I?"

"I miss your parents. Ralph and Naomi were good folks. All the townsfolk hold admiration for them."

Essie sighed. "How's your sister?"

He held the letter upright in his fist. "Which one?"

Essie snapped her fingers. "That's right, you've got two. I don't reckon I know the eldest very well, but I've seen Ava when she's come back to town from up North, isn't it?"

"Yeah, I reckon she likes it just fine in New York, studying and all, and with Abigail still in England, our family feels tossed to the wind. Of course, I've still got Finn over at the mercantile."

"England...New York..." Essie whispered the city names with the reverence of prayer. Pictures from various books flashed through her mind—cobbled streets, tall statues, and brick buildings. She wondered about Ava's school and if the students lived differently than Augusta.

A hand fell against her shoulder and jolted her to attention. She glanced at the masculine digits nudging her bicep and gazed upward to Fletcher's taut face.

He tilted his chin. "Miss Essie, are you okay?"

The foreign images turned to smoke. Squeezing her eyelids, she tried to hold onto them, but they escaped her efforts. Essie sighed and released her visions. *Maybe someday, they'll be more than objects in my imagination.* "I'm sorry—rough night." She pulled up her spine and pointed her thumb toward the envelope in his grip. "Do you want to get that on the next stage?"

Fletcher nodded and placed the letter on the counter. "It's for Uncle Martin."

Essie lifted it and ran a fingertip over the name. "Martin Wylder. Your father's brother in Kentucky?"

His face softened. "Yeah, his younger brother is the sole family survivor. I'm sure..."

Whatever else he said was lost on Essie. She couldn't hold her focus and allowed her mind to wander to the tidbits about Kentucky she'd read from the newspaper articles. A couple of years back, one mentioned the horse racing track that had just opened in Louisville. The reporter referred to the place as the Bluegrass State and wrote about several bourbon distilleries. *I wonder what it smells like there and how bluegrass looks.* "Do you suppose the grass is really blue?"

Fletcher stared. "Pardon me, Miss Essie. Are you sure you're all right?" He peeked around her. "Is Gus here? Should I fetch her?"

Essie stowed the letter beneath the counter. "I'm fine. Gus woke me earlier than normal and after yesterday…" She exhaled loudly, blowing frustration through her lips.

He looked over his shoulder at the still-closed door and leaned in. "I heard. Was that fellow trying to steal the mail? Did he get in here?"

She furrowed her brows. "Steal the mail? Who?"

Fletcher sucked in a breath and stared. "The one who attacked you. He's at the jail as old Hanson arrested him. Didn't you know?"

She winced. "Oh, him. Why does everybody think the man did something to me? I simply helped Sheriff Hanson uncover his crimes."

"You mean, he didn't…" Fletcher's mouth dropped open.

Essie forced a smile. "He did not."

A long exhalation whistled off Fletcher's lips, and he dropped his shoulders. "Well, thank goodness. Talk around town is that Earl was about to gather a posse to go after him."

Laughing, she recalled the way Earl pushed him around. "The town is discounting their sheriff. Even at his advancing age, once he's well-rested, he can still handle the roughest around." She left out the part where she did most of his thinking, and that the promise of receiving the pelts had coerced John Smith. "Earl Hanson shoved him through the door so hard he dislodged another Ace of Hearts from the crook's sleeve."

Fletcher grinned. "I'm sorry I missed such a sight. I'd like to have seen Earl tossing that thief into the jail."

The door pushed open, and Chet Daniels from the livery poked in his head. "Essie, are you okay?"

She groaned. "Oh no." "Does everyone think something happened to me?"

"'Fraid so. How much for the letter?"

"Three cents, please."

Fletcher counted out the coins and tipped his hat. "G'day to you, Miss Essie. I'm glad you're fine." He strolled past Daniels and nodded. "Chet."

Chet held out his hand. "Wait up, Fletch. With the town's sudden traffic, and that fancy couple requesting a carriage, I'll be needing some extra feed."

Essie froze. Although loath to admit it, the elegant pair fascinated her.

Fletcher paused. "Stop by on your way back to the livery. I'm opening early."

"Sure." He closed the door and sauntered to the counter. "I don't have anything to mail, Miss Essie. I just stopped in to check on you after the attack and all."

She threw back her head and groaned, partly from what appeared to be an ongoing misconception about the occurrences on Sunday and partly due to not hearing more about the two people who'd turned heads upon their arrival on the train. "Oh Lord, I have a feeling this will be a long day."

"But good for business, eh? I reckon you've just given half the town a reason to send a letter to a relative elsewhere."

"A letter to a relative..." Essie sighed as she glanced at the desk and its waiting parchment.

Chet jerked a thumb toward the door. "Better get that feed."

She nodded and waved. "See ya later, Chet."

"Good day to you, Miss Essie." He opened the door and slammed it shut behind him.

For a moment, the echo of the door hitting against its jamb filled Essie's head. Wylder was a noisy town compared to the small outpost on Fort Laramie's rim. Most of the sounds she recalled from that tiny house were Augusta's sweet voice or the clattering of her playing with cornhusk dolls and horses she fashioned from logs and sticks. Even if they were back in the house near the fort, she doubted things would be the same.

Gus grew up, as children did, and now Essie realized her daughter needed more instruction than she could give her. She sauntered to the desk and lifted the fresh stationary sheet. *Perhaps I have time to finish Blanche's letter.*

The sound of clomping horses and rolling wheels wafted through the window.

Ignoring them, she settled into the chair and lifted the pen.

Footsteps hammered the porch boards. They grew

closer and paused.

Essie removed the inkwell's cover.

The door groaned open, and the footsteps continued through the entrance. "Miss Essie? You here?"

Essie sighed and stabbed the pen into its holder. She stared at the glaringly pristine parchment. Stolen moments were not enough to allow the focus she needed. The letter would have to wait. "Come in."

Monday was a blur of continually explaining the prior episode with the man calling himself John Smith, the beaver pelts, and the extra cards he held up his sleeve. Everyone speculated about the crook, and the story grew upon itself until it barely sounded like the same events she recalled when she was in their midst.

While flustered with the endless explanations, she was happy with the increased revenue. As Chet Daniels surmised, the event gave the townspeople something to write about in correspondence to their relatives and friends who lived elsewhere, and they were eager to share the news.

Besides, she was willing to withstand the rumors for the chance to find out more about the couple from the train. Every time the door opened, she yanked her head toward it, hoping to see the two intriguing people or someone with information about them. Time after time, her customers dashed her hopes.

Late in the afternoon, Anastasia West, owner of the Vincent House Hotel, swept through the door. She paused just inside its entry, blinked, and exhaled.

Anastasia was a striking woman. She was at least a half-foot, if not more, taller than Essie, with fiery red hair and cobalt-colored eyes which looked particularly large and startled at that moment. "Anastasia? Come on in."

She grabbed her throat with one hand and leaned against the door. Her chest quickly rose and fell. "Is someone behind me?"

Lately, Anastasia behaved strangely. She never appeared fully rested or as astute as she should. That she would ask such a question was further proof of her abnormal conduct. "Just the door and the bar I throw against it when I need to lock it."

She peeled herself from its support and wobbled a bit before straightening. "I'm sorry. I don't know what's happening...never mind. I heard about your little—"

Essie waved a hand back and forth. "The sheriff has the situation under control. But,"—her heart palpitated until she couldn't resist—"I heard Wylder's esteemed visitors are guests at your establishment."

Striding to the counter, she braced against it. "Esteemed visitors?" She patted the bag hanging from her shoulder and then ran her palm around the counter.

"Are you looking for something?"

"A pen. I just need to sign one of these letters, and then I can post them."

Essie thought it odd that Anastasia would leave the hotel with the mail before she'd prepared the letters for posting but said nothing. She also noticed the pen protruding behind Anastasia's ear, but she didn't mention that, either. Seeing as how the tip might bleed ink into her gorgeous mane if she didn't keep it tightly capped, she retrieved the pen and inkwell from the desk and carried it to her. "Here you go."

"Oh, thank you." She took the pen with a shaky

hand, missed the ink bottle's narrow opening on the first stab, and dropped it to the floor. Watching it roll away, she cupped her cheeks with her palms. "I don't know what's the matter with me."

Essie stooped and retrieved the implement. "It's tricky—postal issued—likely not the easiest to handle. Here, let me help." She completed the task of getting ink on the nib, and then left Anastasia signing the letter as she retrieved the blotter.

Anastasia was still scratching her name across the bottom of one of the letters when she returned. As soon as she lifted her hand to dot the i's and cross the t's letters in her name, Essie offered the rocking blotter. "Trust me, this ink requires it."

After blotting and blowing against the paper, Anastasia folded it and inserted it into the envelope. She cocked her head and frowned. "I'm sorry, Essie. Did you ask me about my strange visitations?"

The day had been curious. Essie feared she'd said something odd, although she couldn't recall what it might have been. "Did I say strange visitations? I meant esteemed visitors—distinguished guests—you know—never mind." She held up the stack of mail. "Is this all?"

Anastasia nodded and weakly smiled. "Just these six for now."

"That'll be eighteen cents."

After paying the postage, Anastasia turned for the door. She flung it open and peered left and right before stepping onto the walkway.

Anastasia West's behavior was bizarre. Essie followed her to the street, ensuring she didn't cross in front of a horse and wagon. Although concerned for her wellbeing, Essie was also filled with disappointment. She'd thought for sure she'd learn something about the strangers from the hotel's owner, but sadly, Anastasia was too preoccupied to offer any enlightening information.

Once Anastasia made it safely to the other side, Essie sighed and returned to her post. She listened to the clock ticking away the minutes until the back door burst open.

"Ma?" Gus poked in her head.

"Still at the counter," she yelled.

"Mrs. Hartshorn sent a casserole. Said she heard about your run-in with the crook."

Essie rolled her eyes and stomped a foot. "Lord, help us straighten out the misconception."

Gus clambered through the opening between the back porch access to the storage room, the overhead apartment access, and the post office connection. A covered, deep-dish pie plate rested in her hands. "Want me to send it back?"

The scent of stewed chicken and buttery pie crust wafted beneath Essie's nose. Her stomach growled, and she reached out a palm. "Chicken pie?"

"Her specialty. But if you don't want it…" Gus pulled it backward.

"Are you kidding? I'm starving. That bun I had for breakfast disappeared hours ago."

Gus slumped against the door jamb, one lifted boot heel acting as a brace. "Lock the doors, and we'll dig into this meal. I'm as tired as you are."

Essie didn't argue. She threw the bolts, poured a pitcher of water from the larger urn, and carried it upstairs. As she filled the shallow bowl for washing, she raked a glance across Augusta's dirty cheeks and fingernails. "You'll be wanting a full bath, Augusta."

She kicked off her boots. "No point. I'm going back to the arena first thing in the morning."

Tucking her chin so that Gus wouldn't see her grin, she scraped soap into the bowl and swished it about until it dissolved. "Back, huh? So, you and Clyde must have made up."

"Made up?" Gus's lower lip extended. "What makes you ask that?"

Essie splashed water on her face and patted her cheeks with a hand towel. "Oh, no reason."

Gus grabbed a nail brush from the shelf above the pitcher and ewer and scrubbed her fingertips. "You know something, don't you? Better tell me, or I…"

Her daughter's reddening cheeks puffed until resembling a squirrel's with hickory nuts stored in its jowls. The giggle rushed from Essie before she could stop it. "Have you already forgotten what you told me this morning?"

She twisted her head toward her mother. "About what?"

Essie lifted a finger and rubbed the space between her brows. "Good grief. This morning you were conflicted about Clyde's commitment to the show practice."

Gus blushed. "Oh, that." She stopped the furious scrubbing at her nails and stuck her hands into the water bowl. Cupping them, she splashed water until it not only found her forehead and neck but dripped down the sides of the stand and onto the floor. She grabbed the towel and dabbed. "He's got a job for a few days—that's all."

"See there." Essie crossed her arms over her chest. "I knew it would work out."

Balling up the towel, Gus dropped it beside the bowl. "Who said it worked out? If he…if I…" She frowned. "I don't want to talk about Clyde anymore."

"Oh?" Essie dabbed at the water spills. "Then who has captured your attention?"

"Who said someone caught my eye?" She grabbed a tin plate and turned her back.

Essie suppressed a chuckle. "Has somebody besides Clyde been talking to you?" She knew the answer before asking. Augusta lived in her own world that left very little space for anything besides horses, trick riding, and Clyde Hartshorn.

Gus stomped to the chair and settled her plate against the table. Reaching into the pottery cup that held utensils, she pulled out a fork. "I ain't saying. You'll have to wait to find out, I suppose."

On most days, Essie would have appreciated her daughter's growing independence. However, she now worried she'd waited too long. The need to send Augusta to Boston intensified with each passing hour. *I have to get that letter to Blanche finished tomorrow.*

Chapter 4

Tuesday, June 18, 1878

Essie awoke to full sunlight streaming through the window. It settled on Gus's vacant bed. The spot beside her feather-tick mattress where she stacked her boots and hat was equally as empty. She'd left with a little more stealth than the previous morning, allowing Essie to lie in later than usual. Of course, the busier-than-normal day, and Mrs. Hartshorn's hearty chicken pie aided her sleep.

She checked to see if Gus remembered the hastily scribbled thank-you note she'd left by her boots, and either she had or had kicked it beneath something. Sighing, she realized she'd have to ask later.

After her usual morning ablutions, Essie dressed for the day and grabbed the damask vest before recalling the ink stain from the crumpled letter. She stomped a foot and puckered her lips. *Shoot. I likely ruined it.* Essie patted the new beige as she draped it on the hook where the old garment hung. A visible sign of her sinfulness, she thought back to the day she'd allowed Nancy Finncannon to goad her about her appearance and into investing into a garment that was neither practical nor usable now.

The late May morning had started with promise. Essie slipped into the black vest, stuffed her watch, and the various keys into their pockets. She hardly blinked when the door opened just after she flipped the sign.

Nancy ambled through. She leaned on the counter with one elbow propping her while her cane dangled from the other and lifted a brow as she stared. "Rumor is Phineas Atwater is ordering himself a catalog bride. I said you'd know if that statement is true, seeing as how you handle all the mail into and out of Wylder."

Sighing, Essie gave her the same reply she'd given her the last twenty times Nancy tried to snag private information. "Ain't saying I do, or I don't, and you know better'n to ask. I'm sworn to uphold the sanctity of the mail."

Clucking her tongue, Nancy raked a glance across Essie and sneered. "I'm glad to hear it, because you certainly aren't upholding the standards of fashion or even seasonal attire. I swear, Estelle Baumgardner, that's the same vest you were wearing when you arrived in Wylder. Is it horsehair, or just covered in it?"

Essie had no desire to trade insults, and Nosey Nancy, as she thought of her, was notorious for smarting off whenever she didn't get her way. The cut hadn't bothered her. She merely shrugged. "Makes no difference. What's important is that it isn't covered in secrets which aren't mine to divulge."

Gus popped out from the sorting room and stood behind her mother. "Don't worry about her, Mama. She's just jealous, and I don't blame her. If I were her, I'd be jealous of you, too."

Essie wasn't sure whether to be flattered or appalled. Augusta's short fuse exploded without thought to consequences. As she rushed to her defense, she didn't care who found themselves on the receiving end of her wrath.

Nancy's cheeks turned purple as she pushed from the counter and snagged her cane. She pumped it against the wooden floor and pivoted toward the exit. "Well…I never…" she called over her shoulder as she went. When she reached the door, she gripped its edge, turned to face them once more, and lifted her cane. "You'd better get a hold on that one's tongue or…"

The walking aid hovered horizontally like a long accusatory finger in Augusta's direction. Essie shoved a hand into her pocket, digging for the pistol she kept in her skirt. She didn't come to Wylder to be threatened by the likes of spoiled and pampered Nancy Finncannon. "Or what?"

Nancy narrowed her eyes. "I wouldn't get too comfortable if I were you, Estelle Baumgardner. The office of postmaster is a political appointment."

Essie's jaw twitched as she nudged Augusta behind her. "Good thing you're not me, and I'm not particularly political."

Augusta poked her head around Essie's shoulder. "Rumor is old Stutts was turned down for more than the postmaster position. I guess living on his wife's inheritance makes his new suit of clothes less attractive than my mama's old, reliable uniform."

"The rumors I hear are from Stutts' well-connected friends, and they don't think very highly of you either," Nancy snapped. Her cane beat against the frame as she swept out the door.

The scene stayed with Essie for hours that day, heating her face every time her mind replayed Nancy Finncannon's mocking sneer. Before the day was over, she rushed to the store and parted with precious coins for a yard of damask and matching thread. For good measure, she added a packet of stationery.

As Essie thought about the thinning package of writing paper, she caressed the resulting vest. Since that day, Essie had tugged a sheet from it at least once a week. The third was Sunday, and the resulting stain had likely ruined the vest. The blue ink blackened as it set into the fabric. She hadn't a hope of removing it now. Possibly, she could dye it, but that would be another expense and getting Gus out of Wylder was more critical.

She didn't worry about what Nancy might do to her, but what she could cause against Gus shook her to the core. Images of the way she'd crossed the train worker's palm with enough coins to buy his gruff handling of Meadowlark washed across her mind and settled hard in her heart.

Snatching the black one, she ran a damp, rosewater-scented cloth over it and slipped her arms through it. She glimpsed her reflection in the silver-backed mirror. Despite the darkly faded spots that always reminded her of powdery mildew, she lifted her chin and pointed a finger toward herself. "It's proud I am to wear this vest, and I'll not let the likes of Nancy Finncannon convince me otherwise."

Turning from her image, she stomped down the steps into the storage room. *The people in Wylder depend on me, and I won't let them down because of one hateful old bag of wind and spite.* She gathered each letter and stacked one atop the other, not even pausing to read the addresses and imagine life in each town. *What's the point? I'll likely never see them, but Gus will. I'll give her a better life.*

She stopped and pushed a lock from her forehead. *Not if I don't get that letter written.* Sighing, she shoved the mail in a canvas sack and slipped into the inner post office.

The high temperature immediately hit her. She'd feared leaving the windows cracked with the recent criminal activity and had even secured the shutters. While protecting the mail waiting for the stage, she'd not left an escape for the building heat. John Smith, or whoever he was, could have a partner who'd come to town and think she was easy pickings as the postmistress.

She lifted the bars from the clips across the shutters and peeled them open. From across the street, she saw a hand raised in a wave before she could slither from view. "Dagnabit. Now I have to open," Essie wiped her brow and shuffled to the front. She opened the door and immediately jumped back.

A man in dusty boots with the sides rolling over the soles stood with his nose nearly against the wooden frame. A thin, oversized jacket hung open, revealing the yellowing shirt pocked with reddish-purple stains. He pulled his floppy hat so low that the brim brushed past his ears, hiding his nose and eyes.

She grabbed her heart. "Good grief. You startled me."

"Beg your pardon," he mumbled.

She glanced around him to the spot where he'd been when he waved. "Phineas Atwater, did you run over here?"

He peeked over his shoulder before rushing into the post office. "Quick—shut the door."

Essie reached for the *Closed* sign.

Phineas pushed up his hat's brim with one hand and placed the other on her arm. "Wait. Don't open right away."

Essie wasn't afraid of Phineas, even though he was likely stronger than her, and some people considered him odd. The fact that he had given up on legitimate courtship and taken to answering ads by women offering themselves as brides-for-the-ticket-west-price didn't change any minds. Nosey Nancy's recent inquiries were proof of the gossip circulating through town.

Mostly, she didn't fear him because of the derringer in her pocket. Although she'd never had to shoot anybody before, she wasn't above it. She took her oath seriously when it came to protecting the mail, just as she did the rules she'd sworn to uphold.

Regardless of his plea, she pulled away and turned the sign. "I can't allow customers in the post office when it's closed. But if you'll hurry with whatever business has you in knots, then you'll likely have time to drive home before anybody sees you and your cart."

He balled his fingers into a fist and then stretched them open again. "All right. I came to town yesterday, but even though I watched for the right time to slip inside, you hardly went without a customer."

Despite the heat, Essie shivered. As if feeling the bullnose weapon's metal heightened her courage, she took a backward step and squeezed her skirt. "Let me get this straight, Phineas. You drove into town on a beautiful June day to do business at the post office and merely whiled away the hours watching people enter and leave?"

He winced. "Not exactly. You see, Mama sent me

for sugar. She's making her special plum jam for the Independence Day contest, and—"

Essie relaxed. "That explains the…" She stopped talking before she rudely mentioned his dirty garments, knowing the difficulty in remaining clean and stain-free. Didn't she have a soiled damask vest hanging upstairs to prove it?

"Explains what, Miss Essie?"

Phineas could move fast, but he talked slow, and Essie was eager to start another letter to her cousin. "I think somebody's coming. Better spit it out. What're you here for?"

He shuffled his feet and averted his gaze. "A letter, Miss Essie. I thought…I mean…well…the train came in Sunday, and I wondered if you got any mail off it."

"I'm sorry, Phineas. I didn't, and I won't get any mail until sometime this afternoon. Perhaps you should send another letter. Tell her…I mean…tell whoever it is you're expecting to hear from that you are anxious for a reply."

Phineas nodded. "That's good advice, Miss Essie. Thank you." He made no move to leave.

She exhaled. "Okay, then. Bring it back before Friday afternoon, and I'll get it posted." She snatched the door and held it open, thankful for the soft breeze that swept past. She inclined her head. "Good morning, Sheriff Hanson."

"Sheriff Hanson? Well, I'll just be leaving." Phineas stepped through the held-open door. He pivoted. "You must have been mistaken. I don't see Earl around here anywhere."

Essie closed the door as quickly as she could without slamming it before he figured out she'd only pretended to see the sheriff. Such behavior wasn't like her, but what else could they possibly discuss? He was looking for something she didn't have, and she'd given him an idea on how to spark a response.

She returned to the desk and stared at the dwindling fancy paper stack as she faced another blank page. *This one has to be just right.* Reaching for the pen, she dropped her hand onto empty space—no pen, no inkwell, no blotter. *What the devil happened to them?* She moved the oil lamp and the stationery box but found nothing.

Sweat trickled down her forehead and dotted her chest as the sun streamed in and heated the inner office. She must have done something with it, but what? With a hand on a hip, she swept a glance around the office and saw all three on the counter where she'd left them after she'd helped Anastasia. *She'd acted oddly, too.*

Despite the heat, Essie shivered. The temperature or drought must be getting to people. She felt as forgetful as Anastasia as she carried the implements back to her desk and lined them in the proper order. She dipped the pen into the inkwell, allowed the excess to drip from the nib, and positioned her wrist. Essie had to get a letter posted to her Boston relative, Blanche Davenport, as she feared what might happen if Augusta stayed in Wylder.

Wylder was both a godsend and a curse for Essie and Gus. Until recently, it was much more of the former than the latter. While living in Ft. Laramie, she'd kept a better watch on her wandering child, and even then, she'd slipped from her grip and wound up in places she ought not to have been. The vision of Captain Puckett as he stood at her door with the wiggling eleven-year-old flashed across her mind.

She'd failed Augusta and ached at the thought of what Augustus might say about the way she reared their daughter. Nancy's threats solidified her failings, and she only knew one way to correct her daughter, who was more tumbleweed than a young lady. Gus wouldn't like the change, not at first, but she'd come to see it was for the best in the long run. Essie took a breath and wrote.

Dear Blanche,

You have been on my mind more than usual of late. Your last letter detailing the advantages in Boston for your lovely daughters remains foremost in my thoughts. Since turning sixteen, Augusta has bloomed physically, while her lack of sophistication and elegance is more my failing than hers. If Augustus

As she scratched the name of her long-dead husband onto the letter, Essie trembled. She quickly returned the pen to its cradle, stood, and stretched. Without a steady grip, she'd ruin yet another sheet of stationery.

The sound of swiftly rolling wheels and thunderous horse hooves permeated through the thin glass. Essie crossed to the window and watched as dust clouds settled beneath the stagecoach's wake along Old Cheyenne Road until it halted at the depot across the alley from the post office. Absentmindedly tugging on the watch chain, Essie cupped the dangling timepiece in her palm and glanced—half past noon—right on time.

The driver was likely Cyrus Dunn, or CD as she called him. He was dependable, even if passengers sometimes grumbled about the speed at which he took the bumpy road. Neither she nor CD cared what the travelers thought of the ride as long as he got them and the mail safely from the outlaws lining the rock canyons and sagebrush from Cheyenne to Wylder and back. But from a dead stop, they'd never catch CD as he thundered past. However, they might follow the stage to Wylder and wait for him to unload. If the need arose, she was ready to protect the mail.

Essie stuffed the watch back into its notched pocket in her vest. Wrapping her fingertips around the dangling chain, she glanced down to cram it in as well. Thirteen minutes had passed since she'd spied the stagecoach, and fifteen was all CD ever needed for deboarding passengers and their luggage. A flash caught her eye and yanked her from the ruminations. She lifted the latch and glanced out the now-open back door as the sun glinted off the buckle on one of the bags. From her spot, leaning against the jamb, she watched CD settle satchels beside their owners and deposit feed bags onto the wooden porch boards before retrieving the large canvas sack meant for Wylder Post Office. He peered around the corner, weapon drawn, before lifting the mail sack and tossing it casually over his shoulder.

Essie swiped at the perspiration on her forehead with a palm. The June weather had never been lovelier in Wyoming Territory, even if a bit too dry for the ranchers' enjoyment, and a filmy sheen covered porches and windows and left behind the arid dust's metallic taste. Essie carried herself with authority to the opened frame. Pulling herself away from the door and as upright as possible, she met CD's gaze.

CD nodded and stepped off the boardwalk. He broke the stare and glanced right.

She looked to his left, her pulse throbbing against her throat as she swept the horizon for sudden movements. Seeing none, she gazed upward to the second-story windows, checking for the slightest motion in a curtain or glimmer of sunlight on metal. The time was now if someone intended to jump him for the mail. Her right hand lingered in her pocket, where she gripped a double-barrel, pearl-handled derringer. She'd taken an oath to protect the mail, as had her husband some eighteen years prior. Should anyone attempt its theft, she'd stand behind her word, even if the same fate befell her as had him.

CD marched across the alley between the stage depot and the post office. His slightly bent back absorbed the footfalls, and his hat barely moved. Every step appeared calibrated at a casual gait as if he carried a bushel of corn—maybe just corn husks. He lacked the straight posture generally associated with hauling valuables or a rising puff of dust from a weighted footstep. If not for the routine's predictability and the direction he strolled, someone might suspect him of carrying his laundry to the washwomen.

Essie chuckled. *He'd be in a bigger hurry if he were going to see one of them*. The gossip was that he had a special young gal whose laundry skills suited his tastes better than any other. The sound of hooves pounding the dry earth clipped her giggle before it developed into a full belly laugh. Her focus snapped between the buildings' corners and CD—caught halfway between them and vulnerable in the wide-open stretch. If urged, the approaching horse could easily run over him.

Essie rushed into the back alley and pulled her

weapon from her pocket. "CD," she yelled.

CD dropped the sack in the road and plopped behind it.

The horse thundered closer until it cleared the corner. The rider shouted and fed the reins to his steed. "Hyah, hyah."

As another rider entered the alley, a second horse rushed his heels. They raced straight at him in the center of the dirt lane.

Essie raised her weapon. "CD, get the feller on the left, and I'll get the one on the right."

The first rider yanked on the reins. His horse bucked. As its front hooves left the ground and pawed at the air, its haunches crouched lower.

Essie's nostrils flared along with those of the mount. Everything bloomed in slow-motion detail.

The rider was shabbily dressed and older than she would have assumed from a distance. His fading garments were thin and tattered. A matted beard in flecks of red and yellow hung to his chest. The barrel of a shotgun extended from a side scabbard.

With the reins gripped in his knuckled fists, he yelled, "Whoa, boy." He slid backward as the horse bucked, and his legs swiped the roan, taking a layer of sweat and dust from its sides, revealing the red hair comingled with the white.

The second rider followed the first rider's lead. His saddle had a sack tied to each side. As he neared, Essie had the same visual perceptions. The buckskin, like the roan, struggled to ease up on the hammer-down pace. However, the rider was much more colorful. His curly auburn beard matched the hair sticking out from beneath his hat's brim.

The man pulled his horse in the opposite direction. When it stopped protesting its rough handling, the rider slung one leg behind him and lifted himself off the saddle with the push from the ball of his foot against the stirrup.

Essie aimed and rested her thumb on the hammer. Although her pulse pounded as furiously as the horses' hooves, she held her stance. "You best stay on your horse and keep on a-going. Ain't nothing in that sack should be of interest to the likes of you two ruffians."

The first rider circled back and stared at CD. "Cyrus? What are you doing down there?"

Cyrus eased back the hammer and lowered his weapon. His mouth dropped open. "Fred McDonald? I thought you were prospecting Slingback Creek."

"I was." He jerked his thumb at the other rider. "My boy and me got lucky."

His son cut his gaze at Essie, but he slipped back across his saddle. "Shh, Pa. What did I say 'bout telling strangers the news of our discovery?"

The older man worked his tongue against his cheek until it bulged. He poked a crooked fingertip inside his jaw and flicked out a tobacco plug into the alley. Its ugly, water-moccasin-colored stains splattered the roadbed. "This here ain't no stranger."

The younger man tilted his head toward Essie. "And her?"

Cyrus popped up from the crouched position. He sheathed his gun in his holster and lifted the mail sack. "You needn't worry about the postmistress unless you plan on messing with Gus or the mail. Either mistake will buy you a bullet."

Fred raked wet tobacco strings from his beard and

sucked on his teeth. He spit again. "Who's Gus?"

Despite Cyrus' relaxed position, Essie kept her pistol raised. "Who Gus is ain't none of your business, but right now, you're interfering with the swift delivery of the mail. So, if you two don't mind moseying along, CD and I can get about ours."

CD laughed and took a step. "Essie's right, as is your boy, Fred. Best hold your tongue. No way of knowing who's listening and apt to risk a little lead in exchange for some gold."

The younger man lifted his hat in a salute. "Name's Frank. Pleasure meeting you both." He urged his horse forward. "Come on, Pa. Let's get to the bank and back to our claim before someone stakes it as theirs."

Essie waited until the riders cleared the alley before relaxing her curled fingers and releasing her grip on the pistol. She waved. "Glad that's settled, CD."

He grinned, accentuating the lines in his weathered face. "Howdy, Essie. I brought you some interesting mail pieces today."

A sharp breath caught in her throat. Two fingers latched over her lips as she buttoned off the impending gasp at the mention of exciting mail. Heat burnished her flesh, rushing in through the barely-shaded opening, but mostly from the excitement of the morning and the promise Cyrus made about the sack's contents. Essie exhaled and calmed her voice. "Oh? How would you know what I'd find interesting?"

CD jumped onto the porch boards. He pointed to the boxy corners forming a shape the canvas couldn't hide. "This here package is special."

Essie lifted her chin and retracted her fingertips mid-reach. "All the mail is special, CD. You ought to know that by now. Besides, what right you got snooping?"

Laughing, he dropped the mail sack just inside the back door to Wylder Post Office. "Weren't snooping. I had to hold the coach as the train conductor raced toward me. He said this here package came from France and had to get to Wylder on the next stage."

Essie's heart thumped an erratic beat. *France? That is certainly unusual. Who in Wylder would be getting such a special package?* Her curiosity pounded its rhythm in her mind. Still, she wished to appear calm. To hide her trembling, she clasped her hands together. CD's taunts were good-natured. He knew how much she loved unique mail, especially if coming from faraway places—places she'd likely never see but could hold something from them in the palm of her hand and play an integral part in connecting sender and recipient.

Shrugging and loosening her tightly intertwined fingers, she cast her gaze beyond his head and shaded her eyes with one palm. The gesture wasn't due to the sunlight, but to prevent CD from seeing the excitement that she felt certain glowed from them. "Well, if'n that package is so important, I guess we'd better stop jawing about it and get to the business of its delivery."

CD laughed louder. "That's right, you better, and I better get over to the saloon before my mouth turns inside out. Sure is dry for June."

"Not at the saloon. Betsy'll fix you right up." She waved, making a point of having her arm in the air—and not on the mail sack—when he turned to step off the porch and into the side alley.

Waving back, he shot her one last glance. " 'Til next time, Essie."

Closing the door with no particular haste, she made sure the latch caught before snatching the bag and dragging it into the back chamber. Essie held her breath. *Who is getting such a special package?*

Chapter 5

The back chamber had once served the bank as a vault. Its location was ideal for sorting the contents of the mail sacks so that the public never saw the disorganized calamity of strewn mail pieces laced onto and between one another. Essie recalled her mother's strict lessons of keeping a pleasant appearance. *Am I rebelling against those teachings with Gus? Is that why I've allowed her to float around untethered?*

She pushed the thoughts from her mind and dumped the sack's contents into a hamper. Dust motes sprang to life in the dim light filtered through the back chamber's single window that was too high and too small for anyone to crawl through or to give off much illumination. Since the package had gone in last, it slid out first, the remaining items falling atop it.

Essie bit her lip, and her pulse quickened. She touched the cards, letters, newspapers, and packages from far-off places—a four-by-six postcard to the Wylders from Anna in New York, an official-looking envelope addressed to Anastasia West, two issues each of the *Laramie Daily Sentinel* and *Cheyenne Daily Sun*, and—finally—a package wrapped in brown paper and tied with black ribbon.

"Grosgrain," she whispered. She couldn't recall ever seeing such a fancy adornment used to secure a parcel's wrapping when most folks used plain beige string. Essie stroked its ribbing, feeling the slightly raised bumps of weft against warp, and studied the handwriting in curled and strangely-shaped letters bearing long flourishes. She traced the thickly-applied ink—the kind that dried without the use of a blotter—with a fingertip: *Mlle. Francine Lacroix c/o of M. Pierre Lacroix at the Vincent House Hotel and Restaurant, Wylder Street, Wylder, Wyoming Territory, America.* In the upper left corner, the same artistic scribbling noted it was from *Mme. Caroline Reboux, 9, Avenue Matignon, Paris, France.*

A sharp inhalation whistled off her lips, and she mumbled under her breath as she exhaled. "Paris, France." *What would seeing such a city be like?* Closing her eyes, she envisioned the things she'd read about Paris' wide, tree-lined streets, Notre Dame Cathedral's spires, and the sprawling buildings with slate roofs.

For a moment, she couldn't feel her feet or the wooden floor perched above the prairie dirt and sagebrush that accounted for the biggest part of Wyoming Territory. Estelle Baumgardner had never been farther than Fort Laramie to the north and Cheyenne to the east, but in her mind, she traveled the world, and each item dumped from the mail sack aided in that imaginary journey.

The sound of the door slamming snapped her to attention. She glanced up in time to catch the slender figure of her only child rushing in through the back entrance. A second hinge squeal indicated another entry from the door in the front. Essie reluctantly abandoned the mysterious package that plunged her into another country and culture. Her reality was more demanding than anything she conjured in her mind. Full responsibility for protecting both her child and her position weighed on her slim shoulders. Swiping palms against her thick skirt, she knocked off the dust and rounded the corner.

In a Stetson and brushed-leather coat, a tall, bearded man groped Augusta's shoulders. Fringe hung from his forearms, filling the space between them. In a breathy voice, the man mumbled. "Gus? Is that you, or are my eyes playing tricks on me?"

Essie was in no mood to allow such familiar handling despite the shock in the man's tone. With the derringer still in her pocket for reassurance, she snatched the loaded Winchester she kept beneath the counter for just such an occasion. Lifting it, she steadied the barrel against the cottonwood countertop. Its initial fuzziness was polished smooth with plenty of sanding and oil. "Unhand my daughter, sir, while you still got hands."

Before he responded, the front door pushed open again. A man's silhouette filled the held-ajar opening as he swept a glance over the scene. Backlit from the outer sunlit street, the man practically glowed. His top hat shaded his facial features, but his clothing—fine woolen trousers and coat with tails—indicated he was a man of some means. More than that, they reiterated he was the man from the train, the one who'd raced to the street the previous morning when she'd prevented Nancy's fall, and he'd stopped her from falsely accusing her of causing it.

"*Mon Dieu,*" he exclaimed, staring at Essie. "*Monsieur* Douglas, what have you done?"

The man's voice echoed through the opened

entryway, across the front room, and through Essie's ears until wedging in her brain where she could make sense of his foreign-sounding accent. He was not from Wylder—that much was certain. Essie fought the effects of his charm, cutting her gaze to the man whose palms still rested on her daughter's shoulders. She cocked the Winchester, readying it to shoot if forced. "Now, sir."

The man in the fringed jacket seemed in a trance. He blinked and shuddered. "Daughter? I beg your pardon, madam." He lifted his hands, but they hovered over her.

Trembling, he looked like he intended to bestow blessings upon Gus. Essie had seen Reverend Stillwater use the same stance right before he baptized a parishioner in the name of the Father, Son, and Holy Ghost. But she didn't think this man was here for righteous purposes. "Pardon granted. Now state your business." She kept her Winchester trained on him in the event he made a sudden movement or answered incorrectly.

He blinked. "I thought for a moment he was—I mean she was—Gus Baumgardner."

Augusta Baumgardner lifted her hat, and a single, long, plaited braid uncoiled from around her head like a blonde snake. "But I am Gus Baumgardner, sir. Well, that's what people around these parts call me anyway. My full name is Augusta, after my papa, Augustus Baumgardner."

The man's fingers reached for her chin, but a mere quarter inch from her face, he pulled them back toward his palm and refrained from making contact. His mouth formed a dark hole as it gaped open. "Augustus

Baumgardner was your papa? *The* Augustus Baumgardner who rode with the Pony Express?"

Essie shuddered from the stranger's over-familiarity. She'd read about trickery men sometimes used to get close to widows and their young daughters. The newspapers she received and the alerts for the post office walls mentioned it more than once. "You best get on about your business here. I've no time for useless gabbing."

A smile sliced across his face, separating his heavy mustache from his long, reddish-blond beard. His eyes glinted, and he stabbed at his chest with one forefinger. "I'm Vic."

His tone implied she should recognize him, but she shrugged. Besides seeing him at the train station on the previous Sunday when he collected the strange couple at the platform, she could not recall ever having laid eyes on the man. "I'm Estelle Baumgardner, the Postmistress of Wylder Post Office. So—"

He laughed. "Essie? Little Essie who married my old pal Gus in a prairie church house in the middle of a snowstorm?"

She lifted her chin. Each word made her more suspicious of his intentions. The church wasn't Catholic, but it had been perfect, despite her mother's wailings and subsequent disownment. "How would you know about that?"

The man in the doorway stepped forward, easing the door closed behind him. "Oh good, now we can relax, and you can"—he pointed to the gun still trained on the fringed man who called himself Vic—"lower your weapon."

As Essie's pupils adjusted to the reduced light, she

gradually recognized the top-hatted man's features. He had a twirled and waxed mustache and flesh that seemed naturally tanned. His dark eyes sought hers and held them as he spoke in his sing-song language. Still, she refused to be swayed by his handsomeness. "I'll lower my weapon, sir, when I feel comfortable in so doing."

He clapped his hands and laughed until his mustache wiggled. "This is brilliant, just brilliant. I cannot wait to tell my fellow Frenchmen how I saw the normally fearless Victor Douglas tremble in fear beneath a lady's wrath."

Two crucial details from his statement lodged in her brain—fellow Frenchmen and Victor Douglas. Both shed light on the morning's strangeness. "Wait. You're Vic Douglas?"

"That's what I've been trying to tell you. Although I do apologize for the rough handling of your…young daughter, I hope you can understand how I mistook her—clothing—and swagger for that of Gus Baumgardner. He couldn't have been much older when…" He swallowed.

Essie caught his questioning gaze and shook her head. She didn't need details, and they didn't need her to keep the gun aimed. She released the trigger and settled the weapon back beneath the counter.

Gus, however, brightened. "How'd you know him?"

The Frenchman glanced between them. "That is a story I would rather enjoy hearing myself. However, I can see the postmistress is busy, and we have come for mail services, no?"

Douglas sighed. "Yes, Lacroix."

The name jogged Essie's memory—the box which had arrived just that morning could be his or his wife's most likely. "Lacroix, is it, as in Pierre and Francine?"

A smile cut into his cheeks. "Have you met Francine?"

Blushing at the memory of how she'd groped the package, felt the ribbon, and traced the ink strokes with her fingertip, she glanced into his sparkling eyes and guiltily replied. "I'm afraid I've not had the pleasure of meeting your wife, Mr. Lacroix."

Lacroix laughed and laid a long-fingered hand to his cheek. "Dear lady, like you, I have a lovely daughter whose identity is often mistaken. It aches me to tell you I am a widower since winter before last."

Essie's pulse quickened, and her heart fluttered. Lacroix was undoubtedly the single, most sophisticated man she'd ever met. That he'd found the one link they might share, the one particular thing which they had in common, threaded them together. To hide her excitement, she pulled her postman's cap low on her forehead, smashing her hair to her scalp, and professionally engaged her mind. "Can you verify your Wylder address?"

"*Mais bien sur*, but of course. Francine and I are staying at the Vincent House Hotel and Restaurant on Wylder Street. She is expecting a package from Paris."

"Thank you. I'll just be a moment." Essie reluctantly stepped away to retrieve the item.

"Paris? Like France?"

Gus's excited voice trilled in her absence.

"*Oui, mademoiselle*, the one and only, is it not?"

Douglas's deep chortle indicated he'd finally collected his wits.

"Not so, I'm afraid. There's a little town in Texas named Paris."

"As beautiful as our fair city?" Lacroix raised his voice an octave.

Essie listened to the exchange from the back chamber while she cradled the box addressed to his daughter. Lacroix's accent was the loveliest she'd ever heard. Squeezing her eyelids, she imagined a cacophony of similar-sounding voices chattering incessantly near a little hat shop on a Parisian street lined with chestnut trees. The fallen leaves carpeting the cobblestone walkway muffled the sound of footsteps carrying the boxed hat to the Parisian version of her post office in Wylder—only the season was spring. The leaf litter would be long gone. Every mile between was another thread weaving them together in life's great tapestry. Although she was thrilled to have the man from the train standing before her, she regretted parting with the package so soon.

"What's it like in Paris? Is it like Wylder?"

Gus's curious voice shattered Essie's daydream. Her heart palpitated.

Douglas chuckled. "I don't believe Paris is like anything you or I can imagine, little Gus."

"Nonsense," Lacroix interjected.

Essie gathered her strength. She caressed the grosgrain once more and reluctantly stepped forward with the package. "For you, Mr. Lacroix. I trust you will see to it that your daughter receives it."

Lacroix reached for the item. His fingertips brushed Essie's.

The movement was subtle and swiftly fleeting, but it lingered against her skin. Her fingers quivered. A current, like a lightning bolt, seized her entire body. She gasped and froze.

Pierre Lacroix snapped his hands back to his sides without the package for which he'd reached.

Heat fused her palms to the box. As her gaze met Pierre Lacroix's, she swallowed. The brief connection ignited her flesh and wormed through her veins like a pox.

Nodding, he grinned. "You may ask her yourself at dinner Thursday evening if you would be so kind as to accept my poor offering. It is the least I can do for the person who has taken such pains to see my daughter's new hat is delivered post-haste."

Gus's gaze swept across the Frenchman. "Hat? From France? I suppose she hasn't met our hatmaker yet."

Lacroix bowed. "I would very much like for you to help Francine with these introductions, *n'est pas*?"

"Nest pa? What's a nest pa?" She answered her own question. "Oh, that's you. Like a mama hen, you're a nest pa."

Essie laughed along with the others in the small office. She wasn't sure what he meant either but didn't think it was Gus's interpretation. She opened her mouth to reply to Lacroix's invitation, and the door once again squeaked open, revealing the face of a girl.

She looked about Gus's age, although it was hard to tell beneath the large hat and layered gown. Pea-green silk layers, with lighter green fringe draping the hem, and an emerald lace overlay creeping up her neck and washing over the bustled back that dusted the floor surrounded her. A silk flower garden adorned her turned-up-on-one-side Gainsborough hat, and feathers poked from the brim as though birds nested within it. A long, green ribbon trailed off the back and swept her shoulder when she turned her head, which she did to stare at her father.

"Papa, what is taking so long? The carriage is stifling." Her gaze swept across him and onto the brown paper-wrapped parcel. As she raised a gloved hand to her mouth, her previously hooded eyes widened and sparkled like two amethyst stones. "*Madame* Redoux. Paris. It is for me. It is my hat, Papa."

He wiggled a long finger back and forth. "*Oui, cherie*. But…"

Scampering feet hit the porch, and Clyde Hartshorn pushed through the not-yet closed door. "I'm sorry, Douglas. I tried to keep my eye on her, just like you told me." He held out a dripping dipper. "She said she was thirsty, and I scooped water from the well."

Lacroix took the dipper by its long handle with his middle finger and thumb. His pinkie angled oddly. "*Merci,* young Clyde. But we are just about to finish with our business here and will take refreshment at the hotel's restaurant."

Gus, hands on hips, glared at the two young people who'd just entered. She ground her teeth, then knotted her brows until they formed one shelf across her forehead. "Clyde," she hissed. "What are you doing? I thought you's busy and couldn't ride during the day."

He jerked a thumb at Francine. "What do you call this? I'm watching her, I guess."

"Watching her do what?" she screeched.

Essie balanced the box in one hand and tugged her daughter's arm with the other. "Come along, Gus."

Gus stomped a booted foot. "Not before Clyde

explains what he's doing with that French powder puff instead of practicing for the Independence Day show at a decent hour."

Francine bristled. Her mouth puckered. "Powder puff?

Victor Douglas snickered behind his hand. "Well, it seems we have a little explaining to do, Pierre. Shall we make Thursday's reservation at the hotel restaurant for six—three youths and three adults?"

Clyde grimaced. "What about me?"

"I meant you as one of the youths," Vic added, "but I guess you're an adult now."

He lifted his chin. "I'm nineteen. That's a full man, ain't it?"

Gus's bottom lip drooped. She placed a booted foot behind Clyde's leg. "You ain't answered me yet."

Clyde's knee bent with the threat. He paused and glanced toward Victor. "You gonna—"

Victor chewed his lip and stared at Gus. He mumbled something, but it was not discernable.

Gus appeared more irritated by the second. She inched her shoulders upward as she maintained her balance on one foot before pushing the one directly behind Clyde's knee with added force. "Time's up."

As his leg buckled, Clyde wobbled. "Dagnabit, Gus. Douglas paid me to make sure nobody bothered Miss Lacroix."

Gus snagged her bottom lip with her teeth and dragged it inward. She motioned toward Francine. "How would anybody get close enough to bother her? She's carrying a full poker table behind her."

Francine twisted her head and peered over her shoulder before snapping a narrow gaze at Gus. "Table?

This is called a bustle, you barbarian, and it is the height of fashion. Just ask—"

Laughing, Gus turned toward Francine. "Well, I don't know about fashion, but I'd say it is about the height of the hitching post."

Pierre Lacroix grinned until his eyes sparkled. "Such spirited children we have, *Madame* Baumgardner. I can hardly wait to hear more of their lively banter." He shoved the dipper at Clyde and took his daughter by the arm. "Come along, Francine."

She snapped her focus onto Gus and narrowed her lids but did her father's bidding.

Essie found Francine's mannerisms comical. She fidgeted until her garments' lace, fringe, and silk layers rubbed grouse-like with her weight-shifting. Her squawking at her father in their strange language sounded like a barnyard goose. Although spoken too fast for Essie to isolate sounds, every syllable seemed to jump off the one before it and then run head-on smack into the next. With her head down and a smile tugging her lips, she listened until the door closed behind them and blocked the sounds.

Victor Douglas swept a glance across Augusta before grabbing Clyde by the nape of the neck. "You, too, lad." He chuckled and relaxed his weight on an elbow against the counter.

Clyde stumbled, and the dipper clanked against the floorboards. "Tarnation, Douglas."

The door creaked ajar, and Lacroix stepped back through them. "*Merci,* but it appears in the light of Madame Baumgardner's beauty, I forgot the reason for my visit."

Essie lost feeling in her feet and hands, and her

heart fluttered. She wondered if all her blood rushed to her core to protect her. Staring, she waited for him to explain the reason.

He gestured to the box. "The package, dear lady? It is for Francine, no?"

Looking down, Essie suddenly realized she still held the box from Paris, France, likely for the last time. It wasn't hers except to tend for a few moments. Her fingertips brushed the edge of the ochre postage stamps with two cherubs clasping hands over a globe dotting the upper right corner. Beneath them were the words *Republique Francaise.*

Pierre cleared his throat. "Do you collect the postage stamps, *Madame*?"

Essie lifted her gaze and met his curious stare. She passed him the package and shook her head. "Collect? No, I mean, I do have a few, but none from so far away."

Lacroix peeled a knife from his pocket and popped the blade from its sheath. He edged its pointed tip beneath a corner on one of the stamps. "Would you care to keep these as a reminder of our delightful meeting?"

"Oh...I...shouldn't...I couldn't." Even as she turned down the Frenchman's offer, she salivated at the prospect and swallowed her anticipation.

His mustache wiggled, and he cut the paper wrapping's corner edge from the box. "It is an honor to know such a humble French symbol will accompany that which began with your dear husband's Pony Express rides."

Essie held the paper-backed stamps in the palm of her hand. "French symbol?"

"*Pax et Mercur*—the Greek legends of Peace and

Commerce worldwide." He pointed to their clutched fingers over the interpretation. "Without *Pax*, *Mercur* cannot occur around the world."

Victor Douglas released the counter upon which he'd been leaning and pushed upright. "Well, now, my French friend, with sweet talk such as that, I can see why your country considers you an international ambassador. But as it happens, I've got a little something I believe the dear postmistress and her, umm, daughter, will equally appreciate. Wait here." He tapped the countertop with his palm, which thudded against the cottonwood.

Gus raced after him. "I'll just be keepin' Clyde company."

Essie closed her fingers around the gift. Somewhere in the near past, the stamps waited in a French version of her post office. Perhaps the stamps had lain untended in the Parisian millinery shop cupboard, beneath a layer of brown paper wrapping and spools of ribbon and thread. She wondered what it smelled like in the hat store and if they sipped wine while they tacked adornments and frills to the brims.

"...quite appropriate, would not you agree?"

She blinked and nodded, snapping back into Wylder Post Office from her imaginary romp through the city streets in France. "Appropriate? Yes, of course."

"I suggested to the planning board that I could assist in the design of a newly minted stamp for the World's Fair—or as we say—International Exposition. But alas, such an endeavor requires time and patience, and I grew weary of the exercise." He shrugged.

Her mind whirled with possible scenarios, none of

which she thought to be accurate. "What is it like—the fair—I mean..." The door squeaked open, and she glanced toward it.

Douglas stomped through lugging a set of dusty saddlebags that had a flapped pocket attached to either corner of a long, thick, leather strap. He nudged past Lacroix and slapped it onto the counter. Rubbing his palms together, Douglas focused on Essie's face. "You're going to love this, Essie. It's his...it's Gus's."

Essie blinked at the transition from Pierre's manners and French life to the boisterous Victor Douglas and the item he'd just flung atop the cottonwood. "Gus's what?"

Victor pointed toward the crackled saddlebags. "That's Gus's saddlebags from Pony Express. See?" He pulled up the cut-out in the center. "This fit over the saddle horn." He indicated the four flapped pockets— one for each corner—although one flap was sliced open. "These here *mochilas* contained the mail. This hook through the flap allowed us to lock 'em. I reckon that's why this one is damaged."

She touched the weathered leather. Although the shape and form tugged a memory from a nearly forgotten past, she recalled it differently. "I don't understand how you think it belonged to my husband."

Douglas's mouth dropped open. "I took it off Yellow Hair, an Indian I claimed during my fights with Custer against Sitting Bull's Lakota and the Cheyenne. He had to have been the fellow who struck down your husband, and you'll be happy to know I sent him into the afterlife and recaptured it. I've been hauling it around with me ever since. Might even lure some more of Sitting Bull's tribe just to take 'em out for what they did." He shook his head and stared off into space.

As she didn't want to damage them, Essie carefully laid the stamps into a wooden box she kept for such treasures. Pulling up her spine another inch, she snatched the odd leather piece and strolled to the door. She glanced toward Pierre and inclined her head. "Would you be so kind?"

Lacroix scrambled to do her bidding, snatching the latch and giving it a good tug. "*Mais bien sur*, of course."

With the saddlebags across her forearms, she stomped across the porch and tossed it into the street without concern for where it landed. Wagon wheels and horse hooves could pulverize it for all she cared. Slapping her palms, she turned in time to catch the surprised faces of Lacroix and Douglas.

Victor's cheeks reddened, and he scowled. "What the devil?" He raced into the dirt. Lifting the saddlebags as gently as a newborn, he then jumped left, dodging the approaching carriage just in time. "Essie Baumgardner, explain yourself," he barked.

Essie thought Victor appeared more upset by her treatment of his relic than nearly being trampled in the street. *He would be*. She harrumphed and strolled back into the post office, calling over her shoulder as she went. "There's been enough killing round these parts. I'm not proud of anything that got my husband killed, especially if taken off another dead man." She turned in the doorway to give him one last glower.

Douglas's brows furrowed. "But Essie, the dead man was an Indian who killed Gus."

"No matter," she stormed and slammed the door. Only when she was back behind the counter did she realize her behavior was probably not one bespeaking well of her position. The western territories offered opportunities for women in a few typically male-oriented positions. Getting this appointment was no small victory, and she needed to be careful of her temper. But nothing set her to flaming like talk of further retribution of the Natives, not even Nosey Nancy's insults and threats.

She pushed an escaped tendril off her forehead and glanced up to see both men back in the office. Pointing, she jabbed her finger in his direction to accentuate his fair warning. "Augusta didn't get to know her daddy. Plenty of other babies born to the Arapaho, Lakota, and Cheyenne didn't get to know theirs either. It isn't fair to them to keep this going and will only embitter the next generations."

Lacroix and Douglas exchanged looks. "But—" Douglas protested.

Essie held up a hand. "No buts. I won't hear of it. I won't allow it. If it hadn't been for Tarak and Meadowlark…" When she thought of their kindnesses, she teared, and the weakness such tearfulness dredged stoked her anger.

Victor's nostrils flared. "What about Augustus? What about honoring his name and his memory for his daughter?"

Her face flushed hotter. Air ceased circulating, and the high collar nearly strangled her. If the newspapers' headlines were accurate, the man had a reputation for more than his theatrical talents and killed both animals and humans. "If you want to honor Augustus Baumgardner, Pony Express rider killed in the tour of duty, put him in your show. Put friendly Indians helping their neighbors in your show. Save the buffalo instead of killing 'em into extinction. Do something constructive instead of destructive. Do something for peace and commerce."

Victor Douglas stood with his mouth agape, like he'd stared at Augusta with his palms on her shoulders.

Essie opened the little wooden box where she'd just deposited the French stamps. She held out one to Lacroix. "May I?"

His eyes twinkled. He lifted one brow. "Dear Postmistress Baumgardner, they are yours to use as pleases you."

His tone indicated respect, and Essie nodded. "Thank you." Snatching Victor's palm, she dropped one of the treasured postage stamps from Paris, France, into it. "*Pax* and *Mercur*," she snapped. "Peace and commerce. Learn it."

Victor Douglas stared at the stamp. His face paled, but he didn't reply. He gripped it and nodded before strolling from the post office.

Pierre winked and followed. Before the door shut behind him, he tapped Victor's shoulder. "What a woman," he uttered.

Essie's head swirled with random thoughts. *What does he mean by that? Have I impressed the Frenchman? What about Victor Douglas? How had he remembered my wedding with such detail? And Augustus? What would he think of me if he knew how my heart fluttered every time Lacroix smiled?*

Chapter 6

Thursday, June 20, 1878

Two days later, Essie arose to an empty loft. Despite Gus's anger with Clyde, she'd obviously risen on Thursday—just as she had the previous days—to meet him for rehearsal in the wee early hours. One thing was certain—no amount of frustration would keep Augusta from her trick riding practice.

Although hankering for a bun and a cup of Cissy Arkwright's delicious coffee, Essie didn't want to tell anyone about the dinner invitation and feared it would spew like water from a freshly-tapped well. She ached to talk about Pierre, to say his name, and feel it roll off her tongue. When nobody was close, Essie whispered, "Pierre Lacroix." Then she giggled. The day before, she'd repeated it many times as she stared into the distance and imagined Parisian streets.

She'd hardly slept since the handsome and sophisticated foreigner requested she and Gus join him for a meal at The Vincent House. Of course, the invitation meant nothing. Pierre Lacroix would soon leave Wylder, and everything would return to normal, including Nancy's threats.

As Essie slipped downstairs, she sighed. Whatever respite lingered in the Frenchman's presence would dissipate with his departure. Despite its physical and emotional cost, she couldn't afford to overlook Augusta's education. Lifting the unfinished letter, she read the completed section, took a breath, and dipped her pen.

If Augustus were here, Augusta would receive a better education. But he is not, and I must work for my living. Please do not think me ungrateful.

Essie lifted her wrist and exhaled. She glanced out the window at the stirring townspeople until focusing on one potential customer.

Phineas Atwater crossed the street, his hat brim pumping over his forehead as it flopped in the morning breeze. His arms dangled by his sides.

Her heart palpitated. Even though Phineas' hands appeared empty, she watched his movements and expected a pivot at any moment.

Phineas continued on his way, bypassing the post office door.

Essie held her breath until the possibility of his doubling back slimmed. When no other potential customer strolled toward her corner, she continued writing the letter.

I am thankful to be Wylder's postmistress and have no idea what I would do without the job. Although Wyoming Territory is generous with its opportunities, a woman alone in the west has few choices, and

Attuned to every noise, Essie listened as traffic increased outside her window—clomping horses, carriage wheels, distant laughter, and boots against the porch boards. She lifted her head and stowed the pen. Essie snatched her vest and clamored to her position behind the counter just as the door hinges squealed.

Fletcher Wylder poked his head around the door's

edge. "Essie? You open?"

She waved. "Naturally, Fletcher. Come on in."

He pushed through and ambled to the counter. "Just checking to see if I got anything on Tuesday's coach. I meant to drop by yesterday, but since Wednesdays are slow, I caught up on deliveries instead."

"Just a moment." Essie retrieved the postcard from his sister. "Here you go."

He reached for the mail piece. The door squeaked, and Fletcher turned toward the sound. His hand froze in midair.

Still gripping Fletcher's postcard, Essie peered at Anastasia West as she stood in the opening.

The hotel owner glanced from Fletcher to Essie. She lifted a hand in greeting before hastening away.

"Anastasia—wait." Essie tossed the card toward Fletcher and snatched the letter in the official-looking envelope. She rushed toward the door. "I'm sorry, Fletcher, but she might be looking for this."

Falling into step, Fletcher accompanied the postmistress to the street. He scratched his chin. "Well, ain't that odd? Where do you reckon she went?"

Essie craned her neck left and right, peeking around the porch columns and the wagons tethered to the hitching post. "She must have business elsewhere and just remembered it. I find her a bit forgetful lately."

Fletcher tipped his hat. "She'll be back directly. G'day, Essie."

Earl Hanson's boots hit the porch with a cadence particular to him. His measured steps comingled with his gun belt's slight squeak as he walked.

He touched his hat's brim with a fingertip. "Miss

Essie. Fletcher."

Essie braced herself with the palm of one hand against a post. "Earl, good to see you."

Fletcher stuffed the postcard into his inner vest pocket. "Howdy, Sheriff. How's your guest over at the jail?"

Sherriff Hanson sneered. "He's getting on my nerves. I can't quite figure him out, but I'd be willing to bet this isn't his first brush with crime."

Essie fingered the letter to Anastasia and raked another glance at the few doorways into which she could have disappeared. "That was my take on him, too. He's a little too cocky, isn't he?" Sighing, she caught Earl's eye. "By the way, I looked through the wanted posters. There's nothing that fits his description or method, so he must have an accomplice."

Earl nodded. "I got a gut feeling he isn't working alone, but that's all it is, for now. I'm heading over to the telegraph office to broadcast his profile and don't want to leave him alone too long."

Fletcher patted his back. "I'll walk with you. See you later, Essie."

"Bye, Fletcher, Earl." She marched back toward the post office entrance.

Sheriff Hanson caught her elbow. He leaned close. "Be on the lookout for anything suspicious, Essie. I'll stroll back by a little later."

Essie didn't linger on the street. She returned the letter to Anastasia West to its spot in the divider and herself to the letter meant for her cousin. As her thoughts wandered back to the posters, she tapped the table and sought the words whose meaning might nail her request of Blanche. They failed her. She couldn't shake the feeling the posters held the answer to the sheriff's dilemma.

She snatched the most recent ones from the nail and looked over them once more. Nothing fit the stranger in Wylder's jail, and she couldn't stop pondering on how close he came to succeeding against Tarak and Meadowlark. Enraged, she shook while the hands on her pocket watch rotated to five and twelve. *Finally, five o'clock.*

Essie rose and walked to the entrance, opened the door, and flipped the sign to *Closed*. She dragged the bar into the steel latch against the wall and clamped an additional rod over the edge, preventing anything or anyone from moving it and getting access to the mail. Slipping through the inner chamber, Essie similarly secured the back door and then climbed the stairs to the living quarters above the post office. All thoughts of John Smith, the wanted posters, and Anastasia West's odd behavior dropped with each step she took to the loft. She replaced them with those of the pending dinner engagement.

In the hovering late-day heat, sweat beaded her forehead. The closed shutters kept out the dust but also the breezes. Compromising, she raised the window and pushed on the shutters until air flowed into the room. Turning, she yanked the cap from her head and lifted the tendrils stuck to her neck until relieved and slightly cooled. She didn't recall seeing Gus during the past half hour. "Gus? You up here?"

No reply.

Essie shrugged. "Guess not." She almost giggled for speaking aloud when nobody was there to hear her voice. Essie couldn't remember the last time she'd been as excited to meet someone for dinner.

Tipping the pitcher, she felt no accompanying jostle. Even the ewer was empty. She laid a finger to her cheek. "Hmmm…"

The pounding at the back door wafted to the opened window—*bang, bang, bang.*

Essie tipped the shutters farther and leaned out, noticing a pair of precariously balanced buckets hanging from a pole on her daughter's slender shoulders. "Gus?"

Gus lifted her chin and looked up. "Ma, you locked me out. Open the door before I spill the bathwater."

"Bathwater?" Essie shouted.

"Hush." She tilted her head to the left and then right. "Hurry."

Essie chuckled as she attacked the stairs, unlatched, and yanked open the back door. "Here, let me help."

Squatting, Gus plopped the buckets onto the porch and removed the pole from the handles. "Get 'em inside quick—before anyone sees."

Essie took one and half-dragged, half-carried it into the back chamber where the galvanized tub rested against the wall and out of her way. She pushed the mail hamper into a corner and upended it. As she poured in the first container's contents, she swished her hand through the water, creating waves. "This is quite cool."

Gus dropped the second bucket beside the tub and stowed the pole near the stored churn before bolting the latch. "Turn around, but don't go anywhere. Once I get in the tub, I want you to pour that over my head."

Although Essie turned, she grumbled. "I should be upstairs getting myself ready, not down here playing water games with you." She reached for her pocket watch but realized neither it nor the vest was there.

"Okay, now."

Essie took a cup from the nearby stand and dipped it into the bucket. She pivoted toward her daughter. As she poured its contents over Gus's head, she complained. "Oh, for goodness sake…"

Gus gasped, and her teeth chattered. She hugged her knobby knees and craned her neck over them until she formed a human ball. "More, a-a-and h-h-hand me the s-s-soap."

Essie saw no point in arguing. A sliver from a bar rested in a dish near the pitcher and ewer. Its rosemary and sage scent had nearly faded, but ground, green bits still peppered the remnant. "Should I even ask what has led to your sudden desire for cleanliness? I normally have to threaten you with hiding your boots just to get you dipped beneath water once a week."

Snatching the soap, Gus scrubbed her face. She dropped the soapy bit and feverishly unplaited her hair until it hung down her back in bends and curls from its frequent braiding. She cut a glance at her mother. "I w-wash-up two or three t-times a day, but…" Gus stopped talking and lowered her gaze.

Essie knew her daughter's moods. *Time be damned; something's wrong.* As it no longer mattered what the Frenchman thought of her appearance, she pulled a stool to the edge. Augusta was her main focus—had been since the moment she first felt her move inside her belly. She was all that was left of her daddy on the earth, despite Douglas's braying about saddlebags and rogue Indians. They were only protecting themselves, their families, and property, just as she protected Gus. "But what?"

Augusta continued cradling her knees to her chest while cutting a cursory glance at her mother. She ceased shivering but rocked until she splashed the water. "Did you see how he looked at her?"

Her daughter's voice was soft and low, and Essie couldn't determine her meaning. "Who?"

Gus straightened her spine and slapped a palm against the side of the tub. As she set her jaw and narrowed her eyes, whatever meekness underlined her mood dissipated. "Clyde, that's who. He chased after that French puffball, bowing and scraping like she was the Queen of France."

Essie almost laughed but refrained as she knew how her daughter would perceive it. She would never laugh at her, but with her and at the situation. At least she now knew worrying was unnecessary. Her daughter's was a normal reaction to becoming a woman. "You like Clyde, don't you?"

She wrinkled her nose and blew out a breath. "He's all right, I guess."

"And you want to show him that you can smell just as nice as the foreigner and that you know him better than he knows himself."

"Well…" She stopped rocking and cocked her head to one side. "Can I do that so he notices I'm a lady and not just another horse handler?"

Essie placed her hands on her knees. She pushed herself off the stool, carried it to its rightful place, and stowed it beneath the sorting ledge. Returning to the tub's edge, she handed Gus a soft flannel. "Wrap this around you and come on upstairs. We've both got some primping to do. We can empty the water in the morning. I'm taking what's left in the bucket for my birdbath."

As Essie understood Gus's shyness with her nakedness, she didn't wait. She climbed the steps and retrieved one of the dresses she'd sewn for her daughter in her spare time. It was a simple, pale blue floral cotton with a flounce hem, three-quarter sleeves, a soft neckline with a tatted lace collar, and a matching bonnet. Laying it out, she stood back and gazed at the shape it formed against the quilted bed covering. Nothing about the ensemble resembled Gus.

She stripped away the bonnet, imagining the ubiquitous cowboy hat and boots topping and grounding the outfit. Maybe, if she didn't insist on proper head and footwear, Gus would go along with wearing the dress. While she waited, she emptied the bucket into the pitcher and poured a little water into the ewer with soap scrapings.

With Gus's clothing laid out, she searched for something nice to wear, and for the first time, she regretted not having fashionable attire. Essie understood her daughter's angst better than she dared admit. Scratching through the trunk at the foot of her bed, she carefully tugged the choices from the container, beginning with a black mourning garment. The shape was as severe as the color, and it looked like something from the Civil War era with its thick collar buttoning high around the neck and complete lack of adornment on the sweeping skirt and tight bodice.

Her heart fluttered and then landed with a thud in her gut. Even her breath quickened, and her eyes watered. She held it to her chest as though hugging herself, recalling the last occasion on which she'd needed it—her father's quiet funeral in Laramie. With the reminders too sharp to be worn in happy times, she carefully laid aside the black.

She fumbled beneath an old quilt and retrieved her wedding dress. Her mother had warned her it was impractical, and she'd been correct. Moth holes pocked the white wool, and dark spots indicated tiny flyspeck stains, Despite those unsightly blemishes, she hugged it too, for vastly different reasons. The young girl who'd worn this dress and jacket had no idea of the heartache waiting inside a year. The day, though snowy and gray, had brought smiles and laughter, and they'd danced until dawn in an old barn with potbelly stoves giving off smoke and steaming tendrils from furiously boiling water kettles atop them. Memories swirled like fog from those lost years.

Augustus Baumgardner was a handsome man and one steady on his feet. He carried her around the straw-covered floor as gracefully as if they'd been in the Palace of Versailles. No amount of alcohol turned him sharp. He was tender and sweet, and no man since him—until now—left her giddy. With great care, regardless of the waning time, she wrapped it first in a sheet then in the quilt and laid it atop the mourning gown.

Only one garment remained in storage, as she wore the same twill skirts and plain blouses to the meeting house that she wore for work, with the placement of her vest and hat completing what she thought of as her uniform. She needed to amend that situation, but not today. Even if the color of the prairie dirt, her beige travel dress would have to do.

Gus stomped into their living quarters. Her gaze

swept to the floral gown.

Although she wrinkled her nose, she held it to her body and dropped the flannel wrap. Her lips pulled to one side and then the other. "Well…I suppose it'll do."

Essie donned the heavy broadcloth travel dress meant for withstanding the trials of dragging through dirty streets, over stagecoach steps, and across horse flesh. Sewn for service and not appearance, it was even plainer without the accompanying jacket, but the summer temperature was just too warm. She draped a blue shawl along her shoulders and pinned it with a cameo pendant—one of the few jewelry pieces she owned. As she caught her reflection in the spot-flecked mirror, Essie sighed. "Your dress is better than my option, so count your blessings."

Grabbing a hat—the most bodacious one she owned—she placed it atop her head and hoped it would deflect attention from the rest of her shabby clothing, although she thought it was still missing something. She rolled it around in her hands. Recollections of Francine's Gainsborough hat wafted to her, and she snatched a hat pin and ran it through one side, the crown, and back out the other. If the pin held, at least her hat would appear fashionable.

A set of eyes fell upon Essie as she crossed the room. She turned toward the mirror and laughed. They weren't eyes at all but the circular pattern on a peacock feather's tip protruding from a vase on the table beside the door. "Perfect," she mumbled and stuffed one into her folded brim. She snatched another and offered it to Gus. "One for you."

Augusta exhaled loudly through pursed lips. "Do I have to wear the bonnet?"

Essie quickly returned the feather, threading its pointed end into the collection first. "Of course not, and your everyday boots are fine, too."

Gus scratched her chin. "I didn't notice Francine's boots."

Essie held open the door. "That proves the point. Who's going to look at your feet when they have your lovely face upon which to gaze? Come along."

Augusta slipped on her boots and sighed. "Guess you're right. I didn't notice Clyde staring at her feet." She grabbed her hat from the hook by the door. "Do you want me to hitch Dumpling to the wagon?"

Essie imagined the spectacle Gus would make hitching her old mare to their plain carriage. It would then be like her to attach Lightning—Gus's rodeo horse—instead. "Not tonight, Augusta. The walk will do us good." Essie hoped her excitement at meeting Pierre Lacroix did not shine across her face. Just in case, she dipped her chin and proceeded with her pulse thundering against her veins.

Chapter 7

The walk to the Vincent House Hotel and Restaurant was charming. As businesses closed for the day, shutters snapped, and doors groaned. Townsfolk ambled into the street.

Essie nodded and called greetings to Finn Wylder, Chet Daniels, and Anastasia West.

Chet did a double-take and gasped. "Why, that's Gus."

Gus frowned. "What's that supposed to mean?"

Chet chuckled. "I didn't recognize you for a minute, that's all. I'm not sure I've ever seen you in a dress before. You look quite lovely."

Gus's frown turned to a smile, and she blushed.

Essie noticed but didn't respond. As the thought occurred that Augusta liked the compliment and wished to look attractive, she merely nudged her arm. "Come along, Gus."

As soon as she turned the corner, Essie saw Victor Douglas. He lounged against a column, pulling on a long cigar and exhaling its smoke in circular formations that retrained their shape for a few seconds before wafting toward her. The odor wasn't nearly as disagreeable as some she'd smelled over the years. As summer's heat enhanced everything's scents—good and bad—the aroma actually helped alleviate the stench of fresh horse dung.

Beside him, Pierre Lacroix stood at attention. His watchful gaze scanned the horizon until it locked onto her. He motioned for Victor.

Douglas clamped down on the cigar with his teeth, freeing his hands. He lifted one in a wave and used the other to nudge forward Lacroix.

Essie acknowledged the gesture with a slight nod. She wouldn't openly wave at a man from the street, much less two. She reached for her daughter's elbow but missed.

Head down, Gus swung her arms. She didn't react to the pair of men or the particular aromas.

"Augusta," Essie whispered.

She continued cranking her fists back and forth.

Essie wondered if the motion was the only thing keeping her daughter moving forward. She stretched out a palm, and finally caught her wrist as it flailed backward. "You can slow down now."

Gus pulled to a stop and twisted from the waist. She stared at Essie and wrinkled her nose. "Did you say something?"

Essie's assumption was correct. Augusta was lost in her head, planning some conversation or reliving a recent event. "I said you could slow down. We're here."

Augusta glanced to the porch where Douglas and Lacroix waited. "Where's Clyde?" She jerked her head back around. "He'd better not be lounging with that tea cake, or I'll…" She grimaced and puckered her lips.

Such behavior reminded Essie of her parenting failures. "Remember yourself, daughter. Scrapping over a boy shows poor taste. Besides"—she sighed—"I doubt Francine Lacroix and her father will be in Wylder for very long."

Gus kicked a pebble. "Oh, all right."

Lacroix strode down the steps. He gripped the jacket's lapel edges as he approached.

Victor Douglas stubbed the smoldering end of his cigar into the sand-filled urn before following Pierre into the street. His stride was longer than the Frenchman's, and he overtook him with ease. "Evening, ladies."

Essie paused, waiting for Lacroix to catch up. When he did, she caught both men in a single sweeping glance. "Good evening, gentlemen."

Pierre crooked an elbow and angled it toward her. "As we say in France—*Bonsoir*."

Although Essie had to reach up, she placed her hand atop his forearm. Even through the exquisite fabric, she felt his muscles twitch.

He paused, glanced down, and quickly looked away.

Essie fell into step beside him and motioned for Gus. "Come along, daughter."

Vic scrambled toward Augusta. He offered his arm in a gesture similar to Pierre's.

Gus stomped past him. "I'm not a child. I reckon I can climb the steps without someone holding my hand." She overtook them and stood, arms crossed, in the doorway.

Essie didn't know whether to giggle at Augusta's roughness or kick herself for not teaching her daughter womanly manners. She'd thought it best to allow the toughness Gus displayed to grow in place of tenderness, and now she wondered if she'd made the right choice in the child's upbringing. The letter to her cousin took on greater significance. If she sent Gus to Boston, even for a season, she'd have a better chance of securing a bright future. She couldn't think about it now.

Lacroix turned his head toward Victor. "Would you be so kind, *Monsieur* Douglas, as to hold the door?"

Pierre's accent washed over Essie like an auditory caress. She glanced at him. "Thank you."

He nodded and twirled his mustache.

Victor snatched his stogie from the urn and swiped its tip, knocking off the sand. He gripped the opposite end between his teeth and shoved the swinging door until his weight held it in place.

Gus marched through. She pushed up her hat brim and moved her head side to side as she scanned the lobby.

Pierre stepped behind Essie and placed a palm in the small of her back. "After you."

Although brief, the contact sent shivers to the nerve endings that raced along her spine and trailed off into a dozen spots until landing in her stomach with a flutter. She swallowed and sought something to say. Nothing immediately came to mind, so she merely inclined her head.

Essie distanced herself from the Frenchman. She needed space to regain her composure and feared Augusta might cause a scene if she spotted Clyde with Francine. Scanning the entry, she saw his lithe frame just inside the lobby.

Clyde leaned against the newel post on the sweeping staircase landing. With his head down, he picked at his fingernails with the tip of his pocketknife blade.

Augusta tugged at the dress, holding its hem away

from her boots as she lumbered over. "Hey, are you waiting for me, Clyde?"

Clyde jumped and pulled himself to attention as he motioned toward the staircase with the knife. "Vic told me to watch for Francine in the event she came down before y'all got here."

Laughter wafted from above, joining the clatter of footsteps and glasses knocking together. Pierre said something to someone, and despite Essie's usual joy at the sound of his melodic voice, she ignored him. At the mention of Francine's name, Essie listened in case she needed to intercede. She watched her daughter's posture as she released the handful of the skirt and planted her hands on her hips.

Augusta's lip twitched. "Luckily, we're here now."

Clyde sheathed the blade and shoved the knife into his pocket. "Right." He glanced toward the upstairs landing. "I suppose somebody oughta go tell her we can snag a table now."

Gus yanked off her hat and slapped it against her hip. "And I guess you're suggesting that somebody is you, which says you know which room is hers."

Essie heard every word loud and clear, as she was sure everyone within earshot also heard. She offered Lacroix a tepid smile.

Pierre placed a hand on Augusta's shoulder. "*Non, cherie.* I will retrieve my daughter. Young Clyde is merely standing guard." He jerked a thumb. "*Merci,* Clyde. You and Augusta may join *Monsieur* Douglas and *Madame* Baumgardner now. I will only be a moment."

Victor nudged Essie. "Uh…I was just wondering about the saddlebags. Were you serious about not wanting them back? Should I offer 'em to Augusta?"

Essie took a breath. Victor's comment was just the sort of reminder that took her mind off Pierre Lacroix. "Yes and no."

He grimaced. "What do you mean?"

Stabbing the meaty flesh of her inner palm with her gripped fingernails, Essie metered her words. "I was quite serious about having no use for the saddlebags, nor do I wish to burden Augusta with them."

"Burden?" He snapped. "They belonged to her daddy. I'd think having them back would be a comfort."

With Lacroix taking the steps at a decent clip and Augusta cornering Clyde, Essie had Victor's full attention. She cleared her throat to rid it of any lingering emotion. "I suppose I didn't make myself clear enough earlier. Let's say you gave 'em to Gus. Pretty soon, she'd start stewing over 'em. They'd remind her of the daddy she never had the chance to know. Maybe she'd become a little like you, and the itch to hate people for what they cost her would nudge out the affection for the ones who saved her and me in his absence."

His brows inched inward. "Hate? Who says I hate anybody?"

The laugh that escaped her edged on sarcasm. It didn't sound authentic to her, even. "I hope you do. I hope you aren't going around killing people for sport, same as you did the buffalo."

Vic's mouth puckered. "Sport? Maybe I killed them buffalo to feed both the army and the men working on the railroad."

She shrugged. "Maybe. Maybe not. I doubt the

railroad needed more'n four thousand huge bison, even to feed an army. Besides, rumor out here is that you sat in a rail car and mowed 'em down as they stood grazing the grasslands."

His face reddened. "What are you trying to say, Estelle Baumgardner? Are you insinuating I'm not honorable?"

A door slammed overhead. Essie switched her focus from Victor Douglas to the approaching sound of footsteps on the stairs. As suspected, Pierre Lacroix and his daughter wafted downward. She wanted to end the debate with Vic. "You said it, not me."

He drew his lips inward until his upper ate his lower and practically disappeared. Sulking, Victor practically ignored The Vincent House Hotel and Restaurant's staff.

Victor's lack of attention to the hotel employees appeared to have the opposite effect. The staff worked harder for his attention, bowing and scraping as if Lacroix and Douglas were royalty. They paid Essie little mind and gave Gus and Clyde even less attention. As she and Augusta rarely ate there, Essie didn't blame them. When she glimpsed their prices, she remembered why.

Douglas had been traveling with a theatre company and performing daring acts of pioneer bravery and recreating war battles all along the East Coast, so he was likely used to such overblown dinner costs. He was also something of a star, and he knew it. Although she'd read about his antics from various newspapers filtering through Wylder, she'd not laid eyes on him since the Pony Express days and wouldn't have recognized him in a rodeo poster, even if she'd been told he was in it.

A waiter threaded between Victor and Essie. "Can we get you anything, Mr. Douglas? A drink? A fresh cigar?" He held up a cardboard box and flipped back the lid.

Pushing away the offering, Victor shook his head.

Another attendant held out the latest edition of the *Cheyenne Daily Sun*. "Would you like to read while you wait? You might have some information about the robbery at the general store or—"

Pierre gasped. He turned toward the attendant and widened his eyes. "Robbery? Here?"

As though delighted to have piqued the Frenchman's interest, the employee unfolded the paper and held it up to him. "Not here—not in Wylder—but over in Cheyenne. There's been a rash of such crimes." He pointed to a line. "Says here they're offering a reward—"

Snatching the paper, Pierre stared at the print. "Wylder is an interesting town. I feel as though I am in one of Mssr. Douglas's performances, and it is brilliant." He twisted a section of his mustache between his thumb and forefinger.

The waiter returned and motioned for them to follow him. "This way." He marched into the dining room and stopped at a table large enough for six.

With the paper under one arm, Lacroix pulled out a chair for his daughter and another for Essie. Then he snagged and refolded the newspaper. Sighing, he held it out to the waiter. "How very swift you are. I was just getting interested—"

"You must keep it." He nudged it back to Pierre.

Curling it into a roll, Lacroix stuffed it into his coat

pocket. "You are most kind. When I return to Paris, I will be sure to tell everyone about the first-rate hospitality at this fine establishment in Wylder, and I would love to mention you by name."

The young man blushed. "It's Charles, s-sir…Charles Robinson. I th-thank you." Stammering, he backed from their table, nearly colliding with another employee.

While Victor's appeal mystified her, Essie fully understood how Pierre Lacroix and his daughter could charm everyone within sight or earshot. Even now, he sat bolt upright, confidence and pride oozing from his pores. His smooth, eloquent voice turned simple words into poetry, and the flickering lamplight sparked bright shards of brilliance in his eyes.

Francine's glamorous ensemble was so striking Essie could barely keep her gaze from its golden-hued skirt with a lacey overlay and bolero jacket with embroidery swirls mimicking vines. Her upswept chestnut mane curled around an arc-shaped, hat-like feature that sat firmly attached to her skull, with curls from her hair weaving over it and around it in a complementary fashion to the jacket's embroidery.

Gus flicked a glance over her. She lifted a finger and rotated it near Francine's head. "What did ya call that thing again?"

Francine poked out her bottom lip and pouted. She straightened the utensil edges until they were perfectly parallel. "Why would I tell you when you will just amuse yourself with the name?"

Gus shrugged. "Suit yourself. I only wanted to know so's I could remember what not to order over at the general store."

"The general store?" Francine hit the table's edge with her palm and the carefully-aligned spoon wobbled to the floor. "*Mais bien sur,* I doubt you will have access to anything as refined as this fascinator in your general store."

The waiter just identified as Charles returned with a clean spoon. In one coordinated movement, he laid it beside her knife and snatched the one from the floor.

Augusta snapped her fingers and jabbed Clyde in the side with her elbow. "Fascinator—that's it. I don't know why I can't remember. Guess it doesn't fascinate me all that much." She giggled.

Essie cut her eyes from one to the other of the girls. "Never mind about Augusta, Francine. I think it's lovely."

Francine brightened. "*Merci beaucoup, Madame* Baumgardner."

Pierre patted her hand. "Yes, thank you, dear lady. Nothing wounds a parent more than to hear disparaging remarks concerning a child, and nothing pleases one like a simple compliment."

Essie kicked Gus beneath the table and pulled an expression she hoped reinforced Pierre's statement.

Gus grimaced. "Oww," she yelled.

Turning over the menu, Essie both looked for something affordable and a diversion from Augusta's outburst. She pointed. "Oh, look, they have soup."

Pierre held out his hand. "With your permission, I would appreciate the opportunity to order for the table. I see several interesting things I wish to try and hope I can persuade you to allow me the honor, as a guest in your country, to taste all the flavors of your fine land."

Douglas tossed his menu. "Sure. Be my guest." He

scowled at Essie. "It's been recently inferred that my judgments aren't particularly sound anyway."

All heads swiveled toward Essie in the heat of Vic's gaze.

Essie plopped her menu on the table. "I don't believe I inferred anything. I merely stated the fact that it seems you are having difficulty accepting."

Pierre collected the menus and offered them to the waiter. "We'll have the cutthroat trout and quail eggs to start, porterhouse steaks—not overdone—with boiled potatoes and beans, next, your best cheese and bread, and…" He snatched a menu again and raked a glance across it. "Apple pie with a dollop of whipped cream."

The young man lifted his head from his notepad and stared. His mouth made a great O-shape as he motioned in a circle. "For each of you? You want all that apiece?"

Pierre winced. "Did I order incorrectly? I naturally mean for the table. We will each take the portion which pleases us."

Nodding, Charles continued to stare. "What do you mean by cheese? I might get some head cheese from the butcher."

Victor shook his head. "No. We'll not require such efforts. Just bring us your best butter and some hot bread." He tapped Pierre's arm. "Trust me on this one."

Charles held his pencil at a right angle to the pad. "Beverages?"

Pierre circled a finger and pointed toward the table center. "A nice white wine to start—a *cabernet blanc* perhaps. Then something stronger—*sauvignon*—"

Vic wiggled a finger back and forth. "A pitcher of beer, some lemonade for the ladies, and water for the table."

The young man mumbled beneath his breath, but he paused to stare at Francine before rushing to the kitchen.

Wrinkling his nose, Pierre fixed Victor in his gaze. "No wine? No cheese? *Sacre bleu…*"

Francine giggled. "Don't worry. Papa has excellent taste, for he has dined in some of the world's finest palaces."

Gus leaned closer to Francine, her pinched face looming nearby. "Oh, that's so reassuring. For a minute there, I'd thought we'd all be sipping water and eating hoecakes."

"Hoecakes?" Pierre lifted his chin and winced.

Douglas guffawed. "They're a kind of cornbread fritter cooked on the flat end of a hoe over a fire. That's how it got its name of hoecakes. Cowhands travel light." He rolled his eyes at Francine. "No trunks filled with silly garments and—"

Without appearing bothered, Francine smiled. She captured the corner of her napkin between her middle finger and thumb and gave it a flourish. "I refuse to act like a barbarian simply because I am in a new place where people turn farming implements into cooking utensils."

Sandwiched between Francine and Augusta, Clyde said very little. He glanced between them until the final remark from Francine. "The West can be hard on women—my mama said so. Best let her alone where those trunks are concerned. Besides, look how pretty she is in the items peeling out of 'em."

Gus flamed red in the face. "What's that supposed to mean? Are you making remarks about my clothes, 'cause if you are…" She narrowed her eyes into slits.

Clyde clasped his hands together. He gripped his interlocked fingers until the ridge of knuckles whitened. "Tarnation, Gus. I only mean she looks nice, which, so do you, by the way. I'm not sure I've ever seen you in a dress before."

She looked down and pulled at the too-large, cotton, handmade skirt. "Well, don't go gettin' use to it. It's probably the last time, as well."

The wood floor creaked with the comings and goings of hotel guests and the more affluent residents arriving for dinner at the restaurant. Essie knew most of Wylder's townspeople. At the sound of heavy footfalls punctuated with a thump, she groaned. The sound of the cane hitting the floor bumped between clomps—*clomp, clomp, thump*—could only mean one person, Nosey Nancy Finncannon. Her husband, the long-suffering Stutts Finncannon, was as revered as his wife was reviled. C.D., the stagecoach driver, even laughed about Stutts, declaring he was going straight to heaven when he died, as he lived in hell on earth.

Closing her eyes, Essie silently prayed she'd bypass them without comment. One or two snide remarks shouldn't have mattered, but in such a small town, they always did. *Clomp, clomp, thump*, and then a second *thump* accentuated Nancy Finncannon's progress until right upon them.

"Why, if it isn't Postmistress Essie and her rodeo daughter, Gus." Nancy's deep voice boomed from her extensive bosom. "I almost didn't recognize either of you out of your uniforms, and with such distinguished company, except for you, Clyde. But, Clyde, how is your dear mother? Is she practicing for a new pie contribution this year? Never mind, just introduce me to your acquaintances as I don't believe we've met."

Victor continued brooding. He looked past Nancy and nodded to her husband. "How ya doing, Stutts?"

Stutts Finncannon, a thin, wiry man, was difficult to spot behind his wife's girth and exaggerated bustle layered with folds and ruffles. He stepped into view as though appearing from behind a giant oak, tipped his hat, and took his wife's elbow. "Surely you remember Victor Douglas, my dear. We saw him in the theatre production of *Westward Ho* when we visited your Aunt Clara in Chicago."

"Oh, that's right. I did hear something about you leaving the theatre to come back West. I guess you miss shooting people you don't like and killing animals by the thousands. You just can't do that kind of thing east of the territories."

Vic scowled. "Lucky for you, I no longer kill people I don't like. But I suppose I could make an exception if Stutts—"

"*Pardonez moi,*" Pierre interjected. "As an ambassador for France, I wish to meet as many Americans as possible during my travels." He extended a hand. "I am Pierre Lacroix, and this is my daughter, Francine."

Nancy extended a limp wrist. "Enchanted, to be sure. I am Nancy Finncannon, and this is my husband, Stutts Finncannon."

Essie nearly gasped at Nancy's attempt to fake running across Pierre outside the bakery.

Pierre bypassed Nancy's dangling fingertips and gripped Stutts in a manly shake. "I had the pleasure of meeting your wife on Monday, *Monsieur* Finncannon.

What do you do here in Wylder?"

He coughed and rubbed his face as he cut his eyes at Nancy. "I do whatever my wife tells me to do. But I think it's time we found our table. Come along."

"But…" She narrowed her eyes and thumped the cane.

Stutts placed both hands on her back just above the bustle. "The man is waiting to seat us." He nodded toward the table. "Good to see you again, Essie. I'll be down in the morning with a few items to mail."

Essie lifted her chin. "Come any time, Stutts, but if you make it before noon, I can get it on the next stage. After that, and it'll be the following coach."

They shuffled away, the sound of the cane more pronounced as they departed, meaning Nancy hit the floor with more fervor with each step. Her husband's dismissal clearly nonplused her, and although Essie couldn't make out what she said, Nancy was filling Stutts's ear with a mouthful of whispers.

The scene only added to Essie's woes. Her heart fell into her stomach. The tension among the six of them was palpable and ruining the dinner party as Victor sulked, Francine pouted, and Gus used every opportunity to dig at her, which only deepened her frown.

Caught between the bickering girls, Clyde squirmed. His eyes were round as saucers, and his shoulders pinched upward toward his ears.

As she surveyed her dinner companions, Essie exhaled a deep sigh and focused on Pierre. *I might as well have worn the black mourning gown.*

Pierre rested his elbows against the table. Using the forefinger and thumb of one hand, he twirled the edge of his mustache. A grin teased the corners of his mouth, and the feathery flesh around his eyes crinkled as he appeared to fight back laughter.

Giving him a nudge, Essie leaned closer. "Do we amuse you?"

His hand ceased twirling his facial hair and squeezed hers. "Oh, dear lady, you cannot know how very much I adore this lively banter. It is a rare thing for people to behave so normally—so amusingly—in my presence at least."

Essie recalled what Francine said about her father dining in the world's finest palaces. Wylder sure was a long way from any courts. "Are conversations forced instead of congenial amongst your friends?"

"My friends…" His eyes lost their sparkle, and his mouth drew inward until his mustache covered his bottom lip.

Charles dropped a stack of glasses and a tin water pitcher onto the table with a thud and clatter. "I'll be right back with the lemonade and the beer."

Essie jumped and settled the rocking pitcher. She reached for a glass.

Pierre snatched her hand. "Allow me to serve you." He filled the glasses one by one and passed them around the table.

A chorus of "Thanks" pealed from recipients.

Looking at her daughter to make sure she offered gratitude, Essie was pleased when Gus displayed signs of appreciation with a nod and the appropriate words. Perhaps she hadn't failed her as much as she feared.

Victor twirled his glass. "Pierre, you haven't told me what brings you to America during the great Universal Exposition taking place in Paris. I'd think

112

you'd want to be there, especially after all the work you did in securing its location."

Augusta lifted her chin from the downward position required to stare at her fingers. She hung her hat off the back of the chair, and her hair fell around her face in soft waves. "What's a Universal Exposition?"

Francine raised an eyebrow. She turned her head and angled her half-opened mouth toward Gus.

Her father fixed her in his steely gaze and lifted a forefinger.

Although he said nothing, she snapped back into a relaxed position.

Whatever she'd intended to convey was lost.

Pierre's face softened. "Augusta, do you know what a fair is?"

"Why, of course, I do. Wylder has one every year." She smacked Clyde on the arm. "We've been practicing—Clyde and me." She cut a glance at Francine. "Well, we were until he became too busy with other obligations. Anyway, we are performing with our horses."

Remaining engaged with Gus, Pierre continued. "What else is at your fair? Are there exhibits, new foods, inventions?"

"Well...I don't know about inventions, although I did see some kind of hay-making machine last year. But there are lots of exhibits and contests. Mama runs a booth to capture outgoing mail, and the café has a little cart." She paused but held out a palm. "The cowboys herd cattle through town, and the one with the longest horns wins a prize, plus we have games and competitions between the women for the best jams, jellies, cakes, and pies. Clyde's mama took first place two years in a row for her strawberry-rhubarb cobbler."

Clyde nodded. "Still got the ribbons hanging on the doors to the pie safe." He leaned back, allowing the waiter to deposit the beer pitcher and mugs.

"How long does your fair last?" Pierre asked.

Gus glanced at Clyde. "Well, it's just a day, but it does turn into a dance that lasts until midnight."

Victor filled a mug and offered it to Lacroix. He served another for himself but remained quiet.

Tilting his glass, Pierre tasted the beverage and worked his mouth. He wiped the foam from his lips with a napkin. "That is what a Universal Exposition is, except in a larger forum. Competition isn't just among locals but from people from many other countries. Visitors worldwide gather in the host city to see the newest inventions and taste foods from other cultures. It is brilliant—and long—open more than six months to allow more people to take advantage."

Gus stared wide-eyed at Pierre. "Six months?"

He nodded. "But it takes years to secure the bid just to be allowed the honor of becoming a host city, and then they must undertake lots of construction to build the theatres, fairgrounds, and extra housing."

Francine accepted the lemonade with a nod. "*Merci.*"

A waitress placed a glass of lemonade in front of Gus. She rolled her eyes. "Thank you." She returned her attention to Lacroix. "So, why do all that work?"

"Ah"—he held up a finger—"I am not only a spokesman for my city of Paris and country of France, but I am also an investor. If done properly, the *Exposition Universelle*, uh…world's fair, will draw many visitors to our city. They will need food, housing, and transportation. Plus, they will spend a lot of money buying souvenirs from Paris to bestow on their friends and family members. The return on investment can be astronomical."

Essie was as enthralled as her daughter, although she hated to admit it. She'd read about the World's Fair but had never dreamed of visiting one. "Wasn't there a smaller version, called a Centennial Exposition, in Philadelphia two years ago? I seem to recall something about a display from France—a section of a gifted statue on loan there."

"*Oui, Madame* Baumgardner. It was the torch-bearing arm of *Le Liberte*. Gustave Eiffel is working on the base for Lady Liberty as we speak."

Francine blushed. "The statue is said to be several stories tall. The arm alone measures higher than I am tall. Although Eiffel is not the artist, his vision would not stand erect without the engineering around and beneath it."

Pierre beamed at his daughter. "As our gift to America, *Le Liberte* will unite our two countries in *esprit de corps*."

Francine tasted the lemonade. She tapped the glass. "Most refreshing."

"Those lemons just came in on the stage. It takes a lot of sugar to sweeten 'em up, but a real treat," Clyde said. "I know, cause my mama got some over at the general store before the hotel yanked 'em up."

Victor swigged his beer and refilled his mug. "Who is this Eiffel fellow?"

Grinning, Pierre lifted his head another inch. "Gustave Eiffel is a French engineer. He has worked on many bridges, but his contribution to *Le Liberte* will be his crowning achievement, and I dare say his legacy."

Augusta leaned across the table. "What else do you have at your fair?"

"Well, my *cherie*, Felix de Temple is displaying his monoplane."

She leaned in farther, her attention solely on Pierre. "What's a monoplane?"

"A flying machine."

"Flying machine?" Essie's eyes widened as she suppressed a sigh. "Does it work?"

Pierre shrugged and turned his palms upward. "Apparently. But that's not all. Thomas Edison is there. His displays include arc lighting, a phonograph, and a megaphone, and Alexander Graham Bell brought a telephone. There's a solar-powered steam engine, and the *pièce de résistance* is the crowned head of *Le Liberte*." He spread his arms. "The statue's top section is so large it takes up an entire display section."

The pan-fried trout—head and tail attached—arrived with a flourish on a bed of wild sage. A half-dozen deviled quail eggs surrounded the fish.

Gus licked her lips. Although she swiped a glance across the food, her focus snapped back to Pierre. "What else you got?"

Pierre studied the fish. He lifted a knife and fork. "May I?"

Victor waved. "I've seen your carving skills at work. Please, be my guest."

Working the fork and knife with expert movements, Pierre cleanly sliced each meaty section from the center spine and bones. He trimmed off the head and tail, corralled the discarded appendages onto an extra plate, and proceeded to carve off small sections, which he balanced between his utensils as he placed them along with a deviled quail egg on the plates of the others at the table.

Francine forked a delicate flake from her portion with the manners befitting a princess. "The lemonade complements it. Excellent."

Essie attempted a similar means of angling her knife to balance the flakey fish onto her fork's back tines. Halfway to her mouth, it fell into her lap. Quickly glancing around to see if anyone noticed, she was relieved the spectacle was lost to other important tidbits of conversation if someone did.

Clyde devoured his entire egg in one gulp, his fish in two bites, and poured himself a mug of beer. Downing it, he wiped his mouth with the back of his hand, then looked up.

Francine stared, eyes agog. "*Mon Dieu, Monsieur* Clyde, you must be starving. I fear I have kept you from your meals."

Clyde's cheeks reddened. He unfolded a napkin and dabbed the back of the hand with the beer foam still bubbling against his flesh. "Yeah—hungry."

Gus snapped a curt glance at Clyde. "Are there horses? Trick riders?"

Pierre nibbled at his food and swallowed before answering. "There are some Andalusian stallions and a full animal circus. What is on your mind, young Augusta?"

Augusta popped an egg into her mouth and dumped the fish onto Clyde's plate as she chewed. "Come see us—Clyde and me—tomorrow morning. I bet we can do tricks with horses you've never witnessed, not even in your—what you call it—

Exposition Universelle."

Fearing her daughter's disappointment, Essie rolled the dropped fish into a section of her napkin. "Gus, I'm sure Mr. Lacroix didn't come to Wylder to see people riding horses and performing stunts."

Settling his utensils against the rim of his plate, Pierre once more twirled the curling section of his mustache. "On the contrary, Madame Baumgardner. That is exactly the sort of thing I came to Wylder to see. Will you escort us to the riding ring, *Monsieur* Douglas?"

Victor stared into space. His food remained untouched, but he drained his beer mug a second time and shoved his cigar between his teeth. Although he didn't light it, he chewed one end.

Essie waited for a response from Victor. He seemed a hundred miles away, likely shooting a wild bison or herding escaped cattle from a drive. "Never mind him. If Buffalo Vic over there isn't available, I'll close the office for an hour and drive you over in the carriage."

"Buffalo Vic," Pierre repeated. He laughed and nodded. "I like the sound of that name."

Victor spun around. "What name? Did someone mention my name?"

Pierre's laughter was contagious. One by one, they all joined in the hilarity.

Clyde guffawed. "Buffalo Vic."

Francine giggled. "*Monsieur* Buffalo Vic. What a name."

Douglas joined the laughter but with a sparkle in his eyes. "That's right. Buffalo Vic has a ring to it."

Gus chuckled and punched Clyde. "Almost sounds

as good as the name we gave our show—Wylder's Western Show."

Pierre tapped the table. "Shall I see Buffalo Vic and the Wylder West Show in the morning?"

Victor lit his face with a grin. "Yes, Pierre, you shall. Buffalo Vic and the Wylder West Show. I like it."

Later, Essie lingered over dessert. The freshly whipped cream was a rarity, especially in the summer when heat curdled milk faster than a prairie dog snapped its head back into its den. She'd heard the Vincent House Restaurant had a cellar with a natural spring that kept things cool even in the warmest months. It must be so if they could concoct such a treat on one of the hottest days.

But dessert wasn't the only reason Essie lingered. She had not enjoyed the company of a man as much as she did Pierre Lacroix in a very long time. Plus, Victor Douglas had perked up after the insult she hadn't meant to levy but had landed on him just the same.

Victor switched to coffee and swigged it with equal enthusiasm to match how he'd consumed the beer. Without requesting permission, he snatched a placard from a reserved table and flipped it over to its blank side. He craned his neck, glancing around to his left and right and behind him. "I've got an idea. I need something to write with."

Pierre lifted a hand and swirled it in the air as Charles approached. "Pardon the imposition, but my friend *Monsieur* Douglas requires a writing instrument. Would you be so kind as to oblige him? I wouldn't bother you, but it is important."

Victor looked up and caught the young man's eye. "Slate and board are fine if'n you've got no pen and ink."

When the young man returned with the requested pen and ink, he cleared the dishes and gave the table a cursory sweep to remove crumbs and debris. "My name's Charles," he repeated. He laid the bill of fare on the table.

Pierre scooped it up, dipped the pen in the ink bottle, gave it a sideways swipe allowing the excess to roll back into the bottle, and signed the bottom of the bill with a flourish. "You will add this to my account, *n'est pas*? Naturally, there is a gratuity for your outstanding service, Charles."

Charles snatched the ticket. "Thank you. I hope you enjoyed your meal."

Squeezing Essie's fingertips, Pierre rested a hand atop her flesh as he sighed. "I can say with complete honesty I don't know when I've enjoyed a meal more than the one this evening. Whether the fine fare or the exquisite company, I cannot determine." He swept a gaze over Essie's face.

Her cheeks heated in the scrutiny of Pierre's sated stare. She felt similarly but wouldn't admit it, at least not to him. She smiled and cast a glance at her daughter.

Gus leaned across Victor's arm, eyeing his scribbles. On occasion, she pointed. "Not there—here. Right," she whispered.

Much to Essie's chagrin, Victor and Augusta seemed of one mind. "What are you two plotting?"

Augusta looked up. "The best horse show in the west. Just you wait and see."

Francine cocked her head to one side. "May I be in the show?"

Gus flinched. "You? What can you do?"

"I know how to sit a horse, don't I, Papa?"

Pierre gave his daughter a lingering look and sighed. "You are so like your mother. She adored horses. The first time I laid eyes on her, she was tall in the saddle of an Andalusian mare."

Nodding, Francine stared at Augusta. She lifted a finger and held it to her cheek. If she was about to make another point, it died before escaping her lips.

Gus cut her eyes at Clyde. "Well, I don't know about Andalusian mares. We don't have any around these parts and don't need 'em, do we, Clyde?"

Clyde shifted his weight. "I'm sure they're fine horses, but Gus is right. I've never seen anything called Andalusian in Wylder."

Francine's hand dropped to the table with a smack. "I want to ride a Wylder horse, Papa. You will arrange it, *n'est pas*?"

He shrugged and caught Victor's attention. "*Monsieur* Douglas, you heard my daughter. She would like to ride a Wylder horse, and I would like to make it so."

Victor shook his head but remained silent.

"After all," Pierre continued, "if it is my investment in a show that you seek, how could I refuse one featuring my daughter, *non*?"

Douglas leaped from his seat. "Naturally, I would not disappoint you or your daughter, Lacroix. Clyde will help you find Francine a horse tomorrow." He stood behind Gus's chair. "I'll take care of getting Pierre and Francine to the ring. You two will meet us there."

Essie pushed up from the table.

Pierre held out her chair, steadying it as she rose.

"Thank you, again, for the lovely dinner. I don't know when I've enjoyed myself as much or eaten as much."

He lifted her hand to his lips and kissed the back of her hand. "You honor me with your presence. Shall I see you back to your residence?"

Victor motioned for the door. "No need. I'll drive Essie and Gus home. Clyde's horse is out back, so he'll not need a ride."

Nodding, Essie turned and walked from the restaurant with as much grace as she could manage. Pierre's kiss still tickled her flesh, sizzling throughout her body until weakening her knees. She wanted to look back but resisted. Just at the door, she heard Pierre's voice.

"Until the morrow, dear Madame Baumgardner."

The sound of her name on his lips raked a shudder across her, and she fumbled on the steps.

Victor's arms settled around her waist. "Careful. Watch your step. It can be tricky in the dark."

"Yes. Tricky." She felt the heat in her face and was never happier for enveloping darkness. *What is happening to me?*

Chapter 8

Friday, June 21, 1878

Essie couldn't sleep. She stared into the darkness, reliving select portions of the evening. Pierre Lacroix wasn't like any other man she'd ever met. His bright smile, beguiling accent, and impeccable manners made her heart flutter just thinking about him.

When the first blink of color finally lit the sky, Essie rose, but she wasn't tired or hungry. Having dined so well the previous evening, she had no appetite. She watched Gus gallop off with the dawn and then opened the post office earlier than usual to compensate for the brief closing she planned to make mid-morning.

With the sign switched to *Open*, the grocer popped in. Finn Wylder stopped by to mail a letter.

With each creak of the door, Essie expected to see Stutts Finncannon, but he did not appear. Chuckling to herself, she wondered if his absence was due to a harsh tongue lashing from Nancy or worse. Rumors were that Nancy flailed him with her cane on at least one occasion.

At half-past nine, Victor swung open the door. "Howdy, Essie. Are you ready? I've got Pierre and Francine waiting in the wagon."

"I'll come around from the back." She switched the sign to *Closed*, secured the front door with its double-bolting feature, and key-locked the inner chamber door. After hanging her vest and cap on the hook, she locked the back door and slipped around the front.

Victor reached out and lifted her into the wagon.

Pierre and Francine waited side by side. He stepped forward and scrambled about to assist her with seating. "Good morning, Madame Baumgardner."

She nodded. "*Monsieur* Lacroix, *Mademoiselle* Francine, good to see you both after such a pleasant evening." Francine looked resplendent in a full blue riding habit with its long-skirted jacket that hung low across her bustle and a tall black hat with blue ribbons hanging down her back.

Cocking her chin to one side, she smiled. "*Bonjour,* Madame Baumgardner."

Essie longed to ask how she intended to sit a horse in such a garment but held her tongue. Pierre doted on the child and would be offended at anything he might perceive as negative. "Do you enjoy riding, Francine?"

Francine smiled. "*Monsieur* Montagne says I am a natural. Oh, did I mention *Monsieur* Montagne is my horse-riding instructor? I take lessons in the Tuileries Gardens on Tuesdays and Thursdays. Sometimes we draw a crowd that comes to watch the riders. I have the most beautiful *cheval*—horse, that is. I named her *Lumiere,* because she has light markings on her legs that resemble the effect of the sun on stone."

Unlike the previous night when the girl said little, Francine was chatty. Essie suppressed a grin.

Pierre beamed, as he usually did around Francine. "France is famous for her light, *Madame* Baumgardner. Builders use local limestone for the structures in Paris, and when the sun hits it just right, there is a golden glow that illuminates the structures like a million tiny diamonds adorn the surface."

"A million tiny diamonds reflected in the light." Essie sighed. She longed to see such a sight. "Must be magnificent to look upon."

"Oh, it is, *Madame* Baum—"

She turned a palm toward him. "Essie. If we're going to spend time together while you're here in Wylder, just call me Essie. Everyone does."

"I will call you by your given name, *Madame* Baum...uh...Essie, but only if you refer to me by mine."

"Okay, Pierre." She warmed in the glow of his attention, or was it the way his name rolled off her tongue? Essie couldn't be sure, and she didn't really care, as it felt nice to be so besotted once more. The carriage bounced along until rolling slightly backward before stopping.

Victor leaped from the driver's seat and reached inside. "Give me your hand, Essie. I'll help you from the carriage."

Essie took his proffered assistance and lifted her skirt before descending.

He patted her arm. "This way."

She didn't protest. For once, it was nice to be fussed over and escorted, even if the one doing the fussing was Victor Douglas.

Pierre, sandwiched between her and Francine, jumped down. He turned and assisted Francine then led her to the hastily-constructed board-and-sawhorse seating that cupped the rim.

As soon as they sat, Gus galloped into the ring on Lightning. With subtle cues, Lightning stood on his hind legs and pawed at the air. He bucked and bowed.

Victor and Pierre wildly applauded while Francine watched wide-eyed.

Riding barefoot and bareback, Gus stood on her horse as it galloped around the ring. Only after the uproarious applause of her captive audience did she sit again.

Essie gasped and covered her eyes with a palm. Her daughter's risk-taking unnerved her. "She's just like her father," she snapped.

Pierre tugged her hand away from her face and held it in one of his. He stroked it with the other. "You must miss him very much."

"I...I..." Essie stared at his long fingers with their clean nails and soft cuticles. *What did Augustus's look like?* She couldn't remember. They'd been so young, and she'd lost him so soon that their brief time together sometimes felt more like a dream than reality. "As I'm sure you miss your dear wife."

As he nodded, Pierre sucked in a breath. "Francine is my whole reason for existence, but she is practically grown and will soon leave me to start her own family." He sighed. "Such is life, I suppose."

"Oh, is Francine spoken for?"

"Not exactly, but there are a few acceptable young men who are making their wishes known to me. Perhaps—"

Gus stood again and, without warning, leaped into the air. Lightning galloped from beneath her. When her feet reached for his spine, he would not be there.

"Do not look." Pierre gasped and covered his face with one palm and snagged Essie with the other as he pulled her against his side.

Essie inhaled his aroma of cherry tobacco and bergamot tea. She didn't want to move, nor did she want him to miss the next part of the performance. Reaching upward, she tugged his forearm. "I like this trick. Watch—you'll see."

Francine's face froze in a silent scream. Her mouth hung open, and her eyes widened into saucer shapes.

The sound of hooves thundering against the arid earth mimicked Essie's heartbeat. Pierre still gripped her close, and she palmed his fingertips.

Time stood still as Gus hung in midair. She flipped head over toes. Her horse hugged the outer corral fencing as it circled the rim. If she fell to the ground, she'd be hurt or worse. The descent began as her aerial spins lost their lift from the wind, and she tumbled downward.

Suddenly, Clyde appeared on his steed. His horse raced beneath her, and Gus fell into Clyde's waiting arms. He lowered her to his side, where she dangled like a dishrag. Her feet and legs made running motions, but she was still well above the ground.

Pierre loosened his grip and clapped uproariously. "Unbelievable. I did not see the other rider coming." He nudged Francine. "Did you see that? *Mon Dieu*, what a performance."

Essie motioned. "Oh, but it's not over yet. Look."

Lightning cantered back into the ring's center. His long mane wafted behind him like wings until he met the speed of Clyde's mount. As her horse approached, Clyde lifted Gus a little higher. Finally, Lightning was so close he dipped his head, and Gus's dangling legs landed astride his back.

Francine gasped.

Pierre yelled as he clapped with enthusiasm. "Bravo, bravo."

Augusta synchronized her mount's speed to Clyde's before splitting off into the opposite direction. She rode in a semi-circle until meeting him head to head smack in front of the spectators. Pulling back on the reins, she halted.

Clyde reacted similarly, and his mount lifted both front legs off the ground. Standing on his back legs, he struck a pose with his front hooves. One appeared to point toward Gus.

Facing Clyde, Gus assumed a similar, reflection-like position. As her horse bent his front legs and bowed his head over his knees, she lifted her hat and waved it into the air. The pose lasted a brief moment, but the impact was visually stunning.

As Augusta dismounted, another round of cheers erupted.

Clyde joined her, grabbing her hand and lifting her arm high above her head. They bowed, and on command, their horses joined them in a kneeling position, accepting their small audience's accolades,

Victor stood and rubbed together his palms. "It's my turn." He marched to the edge, rolled barrels into the ring, and erected targets.

Essie had attended a dozen practices before letting her gaze wander from her daughter to the man behind the scene. Now she appreciated the stealth with which he maneuvered his props, so the audience remained continually thrilled.

On cue, Clyde and Augusta walked their horses out of the arena.

Victor raced toward the barrels, yanking his horse

around them in tight figure eights. He barely missed each one, and after the last successful turn, he loosened the reins and tugged his rifle from its leather scabbard. As his horse continued to thunder around the ring, he aimed at the targets with his gun's butt to his shoulder. A successive round of rapid-fire shots resulted in matching pings.

Before the echoing sounds died, a calf rushed the arena.

Vic sheathed his rifle and snatched the rope from his side. He tossed the looped end into the air and fed it a good length before aiming at the running calf. For a moment, it appeared as though the lasso might miss, but the calf turned into its circular rotation. It jolted against the restraint, but as Victor's horse stepped backward, the taut rope pulled against the calf's momentum, and it flopped against the ground.

Clyde raced in and released the restraint, allowing the little calf to resume its running and bucking. He jogged back to Gus, took her by the hand, and ran alongside the arena.

Victor displayed his showmanship. His horse reared, his front legs pawing at the air as Victor lifted his hat in a salute to Essie, Pierre, and Francine.

Essie applauded and whistled.

Francine blinked and stared.

Pierre yelled words in French Essie didn't understand, but she didn't have to interpret his language to know the meaning of his rolling *r's* and the trilling sound of accolades. He was clearly thrilled with the show.

Victor replaced his hat and waved. He dismounted and ran to the bench. "So, Pierre, what did you think about our little western show?"

Pierre raised his hands and threw back his head. "*C'est tres magnifique.*"

Francine nudged him and giggled. "In English, Papa."

"Of course. Thank you for the reminder, daughter. It was magnificent."

Victor fingered his hat's brim. "So…do you think there's a place for it in your exposition?"

Gasping, Pierre slapped a palm against his chest. "My exposition? Dear *Monsieur* Douglas, the *Exposition Universelle* is not mine. It is the collaboration of many, many people. While some share creative endeavors and entertainment venues, I merely offer financing advice and assist with the bookings from participating countries."

Essie squirmed. Hearing Pierre revert to calling Vic by his proper name indicated he interpreted Victor's request as a business transaction. The French Ambassador was unlikely to base such a decision on mere friendship. Victor must have realized it, as well.

He winced and scratched his chin. "Finance, bookings, I see. But if you assist with the bookings, could you give me your opinion on selecting our Wylder West Show?"

Remaining seated, Pierre twisted the edges of his mustache. "I do not think you understand the scope of universal expositions. While your small troupe is quite spectacular here in this…uh…petite arena, I fear the grand theater of the *Palais du Trocadero* would swallow it like a gnat."

"A gnat, huh?" Nodding, Victor pursed his lips and looked over his shoulder. "What would it take? What would I need to accomplish with my show to win a booking?"

Pierre's mouth dropped open. He swiped a finger beneath his nose. "Are you serious? Do you truly want to know my opinion?"

Francine fidgeted with the frills on her bodice. She rose and offered her hand to Victor. "Would you be so kind, *Monsieur* Douglas?"

"Most certainly." He lightly gripped her gloved fingertips, offering more balance than assistance. "Anything for a friend's daughter."

"*Merci*," she said before strolling toward the corral fencing to peer across the dusty bowl.

Although Essie assumed she should join Francine and give the two men a chance to discuss the venture, her curiosity was too great. She tugged at her pocket watch, diverting her attention to its physical reminder she should be at her post.

Vic leaned forward, elbow-against-knee, bringing his face close to Pierre's. "Give it to me straight. I don't need any frills or fancy French words that sound prettier than their meanings. I'm tired of performing in other people's interpretations of the American West. I want to develop something of my own—something people around the world will find amusing and thrilling."

Pierre tucked his chin. "As you wish, but remember that you asked me."

Essie's heart dropped. Pierre's statement carried the warning that it was unlikely to be something Victor wished to hear. She stared into the distance, watching Gus and Clyde brush their horses while keeping enough peripheral vision to catch the taut expressions on

Victor's and Pierre's faces.

Victor nodded. "I'd be more disappointed by a dishonest compliment than a truthful criticism."

"*Très bien*. This morning's performance is but a scene in what would need to be a much larger drama to take to the world's stage. As one act, it is thrilling. As an entirety, it is too little."

"Too little? Huh?" Victor pulled a half-burned cigar from his pocket and chewed the unlit end without striking flint. "What would correct that?"

Essie bit her lip. She fingered the watch chain, feeding its length into the shallow vest pocket. *Gus will be disappointed.*

Pierre inhaled a long breath then slowly exhaled. "You are aiming too low, *monsieur*. Consider the Romans and their coliseum."

Victor hooded his eyes with his lids and frowned. "The coliseum? What's your point?"

Pierre stood. "We would know nothing about it if it were not for the grandeur with which the ancient Romans devised a method to bring the wars over which they celebrated victory to the citizens."

Slapping his hat against his knee, Victor erupted. "Dang it, Pierre, get to the point."

"Think about it. The Romans piped in water from the aqueducts to the coliseum. They flooded the lower level and built model ships like those at sea." Pierre waved his hands. "From this stage, they reenacted battles for their audience. When they weren't doing water scenes, they brought in warriors who were larger and stronger than any ever seen before, and they turned their exotic animals into the arena."

Victor narrowed his eyes and puckered his mouth

until his beard joined his thick mustache. The hairy covering hid his lips but not the bobbing of his Adam's apple. He swallowed several times before speaking. "You want gladiators to face their death at the teeth and claws of lions and tigers?"

Pierre blinked. He offered Essie his hand.

She laid one sweating palm against his and stood.

He then turned back to Victor. "Of course not. You asked what it would take. I am giving you an example. Your audience wants nothing less than the citizens of Rome. They don't want to watch a show; they want to experience the West."

Essie motioned toward the waiting carriage. "I really must be getting back to the post office. People will wonder where I've gone, and the stagecoach will arrive soon."

Victor lifted one hand and laid the other against his cheek. "Yes, but wait one minute."

"Francine," Pierre called out. "Come along."

She spun and walked toward him. "*Oui*, Papa."

Victor visibly struggled with Pierre's response. "Give me a second more. I just want to understand how I'm supposed to take an ancient Roman performance and equate it to myself."

Essie reached for Francine's arm. "We'll be waiting in the carriage."

Pierre glanced across the pair of them and fell into line behind Essie and Francine. "Walk with us, Victor. We promised to return the postmistress to her duties and must not delay."

As she strained to hear what Pierre said to Victor, the noises of everything Essie might not have noticed before seemed uncommonly loud—the rubbing of fabric on Francine's gown, their boots against the dry earth, hooves clomping as Clyde and Gus walked horses in the ring. Pierre's French accent laced every syllable with aristocracy but made it more difficult to understand his whispers.

"You are...famous for your battles...American Indians and the wild buffalo...western plains. If you could...bring those battles alive..."

Tilting her head back, she strained to hear more.

"...reenact them in the center of a huge theater where the pounding horse hooves carry soldiers and savages toward a showdown that reverberates in the chests of every guest, build on it with the animals of the West that people in Paris have never seen before, then we shall talk about inclusion."

Essie's heart plummeted. How could anyone do such a feat? Reenacting such grand battles was impossible, wasn't it? She wished he'd just said no instead of playing along like he would book the show. "Why don't you go to the reservation and see if the Natives are willing to perform with your troupe? They might enjoy a little travel and playacting, as well."

As Victor helped Francine into the carriage, he chewed his lip. He reached back for Essie's hand and snagged it from Pierre's as he aided her next. "An Indian village wouldn't be that hard to recreate, especially if I could get a few Natives on board, too."

Pierre grabbed the edge and pulled himself into the carriage. He sat beside her but poked out his head. "Be careful. With your reputation, they might shoot you on sight."

After settling into the carriage's driver seat, Victor fed the reins to the horse. "Hyah," he yelled before glancing over his shoulder. "The Natives hate one thing worse than me."

Blinking, Pierre lifted his head. "*Oui*? What on earth could that be?"

"The reservation."

Essie shivered. If she knew anything at all about Victor Douglas, it was that he was the most determined man she'd ever met. If anyone could discover a way to bring such a reenactment to people in another country, Victor could. "Don't forget exotic animals. We might not have lions and tigers—"

"But we've got buffalo," Vic shouted.

Dust rose beneath them. "You wouldn't dare..." As she breathed the hot, dry air, her throat closed.

Francine flicked her wrist and snapped open her hand fan in one smooth movement. The tightly accordioned rectangle bloomed into a quarter-circle. She gripped the connecting edge and whipped the painted silk back and forth.

Essie focused on the scene, but its movements nearly made her dizzy. The quick flash of moving air eased the heat, even if only a little, but she ached for the girl to stop fanning so she could see the painted-on images all at one time instead of as broken bits—a dome, people in strange garments, lamp posts, unusual structures, an arched bridge.

The carriage bumped and jolted as Victor rushed the horses.

Essie slid against Pierre, her shoulder touching his. Even through the layers of fabric between them, Essie felt the strength of Pierre's muscle covering the bony joint. A sudden turn in the road pushed Francine against Essie, and the unexpected push shoved her entire right side into the Frenchman's lap. Tingles whipped through her like the wind in the horses' manes. Essie feared he could feel her quickened heartbeat and racing pulse. She peeked at his face as she scrambled back to the seat.

His cheeks were flushed, but a smile tugged the edges of his mustache. *"C'est bonne?* Is everything good?"

Essie's mind went blank. Sweat dotted her forehead, and she swiped at it with first a palm and then a handkerchief. "I—"

Francine righted herself. "I'm sorry, Papa. It seems I rolled around the seat like a bocce ball in Tuileries Garden and knocked Madame Postmistress into you."

"No problem, my darling." He reached down and lifted Estelle's chin with a crooked forefinger. "And you?"

"I…" She swallowed. His touch was featherlight against her flesh. Yet, it carried a charge that surged to her neck and along her spine. Words clogged in her throat.

His thumb stroked her face. "Perhaps you should sit closer. I can steady you."

As if to prove his point, he lifted an arm and draped it around her, clamping her to his side so tightly she could feel his chest expand with each breath he inhaled.

Francine stopped fanning. She snapped the fan closed and offered it to Essie. "Do you need a bit of air, Madame Postmistress?"

Essie reached for the fan she'd admired a few seconds prior, although it seemed much longer now. She eased it open and stared at the pressed ink painted onto the silk, watching the Parisian street scene just as she'd desired at the moment right before the jolt sent them flying across the seat. Time suspended into a strange new reality more dreamlike than real.

Pierre leaned over her, nearly resting his head atop hers. "That is a souvenir from the *Exposition Universelle*." He pointed to the strange buildings. "These are part of the international street scene from the display of nations, and that"—he indicated the railway—"is the innovation portion which covers our newest rail system, Felix de Temple's monoplane, and Alexander Graham Bell's telephone. Of course, the depiction is not to scale but to show the city attractions and our bridges, lamps, parks, and landmarks. Have you been to Paris?"

The carriage dipped suddenly, and she lost the connection with Pierre's comforting grip. "I've never been anywhere outside the boundaries of Ft. Laramie and Cheyenne."

Pierre pulled her against him once more and stared into her eyes. "Well now, we will have to change that, *n'est pas?*"

Essie wanted to change that. She supposed nobody in the world had ever desired travel more than she. The impossibility lost a tiny sliver of improbability with Pierre's assertion. She ached to tell him so and sought the appropriate wording to keep from sounding as desperate as Gus when she needed new boots and begged for them while pointing at the holes in the old ones' toes. "Well, I suppose—" She passed the fan back to Francine.

The horses stopped, and Essie tumbled forward.

Victor raced around the carriage and called to

Pierre. "I'm going to the saloon for a drink. Lacroix, care to join me?"

Pierre leaped out of the carriage and reached up to help Essie first and then Francine. "Not this morning. I promised Francine to find a horse for her to ride while we are in Wylder."

"As soon as he's finished grooming the horses, Clyde will help you," Victor insisted.

Pierre settled Francine onto the ground. "Nonsense. There is no point in bothering the boy. Besides, I believe the morning's show stimulated her desire for a ride."

Francine clapped. "Oh, Papa, *merci.*"

He laughed. "Of course, *cherie*. Perhaps we can convince the lovely postmistress to help us choose. I am quite certain the best horse for Wylder's territory is not at all like the best one for city dwellers."

The sensation of Pierre's hands against Essie's arms lingered. Shivering despite the heat, she paused. The post office's obligations competed with the desire to remain with Pierre and Francine a bit longer.

Victor bounded along the walkway. He glanced over his shoulder. "Whatever you say. Take my carriage. Essie knows the way."

Essie had to return to the post office. Neither the mail nor the stagecoach could wait. She protested. "But…"

Francine grabbed Essie's hand and pressed the fan into her palm. She curled her fingers around Essie's. "You must keep the fan as a token of my appreciation for your kindnesses."

Essie stared into the girl's violet eyes. They practically oozed excitement. She had traveled a long way, and the wrong horse could spell disaster. *How can I refuse?* Gripping the edge of the carriage, she lifted herself back into it. *What's the worst that can happen if I'm only a few minutes late?* "Certainly."

Pierre grinned and climbed into the driver's seat. "I would like nothing more. Besides, you know all about the *chevals* in Wylder, *non*?"

Francine and Pierre looked at Essie as though they respected her opinion. Beneath their admiring glances, she felt important and desired. Heat popped her cheeks. *I know very little about horses in Wylder or anywhere else for that matter. Gus is the expert, but...*

Chapter 9

"*Chevals* in Wylder?" Essie blinked.

Pierre chuckled and kissed the back of her hand. "*Cheval* is French for horse. I trust you know the best location and the best type of horse that will be gentle enough to protect Francine while just spirited enough to make the ride enjoyable."

She pointed straight ahead. "Chet Daniels usually has several. It's not far."

Francine bounced, clapping her hands. "I have missed riding and the liberty it brings me."

Essie wondered if the girl misunderstood the word. "Liberty?"

Pierre steered the carriage in the direction Essie indicated, pulling to a stop behind the livery. "I believe you would say freedom." He winked and helped her from the wagon. "You see, her papa is very protective since losing her mama."

She threaded her arm through his, linking elbows as they walked. "Oh, Papa, you are the best father in all the world."

Watching them both pleased and saddened Essie. Augusta had missed having such a loving relationship. She had never known her father, and Essie had feared bringing another man into their lives. Pierre's softheartedness with Francine told her much about his demeanor, and she thought even more of him for it.

Still, she wrinkled her nose and shivered, despite the heat. Francine appeared to have everything, while Augusta missed out on similar advantages. *I'm not jealous, but...* She chewed a fingernail and spotted Chet approaching Pierre and Francine. While they talked, she strolled around the back.

Chet had two horses tied to the rear hitching post—a roan with a buckskin tethered beside it.

Essie approached the roan and ran a hand along its broad chest. Rays of sunshine lightened the red to a strawberry and turned the white to a snowy froth. Had it not been for the horse beside it, she doubted she'd have considered it the same one she'd seen the day before. But what were the odds two such familiar horses would be tied together at the livery if they weren't the same ones that belonged to the prospectors? "Chet, where'd you get these two?"

He adjusted the saddle for Francine, narrowed his gaze, and lifted it. "An old man and his son dropped them off. Said they were getting a room over the hotel and asked me to clean and feed their horses." He draped another saddle across the mustang. "Expected them back yesterday." He shrugged. "Should be by any time now to pick 'em up."

The image of the two men as they rode into town flashed through her mind. No doubt they were getting the same overhaul treatment as their horses. Maybe even more than that with the Social Club and the ladies eager for a share of their gold. "They'll undoubtedly be as unrecognizable as their horses."

"I hope so," he called back before patting the mustang. "Young lady, you're all set."

Francine clapped. "Papa, can I ride him now?"

Pierre pulled out a watch, glanced at its face, and stabbed it back into its pocket. "Not now, *cherie*. But we will return as soon as we see the postmistress back to her office."

Essie waved a hand back and forth. "Oh, don't worry about me. You two go on and enjoy your day. I've got to get back, and it isn't much of a walk from here."

Pierre took her hand in his, lifted it to his lips, and kissed it. "Dearest Essie, I don't know when I've had a more delightful morning. However, I should not feel good about myself if I did not accompany you to your post."

The sensation of his mouth touching her flesh rushed Essie with a swirling river of emotion. Too tongue-tied to reply, she motioned with the opposite hand toward Francine.

"Look, Papa, I'm riding like Gus."

He sprinted toward his daughter. "So you are, *cherie*."

With a pounding heart and knees weakened from the kiss, Essie slipped out the door and along the street. Her feet barely touched the ground as she relived the moment when he planted his lips against her skin. *How long has it been?* She wandered through the annals of her mind, the dark chambers she'd locked after Gus's untimely demise. Theirs had been a profound, albeit brief, relationship. She'd not imagined another man arousing similar desires until the Frenchman arrived in Wylder and strolled into the post office.

The post office. The thought increased her already thundering pulse. She quickened her pace. What if someone noticed her with Pierre while absent from her duties? *I'm being silly. Who cares?* She rounded the corner and gasped. The stagecoach was parked at its regular spot. *Is it early?*

That would be like CD to arrive early on the one day she would have benefited from him arriving late. She pulled the watch from her pocket. It was half-past noon. "Dagnabit," she exclaimed. *How did I lose so much time?* Essie hiked her skirts and raced for the depot.

Glancing left and right, she raced along the alley, but she couldn't see CD anywhere. She peeked inside the coach, but it was empty. Crates lined the walk. She ran into the mercantile seeking Finn Wylder.

Finn rose from a bent-over position behind the counter with a box of men's work gloves in one hand. He pulled out two pairs and nestled them into the empty slot in the store window before glancing in her direction. "Oh, Essie, hello. You're in luck because I just got—"

Essie hated being impolite but had no time for friendly exchanges. "Sorry, Finn. I'm in a hurry. Have you seen Cyrus Dunn?"

Finn laid aside the gloves. He furrowed his brows, forming a crevice above his nose. "He usually goes straight to the post office. Did you see him earlier?"

She bit her lip. "I missed him…"

Leaning forward, he winked. "Check the saloon."

She could have smacked herself. In all her years as postmistress, she'd never missed a mail drop. Today, she'd nearly forgotten who she was. She ran to the saloon and stood on tiptoes to spy through the doors. Shameful heat blazed her cheeks. Pierre Lacroix and his daughter were in Wylder but for a short time, and she would forfeit her position if word leaked she closed the office while gallivanting with strangers and missed the maildrop. Since the stagecoach hadn't pulled out yet, CD still had to be in town. *Dang, it, CD, where are you?*

Glancing behind her, she saw him tossing luggage onto the roof of the coach. Although already overheated and exhausted from running about, Essie raced back along the street toward the stage depot. The sun bore down, illuminating his silhouette, while he assisted a passenger into the carriage. *Oh no, they'll pull out as soon as the last passenger is loaded—shoot.* "CD," she yelled while waving her arms. "Wait."

CD lifted a hand and cut it across his forehead. "Essie?" he yelled back.

"I'm coming. Wait." For the first time since pulling on her first pair of heels, Essie regretted the tall boots. As she dashed down the street, they pushed into her arches. Her laser focus was on CD and the stagecoach. She couldn't let it leave while she had mail to receive and send.

Essie ran with all her might. Sweat spread from her face to her underarms and in the area beneath her breasts. She hammered her calves into doing her bidding while she ignored her aching feet and scolded herself. *What's the matter with me? Why did I agree to ride out to the ring when I knew I should be at my post? I've managed all these years without a man, and the first one who comes along with a smooth voice and a thick wallet makes me lose all judgment.* Her lungs screamed, joining her feet and thighs. Just as it lifted, she snatched her hat and held it in a death grip.

CD stepped from the shadows and stuck out his

neck. "Essie? Essie, watch out."

In her haste, she focused solely on his bobbing head. She didn't dare take her gaze from him, not even to look left or right at the corner. As if it was hers alone, she raced into the street and dug her heels into the dirt at CD's urgings to watch out.

For a split second, she didn't know what happened. Thick veins pulsed in slick black flesh right before her eyes. Moisture peppered its sides—*a horse*. Its nostrils flared, and its head swung to the side. Its huge dark eyes snapped onto hers. Off-balance, both Essie and the horse rocked and bounced.

The rider bucked against the reins and pulled the horse to a stop so quickly its front feet left the ground. Its rear hooves stabbed at the earth as it both tried to obey and follow its natural inclination to keep moving forward.

Essie saw too late the person was Lionel Peterson. She had a sudden flashback about his mother bringing her a tonic for Gus's sore throat. In a split second between the collision and the eye of the storm, she imagined explaining how they crashed into one another. Would he be thrown? Would he be scarred for life if he witnessed his horse's hooves battering her to death in the street? As her nervous gaze met his, she mouthed, *I'm sorry*. "My fault."

He yanked the horse left and fed it some reins. In one gallop, it gave Essie the space to tumble forward and roll in the opposite direction. Lionel circled back and leaped off his steed. "Miss Essie, are you okay?"

She rolled for a moment before catching herself. As if made of glue rather than salt and sweat, dirt stuck to all her moist places. Essie raised an arm. "Can you help me up?"

Lionel reached down and tugged her upward with one jerk. "Where'd you come from? I didn't see you until you were right there, straight in the path." He shook his head.

CD appeared before her like a mirage out over the dessert.

He smacked his hat against his thigh. "Dang it to pieces, Essie. Where've you been, and why are you running out into the street without watching where you're going?"

Grit and sand turned loose from her forehead and dripped into her eyes. She blinked back tears. "Never mind. Just get me back to the post office."

CD flicked a hand at Lionel. "Good save, lad. With moves like that, your horse will be good for cutting cattle."

Lionel pushed up his hat with a fingertip. "You think so? It's what I've been training him for, but I have to say he obeyed better right then than he ever has before."

CD nodded. "Don't mean to be short, but I've got customers in a hot coach. Get along, Lionel. We'll talk later. Come on, Essie. I'll get you back to the office and bring the mail."

"The mail—" she sputtered, spitting out dirt. Walking made her whole body ache.

Cyrus practically held her upright. "It appears you arrived just in time. I have to admit, though, I was getting worried. It's not like you to miss a drop."

She set her mouth. The little excursion had nearly cost her the reputation she'd worked so long and hard to build. "I won't again, CD. I promise." Essie flipped the

Closed sign to *Open* before brushing the dirt from her clothes. She dabbed at her skinned wrists and elbows with a cool, damp cloth. *I deserve to have my hide skinned.* A postmistress has only one job—watch her post. What if someone needed to get a letter onto the stagecoach? She couldn't think about it. She wouldn't.

All was well. Somehow, she managed to avoid disaster and meet CD, as always and exchange the outgoing mail pieces for the incoming ones.

With the sack tossed over a shoulder, he rushed back to the coach. With one upward heave, he joined it.

Before turning her attention to the mail sack, Essie watched him depart. She'd just sorted the last incoming letter when the door squeaked open. A thump preceded a heavy footfall, and the sound was unmistakable— *Nancy Finncannon.* Essie's jaw twitched. After cautioning herself to be polite, she inhaled a deep breath and squared her shoulders. "Good day, Nancy."

Thump—stomp—thump—stomp. The sounds of her crossing the wooden floor to the counter were the only ones she made. Nancy pursed her lips and glared until she stood within arm's reach. Hooking the cane across one forearm, she reached into the drawstring sack made from the same light gray cotton as her dress and retrieved three letters she laid across the counter in a row. Then she reached into the bag again and pulled out a pendant.

Essie forced a smile that she hoped was congenial. "Do you wish to post these for the next stage?"

Nancy clicked her fingernails together before sliding one beneath the clasp. With one flick, she opened the cover and revealed the clock face beneath the ornate filigree. She tapped it. "Not for the next stage." Her sneer accentuated her bulbous nose and sallow complexion.

"My duties bind me, Nancy, which include the swift expedition of all mail deposited at this office. I can't hold it past Tuesday."

Nancy lifted her palm. "Oh, of course. Nor do I wish you to hold it."

Essie furrowed her brows. She tugged at them, rubbing the space between them, hoping to release the developing tension. The last thing she desired doing was playing mind games with Nosey Nancy. "I see." She reached for the closest. "They are staying in Wylder."

Slamming her hovering palm downward, Nancy trapped the letters against the counter.

The act startled Essie. She jumped and pulled back her fingers just in time to prevent them from being smashed beneath Nancy's palm. She opened her mouth, but words failed.

Nancy leaned toward Essie. "You don't see at all." She stabbed the first letter with the long, hard fingernail on her right forefinger. "This one is going to San Francisco." Moving down the line, she repeated her gestures. "This one is going to Chicago, and this one to Boston."

Raking a glance over them, Essie finally realized what they were—letters to political leaders. Stutts was likely vying for her job. *What if he's successful?* Her eye twitched, and she placed her hands beneath the counter to prevent Nancy from detecting their sudden trembling. "Do you know where these cities are?"

Grabbing her cane off her forearm, Nancy used it to hit the floor for emphasis. *Thump.* "Why, Estelle

Baumgardner, are you insinuating I'm an imbecile? Are you insulting a customer?"

The tremble quickened. Essie could face the most brutal outlaws and not break a sweat because they were direct. They meant what they said and said what they meant. But Nancy Finncannon used words the way hunters used bait, and she'd trap her if she could and had obviously arrived to do just that. "Nancy, I've never insulted a customer, and I don't intend to start today. But I've also never allowed one to waste my time with silly sport. So, if you want those letters on the next stage, we'll get on with it. If not, I've got work to do."

Throwing back her head, Nancy laughed for a full thirty seconds. She stopped suddenly and glared. "Stutts came by at eleven and again at eleven twenty-five. I came back at eleven forty. The post office was closed, uh-huh." She paused. "We want these letters on today's stage, not the next one."

Goose bumps crept along Essie's spine. Her worst fear had just occurred. Not only had she been caught slipping away from her post, but for purely insignificant reasons. She had not been robbed, had not been injured, or taken ill. But letting Nancy find out would be the worst thing. She lifted her chin. "Nothing I can do about that. But I can get these on Tuesday's stage."

Nancy's eyes narrowed. She leaned on the counter with one elbow, its wrist pumping the cottonwood surface. "Today's stage, Estelle Baumgardner, or else."

"Or else what?" Essie snapped. Hot blood coursed throughout her body, and she set her lips in a straight line as heat surged her cheeks.

Nancy Finncannon glared back. "I—"

The door pushed open with a squeak. Essie glanced around Nancy from habit. The anger drained from her head and puddled in her feet, leaving her quaking for other reasons. "Pierre…I mean…Mr. Lacroix…good afternoon."

Jerking her head, Nancy let out a small gasp. "Why, Mr. Lacroix. How lovely to see you again and at the post office, no less." She turned back and sneered at Essie.

Pierre clapped his hands and locked his gaze with Essie's. "Dear ladies, what a treat to find you both here together. Am I interrupting something?"

Essie grimaced. She was both frustrated and glad to see Pierre. Her irritation was certainly not his fault, but she doubted she'd be in the current situation if not for his charms. Yet, his demeanor altered the atmosphere. "Not at all. You might be the right person to settle this dilemma. You see, Nancy wants to mail letters in the past, and I wonder if that exposition of yours has a means of transportation that will allow such a transaction to occur."

Stroking his mustache, Pierre lingered just beyond the entrance. "I am not sure I understand. What does it mean to mail letters in the past?"

Nancy cleared her throat. "Not in the past, but I want them posted today. I want them on today's stage."

As he strolled forward, his fingertips slipped off the edge of his hairy lip-covering with a twirl. "But I saw the stage depart the depot, *n'est pas*?"

Nancy crossed her arms over her chest. "You certainly did."

"Well, then, *Madame* Finncannon, you are asking for the impossible." Pierre smiled and held open his palms while shrugging. "Perhaps you should have arrived with them earlier in the morning."

His comment landed like a punch in Essie's gut. She shifted her weight from side to side until her feet protested. They were sore from the sprint to catch CD, and now her forehead joined her arches in the complaint. She rubbed it with deft fingertips while wishing Pierre had said anything but that.

Glowering, Nancy uncrossed her arms so quickly she wobbled and grabbed the counter for balance. After steadying herself, she slid her hand along the cane's crooked handle. "Oh, I can assure you I did." She shook her cane at Essie. "She closed the office this morning without any prior warning to Wylder's good citizens."

Essie feared Pierre would divulge where they'd been, not that it was wrong or inappropriate, but it was frivolous. The Finncannons weren't the only people in Wylder who might object to her closing during regular hours for anything less than a dire emergency. She was also tired of arguing. "As I told you, Nancy, I can do nothing about that now. I'll post these now or not; it's up to you."

Pierre raked a glance across the two of them and winked at Essie. He placed a palm to his chest. "I am afraid it was my fault." He lifted his hand and laid it across Nancy's, where it rested on the counter. "Whatever can I do to make amends to you?"

"Your fault?" Nancy cut her eyes at Essie. "How on earth is the postmistress failing to open the post office on time your fault?"

"I needed help with some...how do you say?"— Pierre stared at the ceiling and twirled his fingers— "delicate issues. I consider it a diplomatic effort by the postmistress and intend to make that known to your political leaders. She is doing a fine job here in Wylder, no?" He peeked at the letters on the counter and pointed. "May I?"

Essie shrugged. "They aren't posted yet, so they are not officially in my possession."

Nancy nodded.

Pierre lifted them and silently read each name and address of the intended recipients. "Shall I include yours with mine? I also have a few recommendations. As yours are likely similar, you should appear equally knowledgeable of the affairs in your town." He tugged his coat open and poised the letters over the notched pocket along the inside lining.

With her face paling, Nancy snatched the letters. "I just remembered something I need to add—rather, Mr. Finncannon should include. Excuse me, Mr. Lacroix." Nancy rushed for the door. The cane's thumping registered an off-beat, one for every two steps instead of one for one.

Bracing herself with stiff arms against the counter, Essie didn't exhale until the door slammed. The breaths she worked to keep from appearing as labored while Nancy hovered over her, now huffed from her. "I can't thank you enough, Pierre. You saved me from her wrath. But how did you know to come back?"

His smile withered to a frown. "I was looking for Francine and hoped to find her here."

Essie swiped at the tendril sticking to her damp forehead. *Why did Pierre think his daughter would be at the post office?* "Francine? Here?"

Pierre's anxious glances darted around the interior and beyond the window into the street. "Have you seen her since the livery?"

Essie ached to help and wished she had noticed his daughter, but she was so preoccupied with almost missing the stage and the near-collision with Lionel that she drew a blank. "Is the horse still in the stable?"

Pierre nodded and exhaled. "I looked there first. The mustang is tied to the hitching post like she had a second thought at the last minute."

"Perhaps she's in her room."

He rested a finger against his cheek. "Perhaps, but she always responds when I knock, and she was intrigued with Augusta and the young man—Clyde, is it?"

"Well, there you go." Essie patted his arm. "Francine probably ran into them. You know how young people are about such things."

"Maybe." He stepped to the sorting room and out the back door, before quickly returning. "I just do not understand. She was beside me one minute and..."

"She'll be along shortly. You'll see."

He harumphed. "I hope you are right. Francine is out of her element here in Wylder. She is not accustomed to the freedoms afforded your daughter."

"Gus?" Essie laughed. "I don't afford her freedoms. She just takes them where she sees them. She's so like her father." She looked away from Pierre but not directly at anything. A fuzzy image clouded her mind—one of a youthful Augustus Baumgardner and his spur-of-the-moment wild hairs.

"Her father? You miss him still?"

Pierre's voice tugged her from the reminiscence. "I hardly knew him when you think about it. We were so young and so...like Gus, I suppose. We thought we had all the time in the world and burned all the wicks at once."

"This urgency of life pulsates here in the West. The energy is different from any place I've ever visited before. Francine has only joined me on a select few journeys, which is why I am so concerned. She is much more delicate than she appears, and I am to blame. I have shielded her, you see." He covered his face with a hand and inhaled sharply.

Essie patted his arm. "I'm not so sure of that, Pierre. Children often surprise their parents. Your inner strength is within her. She might not show it, but it is there."

His face brightened, and he gripped her hand. Lifting it to his lips, he brushed a soft kiss along her flesh. "How you do soothe me."

The touch of Pierre's moist lips along her palm ignited a firestorm of longing. The sensations pulsed throughout her body. She glanced into Pierre's eyes and felt the heat from his gaze. Essie wondered what he knew that she didn't. Although she'd always yearned to see the world and experience other cultures, she'd only known the West. Was it calmer and more sedate in other places? She slipped her hand from his, although she ached to leave it gripped between his long fingers. "Maybe the spirit of the West only ignites that which is already there."

Shrugging, Pierre placed a finger on his cheek. "You might be right. Francine is taken with Augusta and insists on riding a Wylder horse. Even your ponies are more spirited than the ones in Tuileries Garden, however."

Essie jerked her head and gasped. "Your daughter

is taken with Gus while she is jealous of Francine."

"Jealous?" He dropped his hand and held out open palms. "But—*pourquoi*—why?"

"Francine is so refined and elegant. She has excellent manners, poise, and gracefulness." Essie paused. *Are these attributes the cause of Gus's angst or mine?* She fidgeted with her collar. "You've raised her well, Pierre, but there is the issue of the Hartshorn boy."

Pierre's face blanked. "Hartshorn?"

She fluttered a hand. "Clyde—the young man Douglas assigned to look after her."

Clucking his tongue, Pierre nodded. "*Oui*, yes. I am so accustomed to his ever-watchful eye; I forgot he was not there." He turned and glanced behind him. Bending, he retrieved something from the floor and held it out in his palm. "Someone must have dropped this."

Cringing, Essie immediately thought of Nancy and the trio of letters she'd brought into the post office. She snatched it from Pierre and studied the handwriting. "Must belong to Nancy Finn…no…I think it's meant for you, although the spelling isn't exactly right."

"*Moi*?" Pierre took it back and stared at the front. As he ran a fingertip over the scribbled letters, he called them aloud. "M. P. A-y-r-e L-a-k-w-a." His lower lip trembled. "Do you think…should I open it? There is no street address, and only a semblance to my name is there…"

Essie frowned as she crossed and uncrossed her arms. "You're right, of course. I mean, I know everyone in Wylder, but…" She held out her hand. "As postmistress, I alone have permission to open mail to identify its intended party or parties."

"But, of course." He gave it back to her and sucked in a breath.

Adding to the mystery was the crudeness of what appeared to Essie as a hastily-cobbled envelope. The paper was roughly cut, and the corners tucked into the edges instead of using hot wax. Either the author was in a hurry or lacked the appropriate letter-writing tools. She'd seen it before, especially when travelers passed through town or cowhands stopped in on a cattle drive. She slipped a thumbnail beneath the flap and tugged. The edges sprang open.The writing inside the crudely made envelope was equally as haphazard. Essie glanced over the badly misspelled words. If she understood them accurately, Francine was in danger.

Five thousand dollers to git yer Francy back. No funy bizness. Cash in a mail bag behind the rock canyen chimley rock before sunset tomorrow.

Chapter 10

Essie gasped and grabbed Pierre's arm. "Oh, Pierre."

"What does the note say? Is it about Francine?" His voice quivered.

"I'm afraid so." She held it out.

He glanced over the note and shook his head. "I do not understand the handwriting. It is little more than scribble." He pushed it back into her hands.

"Of course." She fingered the paper, took a breath, and exhaled slowly before speaking. "I believe it to say that someone has kidnapped Francine and is holding her for ransom."

Pierre's chest heaved. His labored breaths whistled through his mustache. "Francine? Kidnapped? We must contact the authorities."

Essie shoved the note into her pocket, turned the sign to *Closed,* and threw the latch. Taking his hand, she tugged him toward the back door. "Yes, Sheriff Hanson and Victor Douglas. One will know how best to handle this situation."

Pierre snagged his hand from her grip. "I'll get Douglas as you must not close again. You heard what that woman—"

She leaned toward him. "Dagnabit, Pierre. Francine is a guest in our country, not a missing cow from a rancher's herd. I'd say the situation calls for extra efforts from everyone in Wylder."

He opened his mouth.

Essie didn't give him the chance to object. She pulled the door closed behind her and half-dragged him across the back walkway. "We'll go to the saloon together for Douglas, and then the three of us can go to the sheriff's office. Hanson has a man in custody at the jail for swindling and attempted theft. If he isn't behind this travesty, I bet he knows who is."

"The card shark? I heard." Pierre's voice trembled. "But kidnapping is quite a stretch from thumbing aces."

A horse galloped past, kicking up a dust cloud in his wake. The legs of its rider's indigo trousers with a yellow stripe down the side were stuffed into tall, black boots. A golden cord rimmed the crown of his felted wool hat where it met the wide brim.

Though she placed a palm over her mouth and nose, Essie tasted the metallic notes in the swirling dirt. Hints of dung and gunpowder filled her nostrils. After glancing in the direction of the cavalry office—the officer's likely destination—she nudged Pierre from the walkway.

As they crossed the street, Essie averted her gaze and tucked her chin. "He's more than a run-of-the-mill thief." Choking on the dry, dusty air, Essie coughed. "He tried to bilk an Arapaho friend out of a season's worth of beaver pelts—practically stole them—and I don't believe we know his real identity yet. Who knows what's he's capable of doing?"

Pierre accelerated the pace, but his pinched face betrayed his worry. He grew more uncomfortably silent with each step. Panic oozed from him in the way he breathed and his unusual leaden footfalls.

Victor's last words from their earlier parting played in Essie's mind. *What if he's already left the saloon?* She walked faster, matching Pierre's steps until she spied the saloon's swinging doors.

Voices wafted beyond them, including Douglas's high laughter.

Essie led Pierre to a bench and settled him onto it. "Wait here. I'll be back in a moment." She pushed through the doors and sauntered forward.

Victor caught her eye and grinned. "Essie'll tell you it's true." He lifted an arm and scooped his hand. "Come over here."

She marched to the bar and leaned her mouth near his ear. "I need to speak with you."

Victor slammed a shot glass against the counter and plunked some change beside it. "Whatever she wants is on me. Go ahead, Essie. Tell the barkeep what you'll have."

His red cheeks were most likely the effect of the sun mixed with that of the alcohol, and his gaiety sent a sharp pain straight to her forehead. She tugged his sleeve. "I'll have you outside immediately."

A loud hoot commenced as the crowd reacted. "You heard the lady, Vic," someone yelled above the din.

He laughed but sobered as his gaze swept across her face, and he lifted a brow. "In that case, I'm coming." He snatched his hat and plunked it atop his head.

Walking ahead of Victor, Essie led him to the exit, pointing to the spot where Pierre sat with his head in his hands. She hated to be blunt, but now wasn't the time to mince words. "Brace yourself, Vic. It's Francine—

she's missing or abducted."

Shaking a forefinger, Victor looked between the two of them and smirked. He pushed up the brim of his hat with the same wagging digit. "That's impossible. Where were they last?"

Essie frowned. "Livery. She was picking out a horse."

"A horse, you say?" Victor stomped through the doors and approached Pierre. He smacked a palm against his shoulder. "See there? She's likely just out for a ride."

Pierre's shoulders shook. He lifted his hand, palm up, toward Essie. "Show…him."

She dug into her pocket and retrieved the note. "Ransom is requested," she whispered.

Victor yanked it from her grip. His eyes moved back and forth, top to bottom. He paled and locked his gaze onto Essie's. "I see."

Essie looked from Victor to Pierre. "Should we notify the authorities?"

Victor handed back the note. "Not yet. Give me a couple of hours."

Pierre glanced up with bloodshot eyes. "A couple of hours? Have you any idea how long a couple of hours is to someone young and innocent and far from her home?" Pierre gargled the words as though they hung in his throat. "Tell me again what it says, Essie."

She'd looked at it so many times she knew it by heart. "Five thousand dollars to get your Francine back. No funny business. Cash in a mailbag behind the rock canyon's chimney rock before sunset tomorrow."

Victor placed a palm against Pierre's shoulder. "I think I already know who's behind this. That fellow

John Smith escaped earlier today."

"Escaped?" Essie immediately regretted revealing the vileness of the man calling himself John Smith.

Vic jerked his head toward the saloon. "A commotion broke out over here, and Hanson came down to restore the peace. When he returned, the door to the jail cell was wide open. The man used some sleight of hand and picked the lock, escaping in plain view during the day."

Lacroix trembled.

Victor patted his shoulder. "No worries, Lacroix. We'll find Francine."

"How can you be so sure? What if…what if…" His eyes darted back and forth.

Essie immediately thought of the officer they'd encountered on the walk from the post office. If the authorities were busy locating the crook, who would help Pierre and Francine? Victor would know. "Did the sheriff gather a posse? Is the cavalry assisting?"

Victor scratched his chin. He tugged his lips to one side but did not answer.

Pierre dropped his head and wept.

Essie had never felt sorrier for anyone. She couldn't imagine having to face such a horrible turn of events. Of course, everyone knew she didn't have five thousand dollars, so it was pointless to ask. "Pierre, who knows you…" The sound of hooves interrupted her. "Someone's coming." She peeked around the building's edge.

Two horses slowed as they entered the town.

Essie recognized Lightning. "It's Gus and Clyde. Maybe they can help."

Gus's laughter wafted over the sound of the

clomping. "I beat you again, Clyde."

Clyde nudged his horse forward and pulled alongside her. "Because I let you."

"Did not. I won fair and square, Clyde Hartshorn, and you better…" She twisted her head toward Essie. "Mama," she gasped. "What are you doing out here? Who's running the post office?"

Essie gripped Pierre's arm. "Should we tell her?"

Pierre's watery eyes searched hers. "But of course, she must know. Perhaps Augusta and…the boy…saw something…heard something…anything…" His mouth continued moving, but sounds ceased emanating.

Clyde pushed his horse forward and leaped off. He tied the reins over the saloon's hitching post. "Is something wrong?"

Gus turned Lightning's head from the gathering, led him to the spot near the post beside Clyde's horse, and tossed the reins haphazardly. "There must be a problem if Mama left the office again." She scanned the faces of the group. "Where's Francine?"

Inhaling for strength and courage, Essie reached for her hand. She'd never found it easy to break bad news to her daughter, yet tiptoeing along the edges of something unsavory never made the occurrences go down any easier. "We aren't exactly sure where Francine is at the moment. She's missing."

"Missing?" Gus snapped. She scowled. "How can she go missing when she rode back to town with you three?"

Pierre lifted a hand to his face. "It is my fault. You see, she admires you so and wanted a horse to ride in Wylder, and…" His shoulders shook, and he covered his mouth with his palm.

Gus blinked. "Admires me? Wanted to ride a Wylder horse after all that talk of fancy mares in even fancier gardens?" She shook her head. "We can deal with that misconception later. When did she go missing? If she's on a horse, maybe she fell off somewhere. Which direction did she go? Clyde and me—"

Essie pulled her daughter close and stroked the dirt from her cheek. "No need. We believe she's been kidnapped."

Clyde kicked a rock. It skipped across the road and landed with a ping against the spittoon on the porch. He spun around. "Kidnapped? Why on earth would you assume that?"

Having composed himself, Pierre lowered his trembling hand and motioned toward Victor. He lifted his chin. "Show them the note. Perhaps one or the other will recognize the writing."

Simultaneously shaking his head and pointing in the direction of the post office, Victor approached his carriage. "Not out here in the open. I think we need to gather at your place, Essie. The culprit could be watching us."

"Good point," Pierre said. "Will you allow us to ride back with you? I'm not sure how much longer my knees will support me."

"Of course. Jump in," Victor said. He braced Lacroix's back and gently nudged him upward.

Essie climbed in behind him.

Gus leaped astride Lightning. "I'll meet you there."

Victor grabbed Clyde's arm. "We need to appear as normal as possible. You and Gus go around back. We'll enter through the front."

As soon as they were in view of the post office, Essie glimpsed two men hanging around the front. She recognized both and doubted either had anything to do with the kidnapping. "I've got customers," she whispered. "Give me a minute and then enter."

Victor nodded. "Go ahead. I'll bring him along in a minute."

Fletcher Wylder and Phineas Atwater stood outside the office.

Essie struggled with normalcy. "Sorry about the delay, fellows. I had to...attend to some business." *That isn't a lie.*

Fletcher stepped forward. An envelope poked from his grip. "Hey, no problem. Just sending a reply to Ava."

"But of course," she replied. She took his letter. "That'll be three cents."

Phineas hung back.

Fletcher was in no particular hurry. He fished about in his pocket and pulled out a penny. "Yeah, Ava's looking to slip home at the end of the term."

Essie's nerves thinned, but she continued with the expected small talk. "End of the term? When's that?"

Fletcher dug around some more and pulled another cent from his pocket. "Late August, I'd say. We'd hope she'd make it back for the Independence Day celebration, but New York is just too far from Wylder for such a short visit." He sighed.

The back door opened, and Essie heard the clanking of the water pitcher-against-bowl. "I'm sorry you had to wait. I trust you told Ava hello from us all."

Fletcher fished out the last penny and slapped it down. He jerked his head at Phineas, who strolled past the window. "I think you've got another customer waiting." He tugged open the door and stepped through it as the next customer approached.

Phineas removed his hat and twirled it by the brim in his hands. "Thank you for not asking me to approach while Fletcher was here. I have something a bit personal and private. I'd appreciate it if…"

"No worries, Phineas. You know I believe in the sanctity of the mail. Let's see what you've got." She extended a hand.

He laid his hat onto the counter and gripped its edge.

He seemed in slow motion. Essie's pulse thundered, sweat beaded her lip, and she resisted every urge to scream. "Might want to hurry before someone else enters."

"Oh, right." He tugged open his thin jacket and reached into an inner pocket with two fingertips, delicately inching the item from its hold. "I don't want to get it dirty. It needs to keep a neat appearance."

Exhaling, Essie waved. "The longer you handle the paper, the higher the risk you'll transfer soil and soot. Best give it a yank."

He did as she suggested but continued to hold the envelope as he stared at the address. "Maybe I should think about it…wait a bit."

Essie snatched the letter and glanced across its address: *Jane Simpson, 12 Water Street, Gloucester, Massachusetts.* The letters were in swirls with curly tails. She ached to tell him he wasn't fooling anybody in Wylder. They all knew he'd been corresponding with a woman he hoped would come west to marry him. Mail order brides weren't as discreet as they seemed, and more than one person had seen the ads in the *Cheyenne Daily Sun*.

She ran a finger across the address. "You sure have pretty handwriting for a man."

He gasped and lifted his chin. "Oh...about that. I...my sister thought it best it has an elegant outer appearance. She has a real gift with a pen; I'll tell you that."

Sister, right. "How is Mary Lou?" While she talked, she tugged a stamp from behind the counter. "That'll be three cents."

"Oh, right." He reached into his coat pocket and scratched around. The coat bulged until the shape of his balled fist poked through the fabric. It receded, and he pulled out a single penny. "She's fine. Still studying. I've never seen a more serious woman where books are concerned." He placed the cent onto the counter. "There's one." Digging back into his pocket, he squirreled around some more.

Essie rubbed her brow to keep him from seeing her natural inclination to roll her eyes at his sloth-like movements. Her heart pounded as if it might explode as he tinkered. "I think someone's coming. If you wish to keep it secret, better hurry if you don't want one of Wylder's residents to see you in here with this." She waved it in the air for good measure.

"Oh, right." He slapped the other two coins on the counter. "Put it in a sack or something. I don't want anybody to know."

She grabbed a mailbag and stuffed it inside. "All done. Anything else?"

"Not unless Augusta is around. I thought I saw her—"

Essie's heart dropped. Suspicion clouded her judgment, and her impatience turned to fury. He was so desperate for a wife that he'd sweet-talk any woman crossing his path, even the young ones—perhaps especially the younger ones. She lifted a finger and shoved it in his face. "You listen to me. If I catch you hanging around my daughter, you'll not need that letter you just paid to post. Dead men don't need brides. Do you understand me?"

Backing away, he held up both palms. "I meant no disrespect, Miss Essie. I just…well…I'll just be going."

She sniffed. Her whole head pounded. "See that you do, and be quick about it."

He turned and bolted for the door.

His movements were the quickest succession of them she'd seen. *I've got to get that letter to Blanche. He's merely one of a hundred men who'd love a chance to get their paws on Augusta.* She swiped at her face. *I can't think about that right now.*

Crossing to the front, she opened the door and peered at Victor's empty carriage. She glanced left and right and saw the pair of them smoking cigars and acting cheerful. It was an act, of course, and her heart ached to think of the pain such pretense must cause Pierre. She stepped outside and snapped open the fan she'd stowed in her vest and whipped it back and forth.

Victor stubbed his cigar's lit end in the sand pot.

Without acknowledging his presence, she slipped inside.

Gus entered from the back. "Heard the door. Is it okay now?"

Essie marched past her and motioned for Clyde. "Guard the back. Let me know the second you see someone—anyone—approaching."

"Yes, ma'am." He yanked open the back door and leaned his shoulder against the post.

Victor entered through the front. "All clear?"

She nodded. "Where's Pierre?"

"Watching the front. Is Clyde…"

"Watching the back."

Standing near the counter with her hands on her hips, Gus glanced between them. "Tell me what's going on. Something bad has happened to Francine, hasn't it?"

Victor pulled out the ransom note and handed it to her. "The spelling is bad, but the message is clear."

Gus's eyes raked left to right. She gasped. "Kidnapped? Someone kidnapped Francine?"

Essie patted her arm. "I'm afraid so."

She stomped a foot. "Well, what are we doing here? We've got to get the sheriff…a posse…everyone in town…"

Victor took back the note and laid it against the counter. "Not so fast. That could cost the girl her life if the kidnapper panics. Besides, Hanson's gone after the escaped crook."

"But…" Gus slapped her hat against her thigh. "What are we doing?"

Essie reached for her daughter's hat and slipped it from her grasp. Placing it just beyond Gus's reach on her opposite side, she nodded to Victor. "What's on your mind?"

Victor tapped the note. "The kidnapper left us some clues." He glanced between Essie and Gus. "They always do. Criminals think they are crafty and smart, but they always make mistakes. Look right here." He tapped the word *mail*.

"Mail?" Essie frowned. "How would a reference to a mailbag be a clue?"

Victor ground his teeth. "It's someone in town—somebody who knows the postmistress would have a reason to meet Pierre Lacroix and his daughter. Who knew she had a package on the stage Tuesday?"

In her thoughts, Essie relived the day she received the parcel from Paris with its swirly writing and fancy trim. She saw the stagecoach driver's smirk and felt the package's weight sliding from his grip into hers. As it had from the first moment CD placed the special delivery in her care, her pulse jumped. "Only CD, but it couldn't have been him."

Victor nodded. "No, it's not Cyrus, but are you sure nobody else saw the package?"

"Wait." Essie closed her eyes. *Think*. As she remembered the conversation, she snapped her fingers. "CD said something about waiting for it. He had to hold the stage for the train conductor. Everybody on the train and the stage would have known."

Victor grimaced. "Okay. That certainly widens the possible suspects. Let's keep narrowing, though." He motioned to her name. "Although they misspelled it, they knew her name." He moved a finger down the page. "They also know the canyon and that the pillar in the middle of the sagebrush is called chimney rock."

Gus flailed her hands. "Everybody around these parts knows that. How does that help?"

He pointed at her. "You said it. Everybody in Wylder knows about chimney rock, but the strangers on the stage likely don't. I think we can rule them out for now."

Essie understood. "That's right. It also has to be someone close to us because they slipped that note under the door without drawing attention and didn't drag her far. But what about that John Smith fellow?"

Victor tapped it again. "He's the most likely suspect. We don't know anything about him, and the note is hurriedly written." He rubbed the paper between his thumb and forefinger. "This is thicker than regular stock. It looks like something from the hotel, but the kidnappers could have snatched a sheet anywhere. I wonder if the general store is selling something like it."

Gus raced for the stationery on the small desk. "Mama got some there not too long ago. I'll grab it so we can compare." She passed the trash bin on the way and reached into it, snagging the wadded letter. "Here you go." She pulled at its crumpled edges. "See…it's…"

Essie sprinted toward her. "Don't…" She saw her daughter's face distort and cringed as she swiped at it.

Gus held it beyond her reach. "Mama, what is this?" She raked a glance across the page and paled. "Are you sending me away? I'm a failure?" She swallowed hard as her eyelids moistened.

Essie cowered beneath the stricken gaze of the one person whose opinion of her still mattered. *How can I make her understand?* Her mouth dried until the words crackled off her tongue. "Oh, honey, it's not what you think. It's not you who has failed, but me. I can't give you the education you need out here. I can't protect you from things like what happened to Francine or from the hungry appetites of desperate men seeking wives."

"But, Mama. I don't need you to protect me anymore. I thought I was protecting you."

Tears slid down Essie's cheeks. She dabbed them with both palms but could not stem the flow.

Victor snatched the half-finished letter meant for Blanche Davenport. "You two can work that out after we get Francine back." He laid the paper next to the ransom note. "Nope, it's not the same." Balling it back into an even-tighter wad than before, he threw it across the room and back into the bin. "For the record, it was in the waste, so it doesn't look like anyone's going anywhere yet." He patted Essie's back.

The gesture comforted Essie. She met Victor's gaze and saw his slight wink. She ached to tell him how much his intercedence meant but could not find the words.

Gus inhaled sharply and placed her hands on her hips. "And I intend to keep it that way. I ain't going east, Mama. I can learn whatever you think I need to know right in Wylder. Besides, who needs a woman out here who prances around in fancy gowns?"

The moment passed. Essie swallowed and glanced at her fingernails. .

"We do, that's who," Victor roared. "You've given me an excellent idea, Gus." He jerked a thumb toward the door. "Gus, get Lacroix and bring him in here. I have a plan."

She crossed her arms over her chest and bellowed. "Not until you promise I don't have to go to Boston."

Essie wouldn't make promises she didn't intend to keep. She assumed a similar stance and shifted her weight. "We'll discuss it later."

Victor lifted his hands into the air. "Never mind. I'll do it myself." He stomped to the door and heaved it open. "Lacroix. Get in here."

Gus glared at Essie. "I mean it, Mama."

"Later, Augusta," Essie said, rubbing her eyes. The headache worsened, and she didn't have any willow bark tea.

Pierre raced inside and shut the door behind him. He glanced from one to the other of them. "What is it? Do you know something?"

Victor massaged his shoulder. "We can solve two dilemmas with my proposition. This one"—he pointed at Gus—"can act as a decoy for Francine. We can dress her in Francine's garments and one of her bodacious hats, and nobody will be the wiser."

Essie chortled. "Victor, have you lost your mind? You'll need more than a dress to make people believe she's Francine. They don't talk, walk, or act alike."

Gus smacked the counter. "But that's what you all want, isn't it? You want me to act like Francine."

"Of course not." Essie furrowed her brows and kneaded her skirt. *It's all coming out wrong.* Her head throbbed. "I only want what's best for you. Can't you understand?"

Pierre leaned against the counter. He glanced between Essie and Victor. "*Pourquoi?* Why would you endanger another child? How does such an act help us find Francine?"

Plucking his cigar from his pocket, Victor grinned. "I'm glad you asked. You see, we lure the kidnapper to the rock canyon with the prospect of having his money. But just outside the chimney rock, we collect Gus pretending to be Francine and turn back for town. They'll be waiting and, upon seeing us leave without dropping the cash, come after us."

Shaking his head and wagging a forefinger, Pierre

objected. "*Mais bien sur*. How can we be sure the kidnapper will not harm Francine or Augusta? It is too dangerous. I don't like it."

Essie didn't like the plan either. "Without Francine, who's instructing Augusta on the proper way to walk and talk and all that fancy stuff?"

Victor grimaced and slammed a palm to the counter. "You've got me there, unless you can do it, Pierre?"

Pierre pointed at himself and shook his head. *"Moi? Mais non*. Being prim and proper requires more knowledge than the way one walks. Undergarments have many concerns and would be too indelicate for me."

"Indelicate?" Victor snapped. "Do you want to get your daughter back or worry about manners?"

He lifted his chin and tugged at his collar. "I'm going to the bank to request a wire—"

"Really? You think you'll get the money by sunset tomorrow?" Victor shook his head.

Pierre jerked his arms high into the air. "I don't know what to think. I'm too distraught to concentrate. I only know I cannot jeopardize the reputation of sweet Augusta for the sake of Francine's speedy return, no matter how much I love her nor how much her disappearance is breaking my heart."

Essie closed her eyes and blocked the noisy protests. She kneaded her skirt with the fingertips of one hand while the other gripped the fan. She recalled the sensation of Francine's cool palms closing around hers as she pressed the gift into her hand. An idea swept over Essie and chilled her to the core. Her head roared. *Keep quiet. Don't speak of the crazy thought*. But she couldn't remain silent if a chance existed of helping Francine. "I know someone who could help if she would agree."

Gus ceased pouting and uncrossed her arms. "Did you say something, Mama?"

"Who?" Victor prodded.

Don't say it, don't say it. As she struggled with her self-preservation, Essie's conscience rebelled. If she agreed, she would demand payment, and it would likely be more costly to Essie than five thousand dollars would to Pierre. But Victor was right. No other person was safe if some outlaw thought taking their children would result in remuneration. "N...Nan...Nancy Finncannon."

Victor's lips slackened until the unlit cigar he chewed dropped to the floor. "You gotta be kidding me? That bag of wind and..." He twisted his mouth into a sneer. "What can that awful woman teach Gus about acting more ladylike?"

Pierre blinked. "The woman with the cane and the terrible disposition? I agree with Douglas."

Essie exhaled loudly. "You are right, of course, about the Nancy Finncannon we know today. But how many times have you heard people joke about Stutts marrying Nancy for her inheritance? Where do you think they got their money?"

Victor squatted and retrieved his cigar. He swiped a dust speck off the tip and rolled his cupped palm over it before sticking it back in his mouth. "Her parents came West with the railroad but sent her back East to school. I do recall hearing something about how light she once was on her feet and how well she sat a horse before getting thrown."

Gus coughed loudly, clearing her throat.

Essie turned toward her daughter. "Are you getting sick?"

She poked out a hip. "Sick of you all talking like I'm not even here. You forgot one thing."

Pierre smiled weakly. "What is that, dearest Augusta?"

She exhaled and straightened her spine, cutting her gaze at Essie. "If I agree to go along with this crazy plot, I want something in exchange."

Crossing to her, Pierre snatched her hands and held them to his heart. "Anything. Name it, and it is yours."

Slipping her hands from his, she patted him gently on the arm. "That is most kind, but you cannot give me what I want." She pointed at Essie. "Only she can."

Essie widened her eyes. *What on earth does that child have on her mind? Now isn't the time for games.* "Me?"

Gus crossed her arms over her chest and tapped a toe. "I want your word in front of these here gentlemen that this talk about Cousin Blanche and Boston and my going east is done. Promise me that you'll forget this nonsense, and I'll be more like Francine than Francine."

Flinching, Essie hated the trap. But Gus was still very young and had a lot to learn. She felt it was incumbent upon her—as her mother—to act responsibly. "Gus...I..."

Pierre took Essie's hands in his. "Why should she go to Boston when she can come to Paris and stay with Francine? After a season abroad, tutelage with my daughter, and exposure to the best academic circles in the world, Augusta will be at home in any city in the world."

Essie's heart fluttered. Pierre's offer was much better than she could have hoped. He was correct, of course. A season in Paris with suitable tutors would do wonders for her daughter. "Your generosity is overwhelming. But we mustn't talk about this now. We have to focus on Francine."

Clyde burst through the back door. "Finncannon's coming with a fistful of letters."

Essie exhaled. "Stutts or Nancy?"

Clyde frowned. "Nancy."

Gus snatched her mother's hands from Pierre's. "Promise. Make me as strong a vow as you made about the sanctity of the mail."

Essie's pulse raced. She'd not considered her daughter's refusal and now faced her absolute determination to stay in an ultimatum whose result could affect Pierre's daughter. She stared into Augusta's determined eyes. *What choice do I have?* She had none. "Oh, all right. I promise."

Victor removed his cigar and waved it around. "Let me do the talking. I'll call on you if I need you."

The sound of heavy footfalls reverberated from the porch.

Each *thump* stabbed Essie's heart, and as she waited for the door to burst open, she held her breath.

Victor pointed from Clyde to the back door. "Head on back. I want to know who you see, even if they're not coming this way, you hear?"

Clyde nodded and raced back through the door just in time.

The front door peeled open, and the *thump—step* sounds that always preceded Nancy Finncannon grew louder. Nancy stepped inside and glanced at the two men. "Well, well. Here you are again. Mr. Lacroix, have you been here the entire time?"

He bowed low and swept his hat across his thighs. "Madame Finncannon, is it?"

She extended the fingertips of one hand. "How gallant of you, Mr. Lacroix, to remember."

He accepted her fingertips and quickly brushed the back of her hand with a kiss. "How could I forget someone of your sophistication?"

Victor cleared his throat. "Yes, Nancy. Lovely to see you again."

She sneered. "I wish I could say the same about you."

Laughing, Victor stepped forward and snatched her hand from Pierre's. "You wouldn't hold a comment made in jest against a man, would you, Nancy?"

Essie struggled with her conscience. *Can I risk sending off Augusta with this awful woman?*

Chapter 11

Nancy raised a brow and withdrew her hand from Victor's grip. "Against a man? Never—but holding a grudge against *you* is entirely different."

Essie feared Victor's comment at the restaurant the previous evening about killing people he didn't like and insinuating she was among them would not make it easy for him to sway her, despite his insistence that he could. She forced a smile. "What can I do for you, Nancy?"

Jerking from Victor, Nancy met Essie's stare. "I thought about what Mr. Lacroix said and have returned to mail the letters. I'm glad to see I didn't waste a trip this time as you're actually in the office and the door is unlatched."

Pierre pushed aside Victor. "About that. I must tell you it was for my daughter and me."

Victor winked at Essie. "Don't do it, Lacroix. Don't tell her. Everybody west of the Mississippi will know about it inside an hour."

Despite the seriousness of the situation, Essie stifled a laugh. Nothing would make Nancy want to know something more than thinking she wouldn't be allowed. "That's right. People talk around these parts. It's not like Paris, France. We don't have the same kind of sophistication as Mr. Lacroix and his daughter."

With a hand to her throat, Nancy gasped. "I'll have

you know I've been in the parlors of the highest classes in America and England. When I was much younger, I seasoned in London as a debutante."

Gus dragged her lips to one side and gagged.

Nancy snapped toward her and raised a brow. "You doubt me?"

She smiled warmly. "No, Mrs. Finncannon. I can see that you have an air about yourself. Mama says I could learn a lot from you, but I don't know if you have the skills to teach me."

Tapping her cane, she sneered. "It isn't a question of whether or not I could teach someone like you, but the amount of time such a task would take. Why I'd likely be in my grave before you even learned a proper curtsy."

Gus brightened. "I'm a fast learner. What can you teach me in twenty-four hours?"

She aimed her cane at Gus. "I couldn't even get all the dirt from behind your ears in that amount of time. But enough nonsense. What is going on? I promise not to tell."

Nancy's actions reminded Essie of the ones that had cost her the coins for the damask and the stationery. She wasn't certain she liked Victor's plan, especially as it thrust Gus into the fray. In hopes of appearing taller, she stretched her spine. "Never mind. Did you want to mail something?"

As her cheeks turned purple, Nancy kept the letters gripped in one hand. She pouted. "After you tell me and not one minute before. You can't leave me dangling like this. It will work on my nerves."

Pierre pressed his palm against the cane, lowering it horizontally. "Only if you agree to help. We are keeping the circle of trust small, and everyone within has a role."

"Well, I suppose." She narrowed her gaze and peeked around Pierre to glare at Victor. "Unless it is dangerous or immoral."

Gus shrugged. "I suppose? That's not a commitment. I think we'll need a firm *yes* before we can let you in on the secret."

"Secret?" Nancy licked her lips. "Fine, yes."

Pierre released his held breath. "*Merci*, dear lady." He grabbed the note and presented it.

Nancy accepted the paper and hooked her cane on the counter's rim. Her eyes moved back and forth until her brows furrowed. "This is gibberish. I cannot possibly understand what this says." She lifted the cane and aimed it at Gus. "Did you write this?"

Gus gasped. "Of course not. I write just fine, don't I, Mama. No, somebody…"

Pierre gently took the cane from Nancy and replaced it against the counter's edge. He then gripped her shoulders as he stared into her eyes. "Someone has…kid…napped my daughter…for ransom. They want five thousand…dollars by sunset…tomorrow."

"Oh, no," she gasped. "Of course, I'll loan you the money until you can get your bank to wire it. Have no worries."

Pierre dropped his hands from her shoulders. "That is very kind…but we have decided not to pay…as we fear giving in to the demands could en…danger other young ladies in Wy…lder." Tears wet his lashes, and his voice cracked.

She glanced from him to Victor and Essie. "What does the sheriff say?"

Victor shrugged. "We haven't told him yet." He shoved the cigar back into his mouth and chewed.

Nancy swayed and grabbed for her cane. "You must tell him right away."

Essie reached behind her and retrieved a vial of smelling salts from the bottom row along the mail cubby. She worried that the shocked expression on Nancy's face indicated she'd pass out and hit the floor. "Alerting Sherriff Hanson was our first instinct, too, but he's not here at the moment."

Gus lunged for Pierre. "Mr. Lacroix," she shouted.

Victor grabbed Pierre as he slumped to the floor. He smacked Pierre's cheeks with a palm. "Lacroix? Breathe, Lacroix."

Essie raced around the counter and pulled the stopper from the glass vial. She waved it beneath his nose until Pierre sucked in a breath.

Blinking, he sat up and looked around. "Francine?"

Gus grabbed the desk chair and brought it to him. "Mr. Lacroix, you must be in shock and shouldn't be standing."

He squeezed his lids until tears wet his lashes. "She must be frightened. I have to find her. I must—the bank—the money…"

"Don't you worry. We'll find Francine." Victor hooked his arms beneath Pierre's and lifted him into the chair. "You just rest a while. I'm thinking of a plan right now."

Pierre grabbed Nancy's hands. "Will you do it? Will you teach Gus to act like Francine?"

Essie groaned. After regaining consciousness, Pierre must have forgotten they'd not reached that part of the plan yet. She glanced over her shoulder at Nancy.

Nancy sucked in her lips and crossed her arms over her chest. She stared down at Pierre and glowered. "What did you say? Oh, never mind. I see what's going on here. You all insult me at every turn until you need my help. I should have realized you weren't sincere."

Victor laid aside his cigar. "Now listen—"

Nancy's face reddened. She puffed her cheeks. "Don't you dare tell me to listen. If you want help, get Hanson. If you're going renegade, which you normally do, you're taking the life of this man's daughter in your hands. I'll have no part of your little scheme."

Essie's fears of counting on Nancy without giving her something in return had come to fruition. She stomped back behind the counter, talking as she marched. "I told them as much. You're merely delaying us now. If you've got business, better get on with it."

Nancy uncrossed her arms and slapped three letters on the counter. "Fine with me. Post these."

Pulling stamps from beneath the counter, Essie laid three in a row. "That'll be nine cents."

She pulled out a small change purse and dug for coins. "I should take them back and add this little charade to the notes. Stutts' connections would love to hear how you're staging a meet-up with outlaws right here in the post office."

Pierre dropped his head in his hands. His shoulders shook. "I have to find her—and get the money just in case. Douglas, the bank…"

As she watched the previously happy-go-lucky Frenchman succumb to grief, Essie's heart broke. Pierre was likely scared, worried, and wounded that he could do nothing to help Francine. She pushed the coins back across the counter along with the letters. She'd known what she had to do the moment Pierre collapsed. "Save your money, Nancy. I'll give you what you want."

"Give me what I want? What do you mean?" Nancy snapped.

Essie took a breath and glanced at Gus. Her daughter was her whole world, and she had no idea how she'd provide for her if she surrendered her position. But it was clear that Nancy was their last hope, and she only wanted one thing badly enough to agree to help them retrieve Pierre's daughter. "If you agree to help us, I'll resign, and Stutts can have the respect of this position as Wylder's postmaster."

Pierre removed a kerchief and swiped at his eyes and nose. "*Non*, Essie, you must not. There must be another way, surely."

Nancy smirked. "This isn't a trick?"

Although bereft, she could not see another solution. The carrot had to be attractive, and the Finncannons had everything except the post office. Essie steadied herself, locking her wobbly knees. "No trick. We'll shake on the agreement right here in front of witnesses."

After collecting the coins and the letters, Nancy motioned for Gus. "Come along, girl. Time's wasting." She patted Pierre's arm. "I'll have your money by the morning."

Gus's enlarged eyes silently pleaded with Essie. If she stared a single moment longer into her daughter's wounded face, she feared she would cave. Turning, she dropped the stamps back into their place, and gripped the edge of the counter. "Do as she says, and be quick about it. Stay over so you can use every minute. We'll be fine." She didn't dare lift her gaze as tears pricked her lids.

"But, Mama…"

Her daughter's low, questioning voice sent a fresh wave of guilt and remorse through Essie. She glanced over her shoulder. "Remember the cost and make it worthwhile."

With her head downcast, she fell into place behind Nancy. "Yes, Mama."

Essie lifted her chin until the door closed behind Nancy and Gus, and then she collapsed into tears. Her daughter's bowed head and soft voice played in Essie's mind. She wrung her hands.

Pierre stood. He wobbled as he walked, but he made his way behind the counter and embraced her. "Dearest lady, what have you done?"

"Your daughter is more important than a job. I'll find another…some way…somehow." She'd made the decision and executed it. Swiping tears from her cheeks with a shaky palm, she pivoted. "So, Vic, what's next?"

Victor stared at Essie. He licked his lower lip and lifted his cigar. "Okay, everyone, enough moping. Here's the plan."

Clyde raced in. "Finn Wylder's coming."

Essie motioned toward the door. "You two best be going. You can put together the plan and tell me about it tomorrow. Business increases around this time every evening, so you'll not have much privacy."

Victor frowned. "Essie's right. Come along, Clyde, Pierre."

Pierre kissed the top of Essie's head. "You are dearer to me than you know. I shall not forget your sacrifice, regardless of how this turns out. I will find a way to repay you."

"Nonsense. Doing what's right needs no

reimbursement. We'll get Francine back, don't you worry."

Victor jerked his head. "Lacroix, now, before we have to explain to another Wylder resident."

" 'Til the morrow, sweet Essie." Pierre tipped his hat, then scrambled behind Victor and Clyde while departing from the post office.

Steadying herself, Essie understood that her days as postmistress were few and wondered if she had another way. Unable to think of one, she sighed. *Enjoy the last moments, and wait on your customers while they're yours to serve.*

****

With the darkness came the knowledge that Augusta wasn't coming home for the night. Essie retreated to the upstairs room and cried. She couldn't eat or sleep.

Fletcher's comment about Ava not returning to Wylder because of the distance played on her mind. Saving the money for the initial trip was all Essie considered. If Gus went east, how often would she visit? Most likely, never. *I can't think about that right now.*

Worries for both Gus and Francine played on her mind, alongside those for whatever plan Victor and Pierre cobbled together. She peeked out the window at every sound, hoping the kidnapper would change his mind and bring back Francine. Another worry stabbed at her heart. *What if the kidnapper injures the girl? What if…*

Don't think about that, either. Essie spread the fan and snapped it closed. Such an attack would ruin Francine. Beneath her haughty air, she possessed gentle sweetness. Francine was unique, and Essie didn't want anything about her altered.

What about Gus? She was one of a kind, too, and even as the watch ticked, she was changing. *Perhaps I've been wrong to think she needed altering.* Who made the determinations about the expectations of a young lady in society? Why did Gus have to change to accommodate others' assumptions?

"Oh, Gus," she moaned aloud. "I've wronged you, too, and I'll tell you after this is over." She recalled the wounded expression on her daughter's face when she spread apart the letter to Blanche Davenport. *"You're sending me away? I'm a failure?"*

The worst part was that Augusta thought she was shielding her mama. Gus had become a tough tomboy out of necessity. *She was only protecting me.* Essie wailed. *I'm horrible, worse even than my mother.*

The sleepless night dragged unmercifully. By morning, Essie was in the window, watching the sunrise over Wylder. Before it set, the ruse would be over. Either they'd be successful, and Francine would be back, or they'd fail, and both girls might be lost. The grim reality stabbed at Essie's heart, as did the prospects of what Gus might be going through at the moment.

What was Nancy inflicting upon her daughter—what tricks, snags, and ridicules? What punishments if she failed? The worries compounded until Essie nearly retrieved her from Nancy's grip. *Surely, she'd not hurt Gus.* A smile curled her lips. *Surely, Gus wouldn't hurt her, but she would if the need arose.* "Gus, you're perfect just as you are," she screamed. Too bad nobody heard the words meant for her daughter.

Wringing her hands, Essie crossed to the ewer stand and drizzled water from the pitcher into the bowl. She splashed it against her warm face with cupped palms and allowed the excess to drip down her neck, forming a rivulet into her bosom.

The weather was much too warm for heating water over a fire. The eggs in the cupboard were likely spoiled, and with Essie's nerves acting up, she doubted she could get one to stay down. Dressing for the day, she rushed down the stairs and opened the office earlier than usual. After flipping the sign, she'd barely made it halfway when she heard the door squeak ajar. Jumping at the sound, she squealed and turned. "Goodness, Phineas, I wasn't expecting anyone this early."

Phineas Atwater pushed through the entry and plucked off his hat. He ran the brim through his fisted fingers. "You're open, ain't ya? That's what the sign says."

Taking deep breaths, Essie calmed herself. She feared the tremble in her voice would trigger suspicion, but with Phineas startling her, she had a good reason to be shaky. "I'm open. What can I do for you?"

He shifted his weight from one foot to the other and took a deep breath. "Essie, I've changed my mind. I want that letter."

Blinking, Essie digested the strange request bordering on an ethics code violation. Phineas normally moved slow, and talked slower, but this time, he spat his request so quickly that his words ran together. *Is he asking me to betray my oath?* She balked and swallowed the knot in her throat. "I'm sorry, Phineas, but you know better. Once a letter is posted, it belongs to the United States Post Office until it gets to its intended recipient."

Phineas slapped his hat against a thigh. "Tarnation, Essie. I—"

The door opened, and Cade Peterson, Lionel's dad, strolled inside. "Morning, Essie. I didn't get to town yesterday. The young'uns wanted to go fishing." He talked as he walked and jerked his chin at Phineas. "Morning."

Phineas nodded and mumbled a thin greeting. His hat fell to the floor. "G'morning."

Essie hid her hands beneath the counter to prevent the customers from witnessing the shake. "Fishing, you say? Any luck?"

Cade beamed. "Caught twelve trout and a snapping turtle."

"Well, I suppose you will be feasting tonight." Essie hoped she sounded more cheerful than she felt.

"Hey, Phineas, how are things over at your ranch?" Cade winked at Essie. "Caught anything or anyone lately?"

Phineas' cheeks reddened. He grabbed his hat and made for the door. "Not that I'm telling you. See you later, Essie."

Cade leaned on the counter after the door closed behind Phineas Atwater. He pointed a thumb over his shoulder. "Rumor has it he's sending off for one of those mail order brides. Reckon you'd know."

Essie lifted one hand and wiggled its forefinger. "Not that I'd tell even if I did." She turned to the sorting cubby, pulled out an envelope, and placed it on the counter. "I suppose you came for this."

He lifted the letter addressed to his wife and tapped it against the cottonwood counter. "You're a real gem,

Essie Baumgardner. Wylder's lucky to have such an honorable postmistress; I'll tell you that."

Tears threatened. Lack of sleep and the perilous situation left Essie shaky. Her usual toughness turned to mercury glass, leaving her a mere reflection of herself. "The pleasure has been all mine."

"Has been?" Cade jerked his chin. He tugged his suspenders. "You're not planning on deserting us, are you, Essie, because we need you looking after things."

She swallowed hard and felt her eyes growing large. "Well...I...mean..."

He leaned closer. "Rumor has it that Nosey Nancy Finncannon is lobbying for her husband to take over things here, and I'll let you in on a secret—the good folks of Wylder won't stand for it."

"Oh?" She blinked. She'd not considered the town's outcry if Stutts replaced her.

Cade shrugged. "They don't need the money. Nancy only wants him to have the post so's she can snoop through the mail and know everyone's comings and goings. She'd know the handwriting of every person..."

Handwriting... "Handwriting of every person," she whispered aloud. Whatever he said next was lost on Essie. She snapped her fingers and bolted from behind the counter as she dashed for the door. Turning as she flung it open, she called back over her shoulder. "Wait right there. I just thought of something. I'll be back..."

Phineas's anger didn't increase his speed. He was barely to the corner where he slumped with his head down.

Essie cupped her palms around her mouth. "Phineas, wait. Turn around."

Phineas turned. "If'n you ain't giving me my letter, I ain't returning."

She had to entice him, but even in her current predicament, she wouldn't lie. "I have an idea. Come back to the office, and we'll discuss it—please."

He pressed a palm against a pillar and leaned into it with his weight. "And then you'll give back my letter?"

Essie had never breached protocol. She'd always followed the rules and obeyed the commands of the service, but what difference did one letter make when a young girl's life hung in the balance? "I can't promise, but I can give you my word that I will accept a formal written request from you and attach the letter while I search for an answer."

He sucked his lips inward and yanked off his hat. "Can't you just take my word, my statement?"

She frowned. "I'm sorry, but it will need to be in writing. Don't worry. I'll tell you what to write."

He shoved the hat atop his head. "Then no."

Suspicion crawled across her flesh until it tingled. "But, why? If it is so important to you, why won't you give me a written request?"

His eyes flickered with glazed sharpness. He glanced left and right. "I'll tell you, Essie, but only if you promise to tell nobody. I mean it. If you take your post so gol-darned serious, then you have to give me your word."

Essie's pulse jumped. The heat and the dust dried in her mouth until she feared she'd not be able to speak. She licked her lips and nodded. *Is he about to confess?*

Snatching her arm, he searched her face with desperation clinging to his actions. "I..." He cut his gaze toward the street.

Essie's heart leaped. "Yes, you…"

His lips moved before sound emanated, but finally, his voice synced with the movements. "I can…not…"

She clawed her neck, scratching at the collar. The heat was stifling. Waiting for his confession was worse. "You cannot…"

Phineas gasped to breathe. He inched closer. "I cannot…write."

"Write?" she snapped. "You cannot write?"

He grabbed her arm and glanced behind him. He held a finger to his lips. "Shh…you swore not to tell."

Essie gestured toward the office. "But the letters…the…" She swallowed the lump in her throat.

Phineas kicked a stone. It hit the wooden boards of the post office with a *plunk*. "My sister wrote them. You won't tell, will you, Essie? I mean, they are my words. I told her what I wanted to say, but…"

"Your sister?" She couldn't quite believe what she was hearing. "I know your sister addressed the envelope but is anything in the letter your handwriting?"

He raised both palms. "Keep it down, would you? Most people don't know. It's why it was so important I get an educated woman. I need someone in my life, Essie. I want a family, but…" He dropped his hands and shrugged.

Essie's heart sank. "Then why do you want the letter returned?"

Phineas inhaled rapidly. His gaze darted from left to right. "I…you…" He crossed his arms and clamped his lips together.

Watching his chest heave reminded Essie of similar reactions from Gus whenever Clyde disappointed her.

She lowered her voice. "You're afraid that once she gets out here and makes the discovery, she'll head back East—is that it?"

He nodded.

If Essie learned anything from her daughter, it was boldness. Phineas needed a good dose of hope and bravery. She gripped his shoulders. "Take the risk. What have you got to lose? If you don't send the letter, she ain't coming—that's for sure."

"But..." His lower lip quivered.

"Get along, now. I've got to get back to the office." She couldn't worry about Phineas and his mail order bride, but she could scratch him from the possible suspect list. She pivoted and marched back to the post office.

Cade stood in the opened doorway. He lifted his hat and nodded. "If you're back now, I'll just be going."

Essie wondered what Cade thought of her sudden disappearance. She wished for a way to explain without jeopardizing Francine and their plan, but none came to mind. "Thank you for waiting. I appreciate it."

He crossed the porch and stepped off the walkway. "Sure, Essie. Anything for our postmistress."

She returned to the counter with a heavy heart and lifted the mail sack. *Handwriting...hmmm.* She thumbed through the few outgoing pieces but found nothing matching the hastily-scratched and misspelled words on the ransom note, especially the one from Phineas to his mail order bride.

Squeak—slam—someone's here. Essie dropped the sack. *What would they think if they caught me pilfering through the mail?* She turned toward the sound of

192

heavy footsteps and exhaled. "Oh, it's just you two."

Essie surveyed Victor. He looked about the same as he had the day before and the day before. A long beard, wide-brimmed hat, and a brushed leather jacket hid many sins, such as over-drinking, over-smoking, and overthinking a lousy situation.

Pierre, however, barely resembled the man she first witnessed on the train's platform. His normally tidy attire was mussed, stubble darkened his cheeks and chin, and bags swelled beneath his bloodshot eyes.

He met her gaze. "I must look a fright."

Victor patted his shoulder. "Anyone would in your circumstance."

"But, Pierre," Essie reasoned, "you must look normal if the ruse is to work. You can't give away yourself. If your daughter is beside you, then why would you appear so rough?"

Gripping an unlit cigar, Victor stabbed at the air. "She's right. I'll help you." He dropped his other hand from Pierre and turned toward Essie. "We are on our way to the Finncannon house with a trunk of Francine's garments and just stopped by to see if there's anything Gus needs."

"No, I..." Essie tapped her cheek and considered what her daughter might want following an evening with Nancy Finncannon barking at her heels. Gus had asked for her promise that she'd cease plotting a trip east, and she'd given it. *But is that really what she wants, or does she want me to appreciate her?* "Wait. Watch the door for me."

Without giving them time to reply, she attacked the steps and retrieved Francine's fan. After rushing back, she slipped a sheet from the stationery pack and dipped her pen into the inkwell. The words she longed to say flooded her heart. As she wrote, tears wet her lashes.

Dearest Daughter,

You have been my sole reason for living since the moment I felt you moving inside my belly. It has been the two of us for so long I cannot remember anything different. I have never thought you were not enough, but that you deserved better than I can give you. Do not absorb too much of Nancy's fancy ways. It is only for the ruse. After that, I want my Gus back exactly as before. No changes. No more talk of cousin Blanche and Boston. You are perfect.

Your proud mama

Essie rocked the blotter across the hastily-penned note and shoved it in an envelope addressed to Gus—not Augusta, and definitely not Miss Baumgardner. She then tied it to the fan's handle. "Make sure she gets this in the folds of a garment so that Nancy doesn't have a chance to intercept it. I want her to know there's only one Gus, just as there's only one Francine."

Pierre whimpered. His hand shook as he reached for the item his daughter had cradled to her chest the previous day.

Victor snatched it. "I've got some work to do with this one. He's wearing his emotions on his sleeve."

Cutting his watery gaze at her, Pierre shrugged. "*Pardonnez-moi*, but she is all I have left...in this...world." His voice crackled, and he coughed. "I cannot imagine what she must be going through...or how frightened she must be." He grabbed Essie by the shoulders. "What if...madam...what if..." He widened his eyes and stared.

Swallowing the words that would likely have

finished his sentence, Essie wondered the same thing. She hugged him tightly, hoping whatever strength she still possessed passed through her and into him.

As he returned the embrace, he trembled.

Essie pulled slightly back. "Hush about that. Nobody's going to hurt her while awaiting payment for her safe return." Pierre's sorrow removed any doubts about whether or not she was doing the right thing She understood too well. Although, unlike Francine, whose actual whereabouts were currently unknown, Gus was at Nancy's and likely equaled as tortured.

He cupped her head with a shaking palm. "Do you believe so?"

"Yes, of course," she answered as confidently as she dared. "If not, I wouldn't have sent Gus to Nancy's. We're in this together."

Victor furrowed his brows and tugged Pierre's arm from her. Dragging the Frenchman behind him, he shuffled toward the exit. "Stop blubbering, and come along before someone sees you in this condition."

"I will make it up to you, dear lady. I swear it on my honor."

Essie ached for him. She looked down and lifted the mail sack. *I almost forgot.* "Wait," she yelled. "I have one more thing you need to know. I checked a few people's handwriting against that on the note."

Victor pivoted. "Now you're thinking. Come up with anything?"

Shaking her head, she grimaced. "Only discounted one or two possibilities. It's not Phineas Atwater, and it's not a half-dozen others we might have thought desperate enough to pull such a prank."

Victor left Lacroix by the door and sauntered back.

"Weeding out people is important. Good job. If anyone comes by…even people you trust like…"

"Cyrus?"

He nodded.

"Yeah, I already thought of him."

Victor's eyes glistened. "You're one heck of a woman, Essie Baumgardner. Augustus would be proud."

She blinked back tears. "Augustus wouldn't have given into Nancy Finncannon's demands, but…"

Victor caressed her cheek with a thumb. "Maybe this position ain't Nancy's to determine."

"But she'd—"

"She'd rather have you in here than face Stutts losing to another Wylder resident. Being passed over twice would practically devastate them both. You keep that in mind—you hear me?" He bolted for the door, shoving Pierre through first.

Is it possible? Could Nancy's attempts to force Stutts into the position fail? As she'd much rather be surprised than disappointed, she shook away the hope. Besides, everybody knew Stutts' best asset was his political connections—Nancy ensured it.

Essie wrung her hands. *I shouldn't have sent Gus with Nancy. Everybody knows she despises the girl and vice versa.*

Her head and heart ached. The occasional interruptions of a customer entering and leaving snapped Essie from her worries. She lumbered through the motions—retrieving letters, selling stamps—but when the door shut once again, loneliness enveloped her. Like it or not, she and Pierre were in this together, each with a daughter at risk.

She focused on Pierre's offer to take Gus back to Paris with him and Francine. It soothed her, even though she doubted Gus would agree to accompany them to France. Her daughter didn't appear to have inherited her own wanderlust. She opened the box with the postage stamps from France. *Pax* and *Mercur* stared upward. All the little pleasures of this position would soon be lost to her, too. There'd be no more letters and packages from distant places she could hold in her hand—no more daydreaming about the lives behind the handwriting.

The clattering of an approaching carriage dragged her back to reality. If the plan was to work, she couldn't give into worries. Gathering her skirts, Essie hustled to the back door. Snagging the chain, she tugged her watch from its pocket and stared—five minutes past one.

Essie watched the arriving coach. She couldn't be completely sure CD had nothing to do with the plot. *Does he know the crook? Has he returned with a carriage full of accomplices? Where's the sheriff? Why did he leave Wylder unprotected? How do we know he is safe? What if he rode into a trap?* Her pulse accelerated. Its hammering beat against her wrists and throat. Her fears for Gus overcame her aching conscience. Still, she felt badly for thinking one of her acquaintances could be the culprit.

She reached into her pocket. Her fingers caressed the pistol's pearl handles. *One might not be enough.* Releasing it, she raced for the counter and grabbed the gun with both hands. *I'll need backup at the ready if John Smith brings his friends back to Wylder.*

Peeking around the wide, pine doorjamb, Essie

stared. Knots in the woodgrain resembled toothless mouths in a full yawn. She'd meant to paint, but first one thing and then another always trumped a brush and whitewash. She sighed. *Soon it won't be mine to worry about. Stutts can paint it or not.*

For a moment, she imagined a layer of fresh pigment crisping the appearance of the wood-frame-and-beam office, the cubbies and locked boxes, the shelves and drawers, and even the textured, cottonwood countertop. Grimacing at the thought, she wondered how long such a coating would last given the dust from the road and the lint from the mail.

While the graying image floated through her mind, another caught her attention. Someone exited. A parasol's peaked tip poked from the interior. It extended an entire arm's length from the opening. A gloved hand gripped the knob of its straight handle while the other pushed it open until a pale blue dome preceded the exiting figure ducking beneath its sun protection. Pale blue silk covered one crooked elbow, bent to hold a fistful of matching blue silk skirt. It was so near the hue of the mid-day heavens that Essie glanced to the sky to see if a dress-and-parasol-shaped portion had gone missing.

Who would come to Wylder on the stagecoach wearing such a lovely garment besides Pierre's daughter? She gasped. *Can it be? Has Francine escaped? Maybe the kidnapper saw the error of his ways and released her.* She stepped to the edge of the porch and stared, but it was impossible to tell with the pulled-low Gainsborough hat covering the lady's face.

Chapter 12

Gainsborough hat? Essie narrowed her eyes and glared. It looked like Francine, but she couldn't be sure from this distance. She watched her simultaneously gangly and poised movements. Francine had never wavered, but an ordeal such as she'd just experienced would naturally stress her nerves. Upon reaching the raised walkway, the woman released her skirt. As she walked toward the depot office, it draped in elegant tiers beyond her feet. The bustle swayed, and its girth accentuated her narrow waist. If the young lady was visiting the depot station, she was likely purchasing another ticket. Wylder was but a mere stop on a long journey west. Essie wanted her to be the missing girl so much she'd allowed herself to imagine the first similarly dressed one to exit the stage was Francine. Still, she couldn't stop staring.

The lady in blue stepped from the depot's doorway and paused at the corner, turning her head in the direction of the post office for a brief moment before quickly jerking it back toward the street. With a pop of the parasol she positioned over her head, she glided into the street. As she strolled to the opposite side and straight up the walkway toward the hotel, she dodged the steaming piles of horse manure.

Sighing, Essie pushed the pads of her fingertips against her raw and puffy lids. Lack of sleep and worry caused them to water and left behind the sensation of sand in her eyes. If the new arrival was Francine, she'd likely suffered little. Her high-hattedness indicated she had not been traumatized or humbled by the experience, so it was unlikely that anything particularly nasty happened.

Gus, on the other hand, was still at the Finncannon house. Lord only knew what she was going through. Essie grabbed a cool, damp rag and held it to her face, elbows against the cottonwood, pressing its soothing moisture into her screaming cheeks.

The creak of the door opening jolted her. She dropped her hands from her face and peered at the tasseled jacket of the entrant. "Oh, it's you."

Victor yanked the unlit cigar from his mouth and grinned. "Why would you greet a friend so churlishly?"

Essie harrumphed. Recalling Nancy's retort to him the previous day, she sneered. "I wouldn't snub a friend, but you are altogether different."

Furrowing his brows, Victor leaned against the counter. He fixed her in his gaze. "Now, Essie Baumgardner, you listen to me. I'm taking care of this little tangle, and when I've restored Francine to her father, you're not only going to thank me but sing my praises to your patrons. You might actually see me in a different light—one that is favorable for a change."

Suddenly, she was wide awake, all remnants of the sleepless night forgotten. Her flaring temper spiked her blood pressure and sent a rush of oxygen surging through her veins. "Favorable? Praises? Ha! You mean Nancy's patrons after Stutts takes office, or did you forget about that little deal with the devil?" His maliciously enticing smile spread slowly, starting at a single corner of his lips where it turned a corner and then kept on widening until the hair from his mustache nearly reached his ears.

"It is not what I have forgotten—which is nothing, I assure you—but what I have learned since our last talk. But, if you're not in a mood to hear what I have to say…" Victor snatched the stogie and stuffed it between his teeth before shrugging and turning for the door.

Essie's pulse surged. He'd raised her curiosity and likely knew it. "Dagnabit, Douglas, you can't leave me hanging on tenterhooks. You came in here for a reason, and as it obviously doesn't pertain to mail, there's only one other thing that can be on your mind. Out with it."

Victor turned. He crossed his arms, and his sleeves' fringe dangled over his midsection like an apron. "You can do better than that, Essie, nicer at least," he muttered between tightly-clamped teeth against the cigar.

Although wincing, she bit back sarcasm and swallowed the insult she ached to hurl. "What have you learned, Victor? As my daughter's life is at stake, I believe I have the right to all the information."

After tugging the cigar from his mouth with the thumb and forefinger of one hand, Victor exhaled. He licked his lips as he strolled back to the counter. "Lacroix and I stayed awake all night going over plans, testing them for weak spots. We had to make sure to be convincing, you see? And…when we settled at the saloon for drinks…we overheard Fletcher Wylder saying he thought Stutts Finncannon was ousting you from this position, and a group is preparing to contest his appointment. You're doing a good job here, Essie, and the people want you to remain as postmistress."

As she soaked in Victor's words, Essie's heart fluttered. *The town supports me. They like my work, and I belong here.* For a moment, she was back in the cabin on Fort Laramie's outskirts, facing Captain Puckett and his ultimatum. Being ousted from the place she and Augustus had called home had been hard. Riding through unfriendly territory toward a strange town about which she knew nothing had taken every ounce of courage she could muster. She played a valuable role as Wylder's postmistress but had not internalized the town's appreciation until now. As the realization settled over her that she had no say, Essie thought she might be sick. She placed a palm against her rumbling stomach and frowned. "Won't matter. Done gave my word, and that's all I got...except for Gus." She reached across the counter and tugged his sleeve. "What do you know about her? Have you heard from Nancy? Stutts? What's going on?"

Victor tossed back his head and laughed.

Essie chewed her lip. She felt her forehead creasing and her mouth twisting but couldn't stop them. She was too tired and distraught to work against her nature. "What's so gol-darned funny?"

He jerked his head in the depot's direction. "Didn't you observe the arriving carriage across the street?"

"Of course, what's that got to do with anything?"

Victor's eyes twinkled, and his cheeks flushed. "Didn't recognize her, did you?"

Her temples throbbed. Victor liked amusement, and he didn't mind achieving it at her cost, but today wasn't the day for games. She clenched her fists and stiffened her arms. "Recognize who? I swear, if you don't tell me this instant, I'll explode."

Leaning on an elbow, Victor dragged his brows together. "The lady in blue with a matching parasol. Didn't you see her?"

An image flashed in her mind—Gainsborough hat, swaying bustle. If they'd found Pierre's daughter, Gus could come home. She clapped. "Yes. I suspected but didn't know for sure. You found Francine?"

He laughed harder. "You saw Francine. You saw her exit the stage wearing pale blue silk and carrying a matching parasol?"

Despite her fears for Gus, at least she knew where her daughter was and that she was safe from actual harm, if not from humiliation. Learning it was indeed Francine whom she'd spied on the stage brought a relieved sigh. She grabbed her head, crushing it between her palms. "Oh, praise be. I'm so glad. But where did you find her? Did the kidnapper release her? Where's Pierre? Oh, he must be giddy with happiness."

Victor pushed his hat brim higher. He lifted his chin. "You still don't get it, do you? That wasn't Francine." He leaned closer. "That pretty lady who was carrying herself with dignity and grace…"

Sweltering heat turned the air stale and intensified the cigar's aroma. That he hadn't lit it didn't prevent it from giving off its perfume. Notes of leather and spice wafted off Victor's breath and lingered beneath Essie's nose. Essie's nerves were too frayed for suspense. She ground her teeth. "Was?"

Victor glanced behind him and then back. He widened his eyes into saucer-shaped orbs. "Gus."

Her pulse jumped against her neck as she pounded the counter with both hands. *I'm hallucinating. I thought he said Gus.* "Did you say Gus?"

He nodded and grinned.

"No," she gasped. "You can't be serious. My Gus flicking open a parasol and gathering her skirts in a gloved fist?"

"That girl can do anything she sets her mind to doing. She's completely amazed Pierre and me. Even he ran for her when she entered the hotel, yelling, *'Francine.'*"

While Victor appeared amused, Essie was more confused than ever. Questions pulsed in her mind. "But why the ruse? Why did you drive her into town in a carriage?"

"Think about it, Essie. If the kidnapper watched your door closely enough to know a note slipped under the door would find its way to Pierre, he likely knew that Gus left with Nancy Finncannon. So, if a lady strutted back to town with her, it could have been a bit obvious that it was Gus. By driving her out a ways and then collecting her in a carriage, she arrived as anybody else might. The name for the room is Wilma Starnsby, a lady bound for Park City. Her chaperone is to meet her here in Wylder. That's the story."

As she digested Victor's logic, Essie rubbed her chin. "I see. When the coast is clear, you'll have her change clothes and ride out to the canyon as Pierre's daughter."

He chuckled. "She's ready. I've every hope this will work."

Essie's heart felt like it might burst. "Can I see her? Will you bring her here?"

"Not yet. Be patient. Trust me, Gus is well and as cantankerous as always."

The door creaked open, and George Hawkins entered. "Howdy, Victor, Essie."

Victor pushed upward from his bent position against the counter and turned for the exit. He tipped his hat. "Thanks, Essie. Good to see you again, Hawkins."

Essie inhaled and steadied her hands. "What can I do for you, George?"

He remained silent.

The door closed behind Victor.

As he walked closer, George's boot heels clicked against the wooden floor. "The missus is expecting a letter. Have you seen one? It would be coming from Denver. Her sister…she's ill…and…" He reached the counter and drummed his fingertips against it.

Essie flipped through the envelopes separated by the first letter of the recipients' last names. When she saw nothing in the *H* section, she pulled the entire grouping and glanced through them. "I'm sorry, George. It isn't here yet."

"Are you sure?" He clamped a hand across his mouth and shook his head. "Oh, of course, you are. What am I saying? It's just that receiving word from her soothes Alice so much. It's proof her sister is still alive and eases her mind for a week or two."

Essie heard the desperate undertone in his voice. He'd been collecting a letter almost weekly since Easter. She also knew the trips into town were costly due to time lost on the farm. "Tell Alice there was a mail delay today and not to worry. If it comes before next week, I'll bring it out myself."

George relaxed his shoulders. He grinned. "Oh, Essie, would you? That would be a kindness, for sure.

You'll bring Gus, and you'll both stay for dinner—swear it."

Relief oozed through every generous word. "You know I'm not a swearing woman, but I'll make an exception this once because Alice's cooking is so good."

He patted the cottonwood, then turned for the door. "I'll be sure and tell her you said so. Thank you, Essie. You're a gem."

She watched him leave, thinking it had better come fast, or she'd not be the one in charge of receiving the letters from Denver or anyplace else for that matter. Essie shook thoughts of George and the post office from her mind and recalled the vision in blue exiting the coach. *What did Gus tell me before following Nancy out the door?* If she'd promise not to send her to Boston, she'd be more Francine than Francine. If she fooled her mama, Gus had certainly fulfilled her end of the bargain. *Why didn't I realize the slight wobble, the gangliness, the signs I attributed to nerves, were simply Gus's natural inclinations overriding those she'd just learned.* Even the long glance toward the post office should have been a sign that she was checking to see if Essie was there at her usual spot by the back door so that Gus would know she saw her.

Victor and Pierre had planned it brilliantly. They must have convinced CD, too, because he gave no sign of recognition. But anybody who knew Gus would have serious doubts about her turning up on the stagecoach in blue silk and carrying a parasol. She laughed.

From the moment Augusta caught Clyde noticing Francine, she'd watched the French girl's movements. Although appearing to be in jest, she mocked

Francine's postures and gestures. Without knowing it, she'd prepared herself for the ruse and was ready long before Nancy Finncannon came on the scene. She'd known it, probably practicing in private, which was why she'd said she could do a better Francine than Francine.

Essie's stomach complained, yet she could not abide food. Her nerves rattled her body, mainly as the need to squelch them arose with each customer. By closing, she'd merely snacked on a handful of grapes and nibbled a piece of hard bread. As she waited for the sound of Victor's carriage to roll past, she assured herself it was too hot to eat anyway. She placed her hand on the latch, and it pushed inward.

Through the slightly-ajar door, Victor popped into view.

The sounds of carriage wheels and horse hooves pounding the packed-dirt street wafted in with him, along with the pungent aroma of cured tobacco. For the first time, the cigar scent that permeated his jacket—which he always wore, despite the heat—reassured her. "News?"

He shook his head. "We can explain the plan, but we can't change it—we won't change it—so it's up to you to know what's going on or stay free of its burden."

Essie stomped a foot. "Free of its burden? Who are you kidding, Victor Douglas? As long as it's my daughter you're using as bait, I'll not be free of anything."

Pursing his lips, Victor shrugged. "I thought as much. I told Lacroix you'd never stand for being left out." He jerked a thumb toward the door. "So, grab your hat, and let's go."

Chills ran along Essie's spine. She swallowed hard and stared. *He doesn't look like he's joking.* "Did you say *'grab my hat?'* You are going to let me come, too?"

Victor held up a finger. "On one condition…okay…ten." He added a second finger. "But, two really matter."

Pressure built. Her head and her heart felt close to bursting. She grabbed a handful of his sleeve's dangling fringe. "What are they? I'll do anything."

Victor cupped her cheek with his free hand and stared down at her. "You can know what we're up to, but we're not taking a consensus. You don't get to vote. So, you have to understand we've made the plan, and it's a go. Two, no matter what happens, you have to do as we say."

The compassion swimming in Victor's gaze alarmed her more than the warning about the scheme. This was a side she had not previously known about the man reputed to be such a great soldier, guide, and hunter. *If he's empathetic, the situation must be grave.* Even as she had the thought and goose bumps prickled her flesh, she had no choice. "You might as well have made it one condition under the second rule. I don't care, though, and will agree to anything. If I stay here, I'm going to explode."

He swung open the door. "Come along. We're waiting."

Essie didn't have to hear it twice. "Meet me around back. I'll bolt the front and head out."

Nodding, Victor left as she requested.

She rushed through the necessary closing rituals and raced out the back. Carriage wheels resounded from the opposite side. Essie wrung her hands into her skirt's folds and craned her neck.

Victor circled the building and headed toward her from a different direction. He pulled his carriage parallel to the porch.

Essie leaped off the walkway and climbed onto the seat beside him. "Victor," she greeted, aware of the stares of several townspeople clamped upon them as though mentally freezing the scene to make the gossip better and more detailed. She could almost imagine the tales but didn't care. Any other time it might have mattered, but not today.

He raked a gaze across her face. "You're looking mighty fine today, Miss Essie."

She noticed his glimmering eyes and smoldering voice. He almost looked besotted with her. *No wonder people say he is a good actor and attended his plays.* She gathered her skirt and swept it sideways. "You say that to all the ladies in Wylder, don't you?"

The cigar slid down his dropped-open lip. He clamped his teeth onto it just in time to prevent it from falling out. "I most certainly do not. I only say it to the ones in Wylder who are attractive—like you."

Wishing he'd prepared her for the ruse, she placed a palm to her cheek. It felt warm beneath her touch, yet, the summer heat and the dire situation spiked her temperature.

"Essie, Estelle Baumgardner," a familiar voice shouted.

Essie leaned over the side of the carriage and glanced in the yell's direction.

A woman lifted a hand, waved, then pointed a cane toward her.

She flopped back around and cupped a hand

around her mouth. "I don't believe it. It's Nancy Finncannon."

Victor groaned. "I can slap the reins…"

Nancy's voice rose higher. "Yoohoo, Essie, Victor. Wait up. I saw you glance my way. I know you see me."

Stifling a scream, Essie laid a hand on Victor's arm. "She'll make it worse if you do. We'd better see what she wants."

He glanced left and right. "We don't have time, Essie. We've got to go. It's a far piece out to the rock canyon—"

A hole opened in Essie's gut. Her heart dropped into it, and her throat tightened. The situation seemed impossible. If they ignored Nancy, she would worsen it in the long run. She gripped the seat's edge. Tears pricked her lids. "I understand. You go on. It was never part of the plan for me to be with you out there anyway. Besides, my presence here might help stave off problems, like Nosey Nancy." She jumped from the carriage.

Lunging sideways, Victor leaned down. He caught Essie's hand before it slipped from the rim and held it. "Are you sure?"

Looking up at Victor, Essie had the feeling he would yank her back into the carriage if she signaled. She freed her hand and pressed it to her chest. "Go." Before she changed her mind, she turned and walked toward Nancy.

As Victor pushed upright, leather crackled and stiff springs complained. He clapped the reins. "Hyah," he yelled.

Whipped into action, the horses bolted.

As the wagon moved beyond her ability to leap back into it, Essie glanced toward the horizon. *Getting out was the right thing*. She fisted her fingers and held them to her chin.

Victor's rig rolled into the soon-to-ripen skyline. Dust clouds rose from both its wheels and the horses' hooves.

Essie sighed. *At least sunsets in Wylder are long, fading events*. She'd read about places where the sun ascended at dawn as if pulled by a fast-moving chariot and dropped at dusk, plunging light into darkness. But in Wylder, the slow, drifting off of the sun's rays gradually narrowed until the halo became a pinprick and lasted for a full hour, if not longer. However, they couldn't outlast Nancy Finncannon's blabbering on about one thing or another, and Essie figured if she was gossiping *to her*, she didn't have someone else's ear talking *about her*. She leaned against the post and waited.

Nancy slowed. She planted her cane and pushed off it, stepping with a pronounced limp.

Essie ground her teeth together but stepped out to meet the approaching woman. *Be nice*. She took a breath and released it through pursed lips. "How are you this evening, Nancy?"

She patted a hip. "Worn to a frazzle, I'll tell you that. I'd forgotten how much work it was to train young ladies in the ways of proper society."

The last thing Essie wanted was for word of Nancy's training Gus to get out before they completed the ruse. She raised a brow. "We'd not want to discuss that out here in public, remember?"

Nancy waved and stopped walking. She reached

into her gown's bosom and retrieved a scarf which she dabbed at her nose. "My goodness, it sure is hot."

Stepping toward her, Essie extended an arm. "Shall I get you some water?"

As she placed the cane on the porch, Nancy leaned against Essie and pushed herself upward. She shook her head. "I can't stay for refreshment. I only need a brief rest. You see, I hurried here and the...well...it's not easy with this knee and hip acting up again." She plopped onto the bench and dragged in a few deep breaths.

Sitting beside her, Essie exhaled loudly. Her nerves frayed. Every word coming from Nancy sent shooting pains into her brain. *I'll snap if she says the wrong thing.* "If you came to discuss my resignation, save it for later. Now's not the time to concentrate on anything besides getting back my daughter."

Nancy pursed her lips. "I never thought I'd say this, but I have to tell you. Augusta Baumgardner..." She made a fist and stabbed the air.

Essie's face heated. She laid sweaty palms against her cheeks. *I'll deal with whatever Gus did at Nancy's later.* "I'm sorry. She's a willful child—always has been."

Wagging a finger, Nancy squirmed. Her shoulder brushed Essie's. "That's just it. I thought as much. But she's also got an iron will and a magnate's focus. She progressed much faster than I dared dream."

The wide-eyed expression on Nancy's face confused Essie. Gasping, she blinked and scratched her head.. *Surely, I heard wrong.* "You mean..."

Nancy plopped her cane into place in front of her and rested both palms against its handle. "Give me a month, and I could take Augusta anywhere and pass her off as a lady of means."

Hearing Nancy speak of Gus like a science experiment saddened Essie. Gus must have felt humiliated when they discussed her abilities in the post office—an object, a tool—not a person with feelings and pride. "Oh, Nancy, I don't want Gus passed off as anything besides who she is and wants to be. This situation is just temporary until we find Francine."

Nancy thumped the cane against the floorboards. "Well, if you change your mind, the offer stands. I'd do it for the challenge, for the self-satisfaction of knowing I'd done a good deed, and not because I have five thousand dollars invested in the return of the French girl."

"Of course, but…the answer is no. If Gus wants it, then so be it. But I'll never ask her to be anything besides who she wants to be again—that is—if I get the chance." Tears welled, and Essie dropped her head. As she sobbed, her shoulders shook.

The bench vibrated, and Nancy squirmed. She patted Essie's arm. "There, there. Of course, you will. Victor Douglas is a smarmy snake, and I despise him. But, he's clever as all get out, and if he has a plan, it's likely doable. I was just telling the same thing to Chet Daniels over at the livery. He was carrying on about the horses he curried and boarded, and now the prospectors are late on paying." She clucked her tongue. "Fools they are, racing into town with bags of fool's gold, accumulating bills they can't pay. Chet's refusing them both horses. Said they'd—"

Bills they can't pay? Essie brightened. "What did you say about fool's gold?"

Nancy picked at a piece of lint on her skirt and chuckled. "That idiot MacDonald and his nitwit son have been mining Slingback Creek. I could've told them they'd not find real gold out there. But, nobody ever listens to old Nancy, do they?"

Essie's head roared. She recalled the roan and the buckskin skidding to a halt in the road over CD's knelt body. The day Francine went missing, she'd seen two identical horses curried and cleaned in the stables. "Fool's gold? Fred MacDonald?"

"That's right." Nancy nodded and huffed. "Now they've accrued debts, and the good people of Wylder won't stand for it. Those two should have made sure before risking—"

Tapping a finger against her cheek, Essie digested the information. *Accrued debts are motives for ransom. Both men knew CD, and both saw him delivering the mail on the day the package arrived. They were in town, and Chet held their horses for nonpayment. Stakes were high for disappointed prospectors without means of returning to their claim.* "Nancy, can you get back home without me? I mean…I need to run. I do apologize."

Nancy lifted her chin. "Well, I suppose. Is it something I said?"

Essie stood. "I'll explain later." Her mind whirled. Perhaps the father-son team targeted CD all along. Maybe they knew something she didn't. She ran through the back door of the post office and fingered through the remaining mail pieces. Everything was normal. Only the typical letters and publications had arrived no additional wanted posters, no flyers of people to be on the lookout for in the event they

214

appeared. After caressing each item, only one remained, and it was addressed to Victor. "Well, shoot," she declared aloud. She studied Victor's envelope and ran a fingertip over the return address—*Office of the French Consulate, Washington.*

Essie's heart sank, and she took off at a dead run. Her feet still ached from the sprint the previous day, but she set her jaw and made for the small field behind the post office where Gus kept their horses.

Dumpling picked at the sparse grass while Lightning pranced the perimeter as though aching for a run.

She opened the gate and rushed in, grabbing Dumpling's halter. The buggy was parked beneath the lean-to, covered in old, sewn-together canvas bags. For a split-second, she raced through the necessary steps to get Dumpling hitched to the cart. So much time had already passed, she feared using more would delay her too long. But her only other option was Lightning.

Closing her eyes, Essie recalled Gus's image atop the horse that carried her at such speed as fit its name. But Gus rode bareback, and he was a good sixteen hands high. Racing back through the gate, she returned with a lead rope draping her neck, a pocketful of grain, and two buckets which she stacked atop each other just outside the gate. After sprinkling some of the grain for Dumpling, she saw Lightning rounding the edge.

He watched her and pawed at the ground..

She kept the grain fisted in her palm.

Lightning whinnied, and Dumpling watched him from the corner of her eye. He lifted his tail and strolled nearer, sticking out his neck.

Essie held out an opened palm. The grain mounded

in her damp hand.

He stretched closer and curled his lips above his long, still-white teeth before snatching a bite.

Her heart pounded, but she kept watch. Standing perfectly still, she had to win his trust.

Lightning chewed and swished his tail.

"You like that sweet feed, don't ya, boy?" She readied the lead rope behind her back.

His gaze returned to the waiting treat. He flicked his ears and stomped a foot.

She didn't move. The next time Lightning neared, she tossed over the lead rope while he nibbled the grain. Leading him out, she closed the gate behind her and took a breath for courage.

The horse seemed to realize a ride was imminent and pranced in a circle while she gripped the rope. "I wouldn't do this for anybody else," she said aloud.

Lightning pulled back.

"Whoa, Lightning. That's right." She rubbed his neck and ran her hands down his back. "You love Gus; I know you do, so I want you to know this is for her. We're going after Gus, okay?"

Lightning blinked. His long lashes framed his large, dark eyes.

The sun mirrored her silhouette into them. Reflected, her eyes inside his looked huge and frightened. She had to calm herself, or he'd know how scared she was and buck. A memory flashed across her mind. It was brief but powerful—her mother in front of the makeshift altar in the waddle-and-daub house in the middle of the prairie, wolves pacing outside the oiled paper covering the holes where glass would go when they could afford some to put there. One claw, one rush at the flimsy covering, and the animals could be inside where she and her siblings cowered beneath the long plank table. Her mother made the sign of the cross and whispered Latin words. As she pulled beads along a string—each tapping its neighbor in the rhythmic cadence, she repeated the strange-sounding phrase.

Essie's heart fluttered. Despite the heat, she shivered and squeezed her lids until the sounds of their voices wafted across the years. Young and small, the children wouldn't understand the meaning of the chant for a long time, but they joined in the chorus—*In nominee Patris, et Filii, et Spiritus Sancti. Amen.* Another call split through the atmosphere like a siren, and the wolves whimpered, then rushed into the woodland.

If the prayer protected them against the wolves, perhaps it also worked with horses. For the sake of her daughter, she'd even forgive her mother and her mother's strict faith in Catholic doctrine. She climbed atop the buckets. "Okay, Lightning, this is for us both." As she touched her forehead, chest, left, and right shoulder, she chanted. "*In nominee Patris, et Filii, et Spiritus Sancti. Amen.*" In the name of the Father, and of the Son, and of the Holy Ghost. Amen." As soon as the last *amen* left her lips, Essie leaped from the stacked buckets onto his back. She fisted the fingers of one hand through his mane while the other twisted the rope around her wrist.

Lightning bolted. He shot from the field at a speed befitting his name, turning first one way and then another with no particular cues.

She hugged his sides with both knees and lowered her body until his ears were higher than her head.

217

"You're not getting away from me." Riding like a jockey, she steered him toward the road leading to the rock canyon, letting him set the pace, which even she realized was beyond her ability to control Lightning.

Chapter 13

Lightning sped along the dirt road.

At times, Essie lifted from his back, sure she'd go flying into the air, but each time she found him again and continued forward into an ever-darkening sky. As the sun paled, she glanced behind her. Its bright pumpkin color faded to a warm glow. Soon, she'd left behind the town, and searing loneliness overtook her. *What am I thinking? What am I doing? What if I'm wrong?*

Despite her thoughts, she charged ahead. Lightning steamed down the road, opening his chest and stretching his legs for the fastest ride Essie had ever taken. He seemed to know that Gus waited somewhere at the end of this trail and that by following it, he'd get to her.

She searched her mind for every recollection about the father-and-son pair—a shotgun sticking out of the side scabbard, the gun belts, and pistols. As gold miners, they'd be willing to shoot on sight or risk getting their claims jumped. Were the MacDonalds trigger happy? Would they shoot their way out of this predicament? How did they know Pierre?

It all made sense. They weren't intending on staying. Yet, the horses were still there. They had bills at the hotel, the saloon, and the social club—no doubt. They'd probably accumulated debt at the general store and definitely at the livery. No wonder they took the opportunity when it arose.

She wished she had more time. CD knew them. He might have some insight and spoken with them, but she didn't have the time to chat now. She glanced backward again, judging how close she was by the sun's progression as it receded. The visual made her appear to have ridden farther than she likely had. She eased her grip on Lightning's mane, and he increased his speed another notch.

Evening breezes carried the scent of sagebrush and whipped the tumbleweeds into a frenzy. They rolled into the road and off the other side. Lightning paid them no mind. He maintained his swiftness, stomping them when he couldn't dodge them.

Dust filled Essie's nostrils and coated her clothes. Even her hair and lashes felt weighted by the excess. Still, she merely blinked away the annoyances. Gus waited at the canyon's rim, and she hadn't far to go now.

Up ahead, a dust cloud sputtered and spun behind a carriage. Essie narrowed her gaze. She couldn't tell from the distance if it was Victor or possibly the kidnapper. Maybe Francine waited in the heft of its inner chamber.

She kicked her heels, and Lightning raced harder and faster. "Hyah, hyah," she called. Dust choked her, and she coughed. A glint caught her eye. She glanced upward to the peak of the canyon's rocky formation. The dusky silhouette of a horse and rider could have been anyone, but chances were good the rider was the kidnapper watching for his money. Unless Fred and his son Frank rode in on the same horse or found another to borrow or steal, only one was likely atop the ridge.

The prospect of a single person waiting for the money should have eased her mind. Instead, knowing how haphazardly the whole affair had occurred, it frightened her more. He was apt to be nervous and eager to level the field between himself and Victor, Pierre, and, of course, Gus. Perhaps he'd think they'd taken out the other one to rescue Francine. She didn't like it. For once, she was ready to admit that perhaps Nancy was right after all. They should have waited for the sheriff, brought in a team of trained soldiers, and not struck out like a wild bunch of hooligans.

Lightning sped up.

He seemed to sense that Gus was nearby. He closed in on the wagon, although it disappeared again into the canyon. Essie once more dropped her head behind Lightning's mane. As he had good instincts, she trusted he was on the right trail. She peeked upward to see if the rider was still in his place above the cliff, but he'd disappeared. *Where did he go?* She couldn't tell, but it was sure to be somewhere he was protected, and Gus was not.

With the setting sun behind her and the dim canyon yawning before her, Essie shoved a knee into Lightning's side and urged him left. He pivoted, and she gripped his mane. If she could get to the top of the pillar opposite the kidnapper, she'd be able to see more clearly.

A path wound around the rocky outcropping, and Lightning slowed. He picked his way around boulders that had fallen from the overhang and kicked up pebbles beneath his feet. He shied, jumping over a ditch in the path, but with a bit of urging, he continued upward until reaching a cleft in the rocky formations.

"Whoa," Essie whispered. Aching to see who waited across the divide, she stared across the cliff. She didn't dismount. Heaven only knew how she'd ever climb atop him again. She urged Lightning around another of Vedauwoo's granite formations the Arapaho called *bito'o'wu*, land of the earthborn spirit. The sunset reflected against the stone, and the blush-colored sky deepened its hue against the rocks.

Lightning, dislodging small stones, attacked the narrow path that snaked between the rock pillars. They pinged against the granite columns, but the horse no longer shied from the sound. He climbed higher and higher.

When she had a clear view of the opposite peak, she sized up the distance. She'd never get there in time to save anyone, and it was too late for her to do anything. Essie screamed into the fuschia sky.

Crows mimed her squawks and took to the skies in a flurry of wing-flapping.

A circling hawk noiselessly ringed the tallest pillar in Vedauwoo.

Essie clasped a hand across her mouth and felt a tug. She groped for Lightning's mane, and the rope slipped from her wrist. But the determined grip against her arm pulled her too far sideways to remain atop Lightning. *Oh no, how will I ever get onto his back again?* Another thought dislodged the first one. *Who's yanking me off the horse?*

Bolting, Lightning disappeared behind a tall formation.

Realizing too late the tug was the result of the hand still grasping her sleeve, Essie's heart thundered. Her pulse raced until she feared she would succumb to its fury. *The jig is up. I've been outsmarted.* The earth seemed to rise up to meet her. She pushed with her feet, trying to find solid ground.

"Shh," the voice of the person firmly gripping her demanded silence. He counterbalanced her weight and pushed her just upright enough to keep from planting face-first in the pebbles.

She nodded and squeezed her eyelids in hopes of preventing tears. The effort only forced them down her cheeks.

"Shh. Little Sister, it's Tarak. I'm going to let you go, and you will not move or scream, okay?" He released his grip.

Simultaneously relieved it was a friend and concerned for his safety, Essie spun around. "Tarak," she whispered. "What are you doing?"

"Protecting you—come." He led her behind one of the columns and pointed to the space opposite them. "Strangers moved into the canyon. Their movements are sly, and quick meetings with others in dark carriages tell me they are up to something."

Essie watched Tarak's stealthy movements as he eased through slits that seemed impossibly narrow and crept toward a ledge jutting from the rocks. Pressing her back into a monolith, she slid around the path behind him. "That last surrey is not one of them. It is Victor Douglas, Pierre Lacroix, and Gus."

Tarak stepped onto the granite shelf. A breeze lifted his hair, and it danced behind him. He knelt and turned his head. "Miss Augusta?"

Essie didn't want to speak too loudly, but Tarak needed to know about the ruse. She gazed into the abyss beyond the shelf and gathered her courage. She stepped down and balanced on a flat rock. Her pulse thumped in her neck and wrists, but she'd come too far to give in to fears. She stuck out her foot.

"Be careful," Tarak warned. "The path can be tricky."

Keeping her gaze on Tarak, Essie took another step. She exhaled, and her foot slipped from beneath her. Although she dug her heels into the path, she skidded on loose pebbles. Essie snatched at rock formations, but the slide had too much momentum. If she slid from the shelf, she'd continue into the abyss. "Tarak," she yelled.

Tarak tossed a rope around a column and tied the other end around his waist. He flattened himself against the stone floor.

Like a huge mouth ready to devour her, the horizon yawned. Essie tucked her head and extended her arms. She pushed the heels of her hands into the stone's bumps and crevices, but her efforts barely slowed her.

Tarak slithered toward her. "Take my hands."

She reached for him, barely connecting with his fingertips. They slipped from his grip, and she stared into his caring face as she neared the edge.

With a great push, Tarak flung his body atop hers. He scooped his arms around her midsection and squeezed. The rope jerked tautly, and his grip tightened.

Essie's hands dangled from the ledge, but the forward motion ceased. Beneath Tarak's weight, she labored to breathe. But when he eased off, she grabbed him to her again. "I'm scared. Don't let me go until I'm back on the path."

"We shall stand together, but stand we must."

His voice was caring but firm. Her nostrils tingled. Although she knew he was right, she feared moving.

With his forefinger, Tarak turned her head from the drop-off. He motioned to his face. "Our bodies follow our eyes. Look at me, not at the canyon. We will stand."

Essie swallowed. "Now?"

Tarak nodded. "Now." He pulled up to a kneeling position while still holding her waist.

She followed his lead, lifting her upper body while struggling to gather her feet onto solid footing.

"That is very good."

"It wasn't as hard as I expected, but—"

"Stand." Tarak leaped to his feet, tugging her upward.

Surprised by the suddenness, Essie had no time for protesting. She followed his lead and righted herself, pushing up through her heels.

Tarak led her away from the rim and onto the area with a sturdy ledge. "Are you okay?"

Despite the fright, Essie couldn't get beyond concern for her daughter. She patted Tarak's arm. "Thank you for saving me, Tarak. But we don't have time to worry about me. Gus needs us. She's..." Her voice cracked.

He squeezed her hand. "You were about to tell me something about her right before you fell."

Essie dabbed at the corners of her eyes. "The last wagon. She's in it—she's in disguise as a lady of means. Do you recognize any of the others?"

He held up one finger. "A couple of men and a young woman."

She gasped. "Woman?"

As a shadow crept across his face, he nodded and swallowed.

Thinking back to Tarak's recent false arrest, Essie knew him as the least likely person to identify someone without enough facts to be solid. "Why did I ask you such a question? Of course, you are. But…it's just…" She searched for another way to ask the same thing, but nothing came to her mind.

Tarak inhaled and pulled back his shoulders. His focus remained steady and narrowed onto the unfolding scene.

Essie winced and patted his arm. "Tarak, can you get me to the other side without being noticed?" Victor's wagon disappeared around the chimney spires.

Tarak turned toward her. He grinned. "The spirits of my people abide here. We often commune below the earth."

Essie squirmed. *Has he smoked too much wild sage?* "I don't understand."

He motioned. "Follow. Do not fear the darkness, for the light shall point the way."

Doing as he suggested, she followed Tarak. The crevices widened, then narrowed, and the hot air scorched her lungs. She dipped downward between clefts in the rocks until doused into blackness. The farther they commenced, the more pleasant the air became—cool and dry. She shuffled her feet quietly in the soft dirt as the path plummeted and finally leveled to a flat surface before reaching the opposite side's incline.

A pinprick of light reflected against ancient carvings into the rock walls. Essie glanced at the scenes—battles, clashes, spirits hovering over the fray.

The bright dot grew more prominent, and undiscernible voices became louder. She crept behind him toward the mouth, where light filtered in at an odd angle.

Tarak slipped out.

Although rock walls still surrounded her, Essie eased from the tunnel. She shuffled to the opening. Voices grabbed her attention.

"We'll have to kill them."

Shuddering, Essie pushed her back against the rocky outcropping. The voice was both simultaneously familiar and unfamiliar.

A man gasped. "Even the girl?"

"Especially the girl. She and Victor Douglas should be the first two taking arrows."

Essie shoved the side of her hand between her teeth and bit until it bled as she forced herself to remain silent. Every part of her ached to scream. Her pulse thundered. The need to run nearly overtook her, and fat tears flooded her cheeks. She stretched toward the opening. Every impulse urged her forward into danger. *I have to save Augusta.*

Tarak snagged her arm, pulling backward. He held a finger to his lips and tiptoed near the edge.

Essie knew she'd heard that voice before, but her blood gushed through her veins with such force that its whooshing sounds diluted all other noises. *Whose is it?*

"We'll make it look like an Arapaho attack," one said.

"Yeah, it's not like anyone's going to care about the postmistress's daughter or the scout who killed enough Indians to have retribution coming to him? It's brilliant." Laughter erupted from the two men.

Forming a fist, Tarak grimaced and inhaled deeply.

Essie glanced past him through the crevice. Victor was the only person she could see from her angled position among the megaliths.

Tied to a rocky column, he struggled to loosen his wrists and ankles from the ropes that bound them and kicked his heels. Dust sprang from his efforts.

Essie longed to step from their protection long enough to see Gus, but Tarak kept a firm hold against her shoulder.

Tarak lifted a hand, motioning for Essie to stay back. He slid with the breeze, making no additional noise as he slipped into the gap between the rock formations. With equal stealth, he slithered back. "I see two men. There could be more."

Outnumbered and without weapons, except for the bow Tarak kept slung across his shoulder, Essie wondered how they'd overtake the kidnappers. "If we could distract them, perhaps I could untie Gus or Pierre."

"I do not know what they did with the Frenchman, but they tied Miss Augusta to the carriage. If anything spooks the horses…"

Essie clamped both palms across her mouth, stifling the swelling screams. Tarak didn't need to finish the sentence. She knew what would happen if the horses bolted and dragged Augusta behind them. An image drifted past her mind. Shaking, Essie dropped her hands and swallowed the growing panic. She could fall apart later, but not now. Gus needed her, and she needed one more ally. "You don't suppose they've already killed Pierre?"

He shrugged.

"And his daughter? Oh, no…" Urgency demanded

action, yet they had no plan. "Ideas?"

The clatter of horse hooves echoed through the canyon.

Someone's coming. What if... Essie couldn't risk the chance that the approaching horse and rider would upset the carriage that held her daughter's fate. She tiptoed closer to the crevice. Her legs felt like soggy sponges, too weak and overloaded to support her weight, and each step took considerable effort.

A face bloomed through the opening. "Guys? Where'd you go?"

Essie held her breath. The angled opening must have prevented the man from glimpsing her and Tarak but large enough to allow passage.

Tarak waited for what he must have perceived as the right moment and lunged.

Without Tarak holding her back, Essie eased forward and glimpsed the melee. She squinted and narrowed her focus but couldn't make out the identity of the person. His agile movements indicated he wasn't the older prospector. *Must be his son.* Essie leaned with Tarak, jabbing at the air. Everything blurred—Tarak's hair, the quiver and bow strapped to his shoulder, arms, dust, the shirt's cuff against the criminal's wrist.

Tarak pivoted and landed a low back kick.

The man squealed and scrambled backward, tripping over a rocky formation poking through the ground. He landed with a thud.

Tarak towered over him as he reached behind him, hand-over-shoulder, and snagged an arrow from his quiver. He threaded it against his bowstring and pulled it taut. "You wanted a massacre that you blamed on my people."

The man crab-crawled over the stony bumps. "Go ahead and kill me, and you'll definitely take the blame. Nobody in Wylder will believe you didn't kidnap the French girl and kill me for trying to rescue her."

As his gaze swept the captured trio, Tarak loosened his grip on the bowstring but kept the arrow in place between two fingers. "Where is she? What have you done with her?"

He laughed. His guffawing filled the air and echoed through the canyon. "Shh…It's a secret. One, I can't tell you if I'm dead."

"Tie him, Essie," Tarak commanded.

Essie inched forward. She reached for the man and drew back as though slapped. The shock made her forget her blistered feet, skinned knees, and tired muscles. "What? You? Surely it's a mistake."

He grinned and twirled his mustache. "Hello, Essie."

Her mind could not process the familiar face and the distinct voice without the first trace of a French accent. *I'm seeing things. Can it be him?*

Tarak, still hovering, turned his head. "Grab his gun. Quickly."

Squatting beside the man she'd thought the most wonderful in the world until just the prior moment, she raked her eyes over his prone body. Her throat closed, and tears threatened. *I was stupid and gullible. I can't believe I fell for his charm and risked my daughter.*

His coat fell open, revealing a gun handle that poked forward from the low-slung belt.

She snatched the pistol and flipped it around to face him. Standing statue-still, she blinked. "I can't believe you'd do this."

Tarak nudged her. "Miss Essie, I will watch him. You had better untie Gus and Victor before the other man returns."

The reminder jolted her into action. "Right." She raced for Gus and grabbed the restraints from her ankles and wrists before hugging her to her chest. "I've been so worried. I suspected the MacDonalds, but…"

Gus twisted her wrists and ankles. "Thank goodness you came." She furrowed a brow. "Mom, we left you behind. How did you get here?"

She patted her daughter's face, feeling the life inside her rise with each inhalation. "It's a long story, beginning with Lightning."

Gus gasped. "No way. You'd never…"

Victor kicked at the ground with the heels of both feet. He grunted and squirmed.

Essie pointed across the canyon. "Lightning's over there. Tarak brought me through an underground passage. We'll get him later. Right now, we need to free Victor."

Gus ran to Victor, yanked the gag from his mouth, and cut him free.

Jumping to his feet, Victor glared at Pierre. His face puffed with rage. "I was duped. Who would have thought Pierre would have been behind this?" He rubbed his purple wrists and wiggled his fingers. "I let him walk right up to us. I never suspected a thing. Had no idea." He shook his head.

Essie handed him the gun. "Looks like yours."

Victor trained it on the man they'd thought to be Lacroix. He grabbed his belt and draped it over his arm. "Think you could just ride in here and trick us all, didn't you? Well, I've had enough. I'm with Tarak and say we hang him as a sign for others wishing to come to Wylder and make fools of us. Tie him up, Augusta."

Essie peered into the carriage. "So, where's Francine?"

The man who passed himself off as Pierre Lacroix rolled his eyes. "Ask her yourself."

He sounded calm—much too relaxed for a man about to lose his life at the end of Victor's rope.

"Ask her? Well, I'd be glad to if I knew where she was."

The sound of a hammer cocking back echoed.

Essie glanced over her shoulder and gazed into the face of the violet-eyed girl—only she looked a lot less like a girl and more like a female rodeo rider she'd seen in a passing show.

The woman smiled. "Now you know."

Essie turned and grabbed Augusta, tugging her from the hastily knotted ropes around Pierre's ankles toward the opposite end of the opening.

A man stepped from the growing shadows. He twirled a rifle by its butt and slapped his palm against its shaft. "Since you cost me the beaver pelts, I'll feel a lot less guilty about this."

Gus leaned against her mother, and Essie shoved her between her own body and a megalith. If one of them shot Augusta, they'd have to do it through her. She stared at the man's slicked-back hair and broad grin that took her back to the first day she'd laid eyes on the couple from the train. "You again?"

He motioned the gun toward Victor and Gus. "Tie them back up, and make it tighter this time, beaver-trapper."

Tarak crossed his arms. He sneered. "Make me."

John Smith shoved the barrel into Tarak's gut. "How's this?"

Without as much as a flinch, Tarak held his posture and glared at Smith. "How did you escape?"

Smith laughed. "That was easy enough with Pierre dropping by with a key." He leaned down and cut through Lacroix's bindings. "Been meaning to ask how you got it."

Essie could barely absorb the treachery. She'd known something was amiss from the beginning. Strangers rarely made such a fuss when they first dropped into a town. She should have known then, but with Augusta's future at risk, the Frenchman showering her with attention, and the letter to Blanche… *Despite her protests, I should have finished it and sent Gus to Boston. Now John Smith intends to kill her.*

Released from his restraints, Pierre brayed and clapped a palm against Smith's back. "I told you to make a ruckus, and I'd free you. After Hanson left one afternoon, I marched into the office, pressed the key into a mustache wax form, and had its match made. As a French Ambassador, there's not a shred of evidence to connect me, and even if there were, I'd claim immunity."

Victor sneered. He hovered a hand above the gun belt. "What about the money? Why would you need five thousand dollars?"

Essie's stomach rumbled and rolled. The metallic taste of nauseaus fear permeated her mouth. "Don't you get it, Victor? This man is a fake—a phony. He's no French Ambassador to the United States. The real French Ambassador to the United States doesn't live in France. He lives in Washington."

Pierre winced. He cut a glance at Smith.

Essie had nothing left to lose. She retrieved the letter from her inner pocket and ran a fingernail beneath the wax-sealed flap. "Forgive me, but considering the circumstances, I brought it along."

Gus widened her eyes and gasped. "Ma? What about the sanctity of the mail?"

Her daughter's shock was understandable. Even in the most dire situations, Essie had maintained the privacy and security of every mail piece coming through Wylder's post office. "It's still sanctified as the postmaster or postmistress is the only person besides the addressee who can legally open the mail."

"Under what circumstances?" Pierre snapped.

"Ones of deception." She raked a glance down the page, her gaze moving left-to-right. "Just as I thought. You see, the Ambassador to the United States from France responded to Victor's inquiry."

Victor slid his hand downward and reached for his gun.

"He did?" Pierre's voice trembled. "I mean, of course, I did." He smacked away Victor's hand and retrieved the weapon for himself.

John Smith sneered. "Enough talking. The sun is setting, and we've got to make tracks. Francine, I mean Lula Mae, better tie them tightly."

Gus wrinkled her nose. "Lula Mae? That's your name? I knew something was amiss with you the whole time."

She laughed and pointed her gun at Augusta. "Since you'll be dead before the sun sets, I don't mind letting you win this one. I say we shoot them now. Why bother tying them?"

Pierre tossed a spool of rope to Lula Mae. "It's easier to tie live people than dead ones. Besides, they make less mess when restrained." He laughed.

She caught the rope one-handed, formed a loop in its end, and lunged for Victor.

Essie could hardly believe the situation. The man she thought would take her to Paris and show her the world intended to kill them. Panic seeped through her veins. Her flesh crawled, and her heart pulsed with urgency. She could not offer assistance to anybody, least of all her daughter. Not even Victor nor Tarak could help her now. "But…how did you know about the world's fair…the details about the exhibitors…Gustave Eiffel?" She recalled the morning they'd ridden to the arena and his description of French light. "A million tiny diamonds reflected in the stone?"

Pierre strolled toward Augusta. "Newspapers," he called out. "Specifics are necessary for a convincing ruse, and reading the papers not only provides those details but informs me of the authorities' progress. But, now that you know…"

Surely, I can reason with him. Without a thought concerning her own safety, Essie again leapt in front of Gus. *I have to stall.* "How did you learn so much about food, how to carve a fish, and speak another language?"

Lacroix stepped closer. "My mother was French, and I worked in a restaurant when I was young. However, my time in the theater served me best. By the way, that was how I met Victor and learned of his request for inclusion in the World's Fair. He made it easy for me—you all made it easy. You see what you want to see even when the truth flutters beneath your nose."

Essie's stomach roiled until she thought she'd be sick. He was right. She was so impressed with his appearance she'd looked no deeper than the surface, and that miscalculation would likely cost her everything. She dug her heels into the dirt and spread her arms in front of Augusta. "She's just an innocent girl, for heaven's sake. How can you even dream of doing her harm?"

He cut a glance at her and then Augusta. Working the corners of his mouth, he smiled crookedly and twirled his mustache with one thumb and forefinger. "You make a good point, Essie. The girl shouldn't die before she's had the chance to live." He raked a slow stare from Augusta's head to her feet.

Sweat pebbled Essie's brow. She'd seen the look before and knew what it meant. Unwanted male attention was one of the things she'd hope to prevent by sending Gus to stay with her cousin.

Lacroix inched closer. He motioned. "John, since Lula Mae is busy tying up Victor, come over here and remove the postmistress from my sight."

Smith grinned. "Gladly." He pointed the gun at Tarak. "You stay put. He sauntered backward, staring at Tarak as he closed in on Essie.

Essie squinted. "I won't budge."

While he reached for Essie, Smith kept his weapon trained on Tarak. "Don't make this harder than it has to be." He encircled her forearm with his damp palm and yanked.

Despite grinding her heels into the stony earth, she nearly flew toward the greasy criminal. "Stop. Let me go." She wiggled her wrist.

"Thank you." Pierre closed the distance between

him and Gus. "Augusta, I could keep you in fancy dresses like the one you're wearing, and you could keep me in warm embraces. What do you say, girl?" He laid a palm against her cheek.

Essie bolted for him, but John's grip prevented her from breaking free. She swept a gaze around the rocks. *Where's Tarak?* Her mouth dried. *Did Smith do something with him? Did he shoot him when I wasn't looking? Did Lula Mae tie him to a carriage?*

Gus purred and tilted her head into his hand, rolling her cheek against his digits. "I wondered if you noticed me."

All thoughts of Tarak left her mind. Gasping, Essie stopped wiggling. She blinked. *I didn't just hear what I thought I heard.* "Augusta," she squealed. "What are you saying?"

"Well, I'm saying…"

In the distance, a coyote yelped and howls lifted.

Their calls raced like the sound of the train's screaming breaks and pierced the nerves in Essie's spine. Whatever else Gus said, she couldn't hear. "Would you repeat that?"

Gus glanced around the circle and giggled.

Pierre's eyes sparkled. He swallowed and stepped closer. "Please, repeat, dearest Augusta. If you said what I think you did, we might make an arrangement that will allow you to have a long and pleasurable life."

Gus looked at her feet and then slid a hot gaze upward until it landed on his face. "My mother's right here. I can't say it out loud."

Biting his lip, he leaned closer. "Whisper it in my ear, darling."

She smiled and batted her eyelashes. "Okay."

He sheathed Victor's pistol and reached for Augusta. Balancing his hands on her hips, he slowly lowered his ear to her mouth.

She tilted her head. As she moved her lips, she shifted her gaze to Essie.

Essie narrowed her focus. Augusta said something, but she couldn't make out her daughter's whispers over the pounding of her own heart.

Pierre laughed.

Gus lowered her chin to Pierre's shoulder and nuzzled his neck.

Sucking in a breath, Pierre relaxed. "Ahh, sweet Augusta."

After tying off another round of restraints against Victor's feet, Lula Mae pivoted and smacked Pierre's arm. "Take your paws off the horse-girl before I put a bullet in your back."

He shoved Lula Mae from him. "I'm warning you. I'll take you back to Kansas City."

She sneered. "I doubt that. It's not like they'd welcome you with open arms."

Essie couldn't concentrate. She glanced around. *I've been a fool, and I'll pay for that with my daughter's life and my own.* She wished she could go back in time and make different decisions, but it was too late. All she could do was watch the disaster unfold.

Lacroix peeked over his shoulder. "Be quiet. I'd rather listen to the breath of an angel than the threats of a devil." He turned back around and rested his cheek against Gus's. "Tell me that again."

Augusta grinned. "Gladly." She brought her lips near his ear.

"Oh, Augusta," Pierre purred.

"You…" She sank her teeth into Pierre's lobe and kneed his groin.

Screaming, Pierre doubled over and fell against Gus. "Bitch," he yelled. He straightened and swiped at his bleeding ear. "Augusta, I'll teach you what it means to feel a man's wrath instead of his kindness." He drew back a hand.

How dare he threaten my daughter? Essie's body seemed afire. Bile swelled from her gut into her throat. *I have to get to Gus. I have to break loose.* She struggled against Smith's grip until she thought her arm might dislocate from her shoulder.

The horizon turned magenta, and time slowed. Essie seemed both a watcher and a participant in an out-of-body perspective.

Pierre swung his arm.

"No." *No, no, no…* Essie's screams echoed through the valley. Resisting, she twisted and kicked.

Smith wrenched her wrist. His face reddened. "If you don't stand still—"

Essie stopped listening. Something flashed. It was brief and just from her peripheral vision. She glanced at Smith. Either it was another of his gang members, or he was too busy keeping her under his control to pay attention to anything else. *I have to do something. I have to get to Gus. What do I have to lose?* She lifted her foot and drove a heel into the top of his boot.

"Oww," he squealed. "I'm tired of messing with you." While Smith hopped on one foot, he flipped the gun around, holding it by the barrel. He hovered its butt over her head. "One swift blow should take care of you."

Essie flinched. *If he smacks me in the head, how*

will I help Gus? She saw the flicker again.

Tarak reappeared from behind a megalith. He held his forefinger to his lips and motioned for her to draw closer.

Summoning her strength, Essie lunged toward the stone pillar. Her wrist remained in Smith's grip, but the distance prevented him from using his other arm as a hammer.

Smith closed the gap. "Like I said…" He lowered his arm.

Essie watched Tarak's face, trusting him with her life. *He won't let him hurt me, but if he does, Tarak will save Gus.*

He nodded.

His confirmation was all she needed. She ducked and dove for the ground. Essie didn't care if she busted her nose or if Smith broke her arm—bones healed. Even if Smith shot her, the melee might give Gus time to get away.

Tarak sprang from his hiding place like a cougar. He pounced on Smith, and using both hands, landed an upward punch.

Grunting, John Smith crumpled backward. Arms flailing, he stumbled and dropped both the gun and his hold on Essie.

The release happened so suddenly Essie didn't have time to brace. Her skirt billowed, and she fell hard against sharp rocks that pierced her flesh and skinned her knees and shins. But she couldn't waste time nursing wounds when her daughter's safety was uncertain. Spitting the metallic-tasting dirt from her mouth, she leaped up. "Gus!"

Chapter 14

Lula Mae ignored the melee with Smith. Hat askew, she sprinted toward Pierre. "Devil?" She caught her toe on a half-exposed rock and careened off balance. Faltering, she dropped her gun, and it skidded between the megaliths. Red-faced and scrambling from her stony landing, she lifted a rock and stood. Drawing back, she swung at him from behind and smacked Pierre's head. "I'll show you just how devilish I can be."

Pierre's arm sprang forward, then lost its velocity. Only the tips of his fingers grazed Gus's cheek before he hit the ground with a thud.

With her hands on her hips, Lula Mae stood over Pierre. "Breath of an angel—ha!"

While Lula Mae yelled at her unconscious partner, her other criminal cohort wrestled with Tarak. "Lula Mae, get over here and help me."

Ignoring his calls for assistance, she continued her tirade. "'Learn to speak French,' you said. 'Act like a lady.' What did that get me?"

Gus knelt beside Lacroix and laid a palm against his neck. "He's still alive," she yelled.

Lula Mae spun around. "Get away from him."

Essie scrambled closer. "Listen to her, Gus. Don't worry about that scoundrel—just get over here."

Gus slid her hand from Pierre's neck, allowing it to

rest against his back. "Sure—whatever you say." She half-stood before snatching Pierre's gun. With one glance behind her, she tossed the weapon. "Mom—catch."

The flash of the setting sun's last rays glinted off metal. Essie squinted. She didn't know whether the pistol was cocked or loaded, and feared both. If she didn't retrieve the gun before it made contact with one of the boulders, it could discharge indiscriminately. Unable to trust her small hands, she lifted her skirt and held it like a basket. Flipping end—over—end, it appeared suspended in midair.

Looking up, Lula Mae cupped her palms around her mouth. "John, grab it."

He sprang but was too slow.

Tarak squatted and spun a leg. He made contact behind Smith's knee and knocked the criminal off his feet.

As John Smith writhed against the ground, the setting sun's last rays glinted off metal.

Turning, Tarak glanced upward. "To your left, Miss Essie."

Scooting sideways, Essie tightened her grip on her skirt. Sweat pebbled her brow. She had to snag the weapon. Their lives depended on her. The gun picked up speed in its free fall to earth, but she was ready. It barely missed her nose as it wobbled past and landed in her skirt with a bounce. "Got it." She gazed beyond's Tarak's shoulder. "Watch out."

With Tarak's attention off him, John Smith retrieved his pistol. He placed it between his chest and Tarak's.

Staring at the barrel, Tarak stepped backward and

held up his palms.

While Essie ached to run to her daughter, she couldn't leave Tarak in imminent danger. Trusting Pierre kept his pistol loaded, she aimed the gun at Smith. "Put it down."

He sneered. "Make me, but you better do it fast. I've no intention of letting this one live. After all, the good citizens of Wylder know this place is crawling with nasty injuns, and they know you're an Indian lover."

Essie narrowed her gaze until everything blurred around her except the weapon trained on her friend. He was only here because of her and Gus, and she couldn't let Smith kill him. *But can I stop him?* She cocked back the hammer. "You're right. I do love my Arapaho friends, and I will do whatever it takes to keep them safe—including pulling the trigger."

Smith cut a glance in her direction. "You'll never convince Wylder's citizens this wasn't another massacre perpetrated by the Arapaho—and it will be a massacre. Lula Mae, now." He wiped his bloody lip with the opposite elbow, threw back his head, and laughed.

Knowing Gus was still cornered by Lula Mae brought a gasp from Essie. She looked behind her where Gus wrestled with Lula Mae. Neither seemed to have a weapon.

The pistol suddenly flew from John Smith's hand, going airborne.

Essie turned toward the person whose foot had sent it sailing in one long kick. "Meadowlark? How did you…where did you…"

"Mom," Gus yelled.

Essie spun and ran toward her daughter.

Smith's pistol clanged against the rocks, falling into a crevice.

Lula Mae leaped off Gus and grabbed it. She smoothed her skirt. "Stop."

Augusta acted quickly. Mimicking Meadowlark, she drew back a foot and released the kick, making contact with the back of Lula Mae's hand.

"Owww," Lula Mae screamed and dropped the weapon. She lunged for Gus's throat, wrapping both hands around her neck. "I've had enough of you."

Gus wiggled free of Lula Mae's hold. She leaned left and then right before landing a punch in the woman's gut.

Bent double, Lula Mae coughed and gagged.

Gus threw one more punch, landing it on Lula Mae's chin.

Lula Mae's head snapped backward, and she fell to the ground.

Without pausing, Gus tied Pierre's hands and feet, and pushed a bandana into his mouth before he could regain consciousness.

Meadowlark delivered another kick, one that made John Smith's arms go limp.

Tarak grabbed his wife and embraced her. "How did you know?"

Meadowlark squirmed from the hug and placed her hands on his shoulders. "After the last incident, I kept an eye on your wanderings. I hope you are not angry."

He held her at arm's length and then back against his chest. Stroking her head, he rocked side-to-side. "Angry? You've just saved us all."

Essie ran to Victor and cut the rope from around

his wrists.

He grabbed her hands. "Thanks, Essie. I thought we were all doomed. I couldn't bear watching…it was…you were…" His voice quivered.

The past couple of days had been too emotional for Essie. She was suddenly the most tired she'd ever been. Swaying, she leaned against him, but she couldn't process another person's feelings—not now, anyway. She patted his shoulder. "We all feared the worst, but thankfully, we pulled through. Come on. Help me tie up these three, and we'll get them back to town."

Victor furrowed his brows and stroked her cheek with his thumb. "Hey, are you okay?"

She nodded and swiped the perspiration from her forehead. Breathing heavily, she gestured toward Meadowlark and Augusta. "I should help them secure the criminals."

He hooked an arm around her and practically carried her to the carriage. "You should rest. I'll help Tarak get them loaded, and we'll get back to town." Victor grabbed his canteen. "Here's some water."

The heat, stress, and lack of sleep caught up with Essie. She accepted Victor's offering and took a long sip. "Thank you. It's been a long day. But I'm not resting when there's still work to do."

Gus looked up. She bit her lip. "Mama, are you all right?"

Essie heard concern in her daughter's voice. "I'm fine—just catching my breath." She laid aside the container and took Victor's hand. "Come on. Let's get 'em loaded and back to town."

Victor squeezed her fingertips and grinned down at her. "Sure."

As she walked, Essie marveled at his warm, but gentle, touch. Coming from such a boisterous man, it said a lot for his feelings. Still, she felt slightly uncomfortable with the sign of affection in front of her daughter. When they rejoined the group, Essie slipped her hand from his and grabbed Augusta. She held her tightly to her chest. "I'm so sorry I put you in harm's way."

Gus wiggled free. "Aw shucks, Mama, I wasn't hurt. I'm confused, though." She scratched her head. "If Miss Fancy Pants isn't Francine but someone named Lula Mae, I'm guessing her two partners aren't Pierre Lacroix and John Smith."

Victor grabbed Pierre's shoulders. "Search him."

A memory slipped across Essie's mind of his hand reaching into an inner coat pocket. "Allow me." She snagged a wallet, pulling it from its cocoon. She thought of the times she'd seen Pierre snag it with pizazz and the flutter it triggered. Suddenly, she hadn't the heart to peel it open. She held it out to Victor. "You look."

Victor flipped it open and peeked inside. He pulled papers from its inner fold. "Got a receipt made out to Charles Matheson and another to Jeremy Johnson."

The names ricocheted around Essie's mind. *Charles Matheson...Jeremy Johnson.* "I've seen them somewhere."

Meadowlark jerked her head toward Essie. "Where?"

Essie couldn't be certain. She saw a variety of names every time the stage brought a new batch of mail to the post office. Perhaps she only thought the names were important. She shook her head. "It's just a hunch,

246

but when we get back to Wylder, I'll know for sure."

Gus jabbed two fingers against the corners of her mouth and whistled.

A dust cloud lifted, and the sound of hooves pounding dry earth grew louder as Lightning sped toward her.

Essie trembled. Just when she thought the worst was behind her, she remembered how she'd gotten to the desert. She groaned. "Lightning?"

Gus tugged at the dress. "Mom, why don't you ride back to town in the wagon?"

The thought of having to mount Lightning brought a shudder. "Gladly."

Victor motioned for Tarak. "Help me lift these three criminals and toss them in the wagon." He hoisted Pierre's shoulders.

Tarak lifted Pierre's feet. He swung him like a sack of cabbages and repeated the effort with Smith and the woman now called Lula Mae.

Victor smacked together his palms. "This ended better than I imagined." He sighed and held out his arm. "Essie, let me help you up."

After accepting his assistance, Essie waved to Tarak and Meadowlark. She pointed toward the back of the carriage. "It could have been worse—much worse."

Victor nodded but said little. He hung his head and fiddled with the reins. "Let Augusta lead since she can get there faster on Lightning than we can in this buggy."

"But..." Essie protested. She'd just gotten her back from what felt like the brink of near death. She leaned over the edge. "Stop by the post office and grab the wanted posters."

Gus smiled. "Don't worry. We done got the bad guys, Mama. I'll get the posters." She pressed on the sides of the skirt and then the front. "Lightning, bow." She bent from the waist and bowed deeply.

Lightning dropped his head and leaned back on his haunches.

Gus rubbed his neck, hiked her skirts, and leaped astride. "Good boy, Lightning. Hyah." She glanced over her shoulder. "See you at Sheriff Hanson's."

Essie stared at her daughter's dimming silhouette until she couldn't see her. Lightning's hooves tapped an echoing cadence that matched her heartbeat. *What if more gang members hid in the shadows or waited in town?* She placed a trembling palm against Victor's arm. "Let's go."

****

As they pulled up to the hitching post, Essie noticed Tarak and Meadowlark. She leaped down. "I'm glad you and Meadowlark are here. The sheriff might need your statements."

Tarak patted her back. "If he does not, it is okay. We only came to help Victor unload."

She knew what he meant. Given Earl's previous dismissal, the couple likely didn't hold expectations for anything better. But Essie still believed the best of most people. She hoped this event might change something in the relationship between the Natives and the authority figures. "Wait for me. I'll go in and get Hanson. We'll let him decide what he needs after he sees who we've captured." Racing across the porch, she didn't give Tarak a chance to change his mind. She grabbed the handle and swung open the door.

Sheriff Hanson glanced up as soon as the door

248

creaked. "Hello, Essie. Come on in, and tell me what brings you over here."

Essie ran toward him. "Glad you're back. I've something important to tell you." She leaned on the desk with one hand and pointed to the street with the other. "I need your assistance. Got a wagon full of criminals."

Earl rested his elbows against the desk and grimaced. "Criminals? That's a serious accusation, Essie."

She nodded. "I realize it. However, your escapee is one of them."

"Escapee?" He leaped from the chair and scowled. "You found that scoundrel?"

Straightening, she crossed her arms. "Him and two more. But I should warn you their identity might be shocking."

Hanson grabbed his hat. He took long strides toward the door, snatched the handle and held it for her. "I doubt you can shock me, Essie. I've seen more than my share of crooks and villains."

Essie strolled through the opening. As she passed the sheriff, she harrumphed. "So you say." She crossed the porch and stepped into the road. "Vic, Hanson's here."

Victor shuffled around the back of the wagon. "Better bring cuffs and chains. We've got a gang right here, and they're rousing."

The sound of hooves approaching sent Essie's heart plummeting. *Can there be more? What if they've ridden in to free their buddies?* She stared into the darkness. Two blonde pigtails escaped from beneath the Gainsborough hat and flapped behind her. Essie relaxed. "Gus—over here."

Skirts flying, Gus leaped off Lightning's back. She held out the stack of wanted posters from the post office wall. "Here you go, Mama."

Essie flipped through the first two pages. "Just as I thought." She smacked one. "This victim is a Matheson, and we found a receipt on the man calling himself Pierre Lacroix with that name." She thumbed the edges of the remaining pages and tugged out another. "And this one here is a rancher named Jeremy Johnson. He had a receipt on him by that name, too."

Victor stuffed an unlit cigar between his teeth and chewed. "Yep, Sheriff, you probably want to get over to the hotel and bring in their traveling trunks. I'll be willing to bet you'll find a lot more evidence."

Sheriff Hanson blinked and scratched his chin. "Yes, of course, I'll send a deputy. I'll need to get word to the cavalry officer, too. This trio caused a lot of damage across Wyoming Territory." He lifted Pierre by the shoulders. "Someone want to give me a hand?"

Tarak stepped forward. "I will." Grabbing the Frenchman's legs, he helped Sheriff Hanson unload the perpetrator and carry him into the jail. He returned and snagged Smith's ankles.

Meadowlark slung Francine over her shoulder. "I'll take care of this one."

Victor reached under Smith's arms. "I can't get a firm hold."

Sheriff Hanson tapped Victor's shoulder. "With those swollen wrists—no wonder." He nudged aside Victor and shook his head. "They certainly went to great lengths to perpetrate this crime. You were right, Essie. I never suspected a thing."

Although his admission made Essie feel slightly better, she still winced. "None of us did. At least you didn't make a complete fool out of yourself."

Victor rested his palms on Essie's shoulders. He leaned forward until his lips touched her ear. "Now, you listen here. The only people making fools out of themselves are facing jail time. You've got a good heart, Essie Baumgardner, and I told Augustus that more than once. I thought he was crazy for leaving you to relay the mail, but he had a calling, and for that, I respected him."

Gus tugged Victor's sleeve. "Tell me more about my mama when she was young. Was she like me?"

He raised his head and laughed.

For a moment, he gazed over her head like a mirror into the past was just beyond her shoulder.

"Your mama wasn't like anybody I've known before or since. I'm crazy about her—always have been."

Essie, mouth agape, stared. She barely focused on Victor's face. Her brows inched inward, but she couldn't stop their progress. "You're crazy about me?"

Victor drew his lips inward and shrugged. "I'm crazy about you. I'll repeat it as many times as you need to hear it, but think about it, Essie. You're more like me than you'd ever have been to Pierre, even if he was really who he claimed. We share a past, a present, and a future, if you allow it. I'll take you places, Estelle Baumgardner, maybe even Paris, someday."

Augusta gasped and lunged toward Essie. She grabbed her mother and hugged her. "Mama, I'm so happy for you."

Essie's thoughts spun. She recalled the first day

she'd seen him with the man she believed to be a Frenchman. Victor was right about Pierre. Even if he had been the French Ambassador, he would not have made a good match. Everything made sense for the first time in days, but she'd never let Victor Douglas know it. "Can we talk about this later?"

Victor grinned. "It's not a rejection, so, of course, we can." He offered his arms—one to Essie and the other to Augusta—sticking them out at right angles. "Let's go see if Hanson needs help."

Inside, Earl slapped one cuff on the wrist of each of the three. He attached the other against a portion of the iron bars and crooked a thumb over his shoulder. "Come on, Essie. I need statements."

Essie bit her lip. She took a breath and motioned toward the corner. "Can you take Tarak's and Meadowlark's first? They likely need to get back home."

Sheriff Hanson raked a glance across the Arapaho couple. He tossed the key on its large, round hook onto the desk. "That's all right. They can get along home now."

Tarak stepped toward the door. He cut a glance at Essie and lowered his chin.

Essie understood what Earl's dismissal communicated. They might as well have left the minute they arrived. No white authority figure had ever taken a statement from an Indian against a white man, at least not one that stood the test of time. Essie thought it was time to set a new justice standard. She caught his arm. "No, Earl, they need to give their statements first."

Victor leaned against the desk. "That's right. They're heroes. None of us would have made it out alive if it hadn't been for them. I'm"—he inhaled and stuck out a palm in Tarak's direction—"grateful."

Earl lit a couple of oil lanterns and rummaged desk drawers until he found what seemed to please him. He snagged a few sheets of paper and glanced from one to the other, but he finally nodded. "Okay. Shall we begin?"

The night dragged on. Essie thought she was no worse off at the jail than she'd have been at home. She was too excited to sleep anyway.

Tarak and Meadowlark gave their accounts of the events that had transpired that evening. Their voices rose and fell with each of the sheriff's questions. Before leaving, the Arapaho couple paused.

Meadowlark nodded in her direction.

Tarak pointed and made a fist which he held to his heart.

Smiling, Essie waved. She wondered if Earl even knew what he'd done by allowing the Indians to file complaints. His actions had just restored a bit of lost dignity to previously disrespected Arapaho Natives.

Hanson motioned for Victor. "You want to go next?"

Essie stood in the corner with Gus. One by one, they gave statements.

Two hours later, the door burst open, and the unmistakable sound of a cane hitting the ground thumped toward them—*Nancy.*

As she staggered to the desk and tapped her cane, Nancy's scan seemed to miss the cluster of victims gathered together.

Sheriff Hanson glanced up. Upon seeing her, he immediately snapped backward. He swallowed hard.

"Nancy?"

Nancy Finncannon hooked the cane against the desk's edge and leaned against it with both palms. "Surprised to see me?"

"Well...I'd not...I mean..." He cleared his throat.

"Rumor has it you've arrested the man who tried to steal five thousand dollars from me. Any truth to it?" Her voice was intense and gravelly.

Earl slipped the pen into its holder, tidied the array of papers scattered over his desk, and crossed his arms. "I have. We haven't discovered the money yet, but we'll let you know as soon as we do."

Essie braced for the full brunt of Nancy's wrath. Although she'd offered the money of her own accord, she'd brought her into the scheme. She exchanged stares with Victor, whose eyes—pupils dilated from the dimness—seemed unusually large.

Turning in her direction, Nancy scowled. "Eavesdropping? I'd expect no less from Wylder's postmistress, which is a position for which I suppose you'll have no competition any time soon—that is, if the terms of our agreement do not become public knowledge. I don't want anyone to think I am not a good judge of character, and letting myself get swindled would indicate otherwise, wouldn't it?"

Victor nudged Essie. "We'd never dream of exposing your involvement. Nobody needs to know." He pointed to the jail cell. "I certainly doubt those three will speak of it."

Nancy nodded. "You see, Stutts doesn't know I leant the money, so I'd appreciate it if you could return it with subtlety. With Stutts making a bid for mayor, I think it best to keep some things quiet. Now that it's settled, good evening." She stomped through the opening with her head held high.

Victor pressed his palm against Essie's. "Well now, it appears all is well. You won't have to sacrifice your position after all.

Earl snatched the forms and slipped them into a drawer. He removed a key and twisted it in the lock. "I have all I need to keep them here until the marshal arrives. Why don't you get on out of here and get yourselves a good meal?"

Essie hugged her daughter. "I'm not very hungry at the moment."

Gus wiggled from her embrace. "I'd hoped to see Clyde. Does anyone know where he is?"

She cupped Gus's elbow. "Come along. We'll find him together." Although she felt Victor's questioning gaze searing into her spine, Essie didn't look back.

"Hey, wait up. I'll see you home."

Victor's voice wafted over her but she didn't slow. If desired, he could catch her easily enough.

In a matter of seconds, he was beside her in his surrey. "Hop in. I'll drive you."

Gus leaped in first. "Thanks. These shoes aren't meant for walking—I'll tell you that."

Seeing no other option, Essie exhaled loudly. "Oh, all right—might as well." As she scrambled in, she caught a glimpse of Victor's pinched face. "What's on your mind?"

He turned toward her. "What makes you think there is?"

Essie crossed her arms. "Really? You're going to make me describe your current posture and studious brow?"

Victor snagged an unlit cigar from his pocket, jabbed it into his mouth, and held it tightly between his teeth. His jaws remained still, but his lips moved. "I've been thinking about something you said, and Lacroix confirmed." The tightly-gripped cigar muffled the sound of his words.

She bristled. "Something I said? Do tell."

Snatching the cigar, he pointed it in her direction. "About the Indians. You might be right. There was such balletic beauty to Tarak's movements tonight. Did you notice?"

Has Victor Douglas lost his mind? "Balletic beauty?"

"Pierre—or whoever he is—might be right about something, too. I need them for the show. I want to put Indians and buffalo and battle scenes in the show."

Essie couldn't believe her ears, but she was too tired to be diplomatic. "What makes you think they'd agree to help you make more money off them? Haven't you done enough to destroy their people and their way of life?"

He hung his head. "I have, Essie. I surely have done too much to them and their hunting lands." Victor snapped his head toward her. His gaze sought hers. "But have you seen the reservation? It's not any kind of life for people with the talents of the Natives. If I put them in my show, they could earn a living reenacting what they love doing—riding, roping, honing their combat skills. Heck, Essie, you could be in it, too—you and Gus."

Gus bounced against the seat. "Really? You'll make me a permanent part of your traveling show?"

Gritting her teeth, Essie bristled against his false

promises. "He says that now, but when the time comes…" She shrugged.

Victor shoved the cigar back between his teeth and used both hands to navigate a turn. "That's not fair, Essie, and you know it. I want to take my show international. To do that, I need something authentic of the American West. The Wylder West Show can do that. It can be a starring feature in the next Paris Exposition."

Essie blinked. "Did the real French Ambassador promise this?"

After finishing the turn, Victor pulled the cigar from his lips and held it between his thumb and forefinger. He stabbed at the air. "Well…he…not exactly, but I know…if the show is big enough and bold enough."

It wasn't a bad idea. Essie tapped her cheek with a forefinger. "Plus, it doesn't hurt that Tarak and Meadowlark likely saved your sorry hide from the gang set on killing you and Gus."

He pulled the surrey along the walkway. "Come with me. You don't have to answer me now, but think about it. Let Nancy have the post office, and you and Gus join me on the road."

Gus leaped from the carriage. Her skirt snagged on a board, and she yanked. As soon as it gave, she held together her palms in a prayer position. "Oh, please, Ma, please say we can do it. I want to go to Paris but only if I can take Lightning. I want to ride a Wylder horse in Tuileries Garden. That'll show Clyde, especially when he sees I am the real deal and not some fake like Lula Mae."

Essie wanted to laugh, and she might have had it

not been for wondering about the Hartshorn boy. She held the seat's edge and lowered herself to the step. "By the way, Victor, do you know what happened to Clyde?"

"Clyde?" Victor repeated. "Nobody has seen him recently."

The sound of hooves thundering against the road echoed down the street. Essie paused at the back door to the post office.

Gus adjusted the bustle in the back and the overlay in the front. She craned her neck and twisted her shoulders while puffing. "I can't tell if I'm wearing this gown or if it's wearing me."

Victor stepped down and snagged a lantern from the post beam. He held it out to Essie. "Here. The light ought to help."

The lock gave, but she paused. The horse and rider neared.

"Gus," the rider called out.

She stared at the dark figure. "Clyde?"

He leaped off his horse, raced toward her, and grabbed her shoulders. "Oh, Gus. I'm sorry. Mama's canning pot exploded, and she got a glass shard in her eye. I had to fetch the doctor and then clean the broken glass and slippery jam mess. I couldn't leave her alone with her eyes bandaged until it was all cleaned."

Gus took the lantern from Victor. She picked at Clyde's shirt and laughed. "You've not changed clothes. You're still covered in preserves."

Clyde followed Gus's movements with his gaze. "I didn't take time. I feared you were in danger." He turned and grabbed Victor's arm. "Francine? Did you find her?"

Essie paused in the open doorway. The glow from the lantern flickered across her daughter's face as her smile took a downward turn.

Gus shoved the lantern back toward Victor. She gathered her skirts and hiked the hem above her ankles. "So that's why you came riding into town in such a hurry. You're not worried about me. You're worried about Francine."

Fidgeting with his hat brim, Clyde frowned. "Francine was kidnapped. Of course, I'm worried about her. I was worried about my mama, too. Can't a fellow hold concern for more than one person at a time?"

Victor spread his arms, corralling the youngsters. "We're all fine, Clyde. Francine isn't—"

Gus jerked her chin and met Victor's gaze. "Francine isn't in danger any longer." She bumped Clyde with her elbow. "You don't need to worry."

Essie understood more than Gus thought she might. Her daughter didn't want to win Clyde's affection by his discovering Francine's schemes. She wanted him to desire her more than the person identified as the French Ambassador's daughter. "It turns out that our own Augusta was the hero. She figured it all out, but I guess she'll be wanting to tell you about it."

Clyde yanked off his hat. "As long as you've found her, and she's home with Mr. Lacroix, then I don't reckon we need to spend any more time discussing her." He grabbed Gus's hand. "It's you, Gus—you and me—that I want to discuss."

Victor smiled and pulled open the door. He swept a hand forward, motioning for Essie to enter. "Let's leave these two to sweet talk on the back porch, and you and I can get down to some details."

She stepped through the entryway without acknowledging her acceptance of his invitation. "Details, huh? I don't suppose they'd be about your Wylder West Show."

He tossed back his head and laughed. "Of course."

His hopeful tone piqued her interest. Still, she was careful to keep her hopes low. Essie had been disappointed too many times to allow herself to expect much. "What's on your mind, Buffalo Vic? Am I going to like it?"

Chapter 15

The sun was already up when Essie roused. She crossed to the window and threw open the shutters. Light streamed across the floor and hit the bed where Augusta still lay curled into a tight ball.

How many more mornings would she have with her? The thought simultaneously saddened her and gave her a sense of pride. "I did it, Augustus," she whispered into the dawn. "I somehow managed to raise our girl." As if he'd heard and approved, a sense of warmth enveloped her.

She stood by the window, soaking up the rays and wondering what Augustus would say if he were alive. He'd love Gus's spirit, her vinegar-tongue, and sharp wit—that was certain.

"Mama?"

Essie turned. Gus wiped the sleep from her eyes with the back of one hand as she'd done when just a baby. "Yes, darling girl."

She blinked and yawned. "I had the strangest dream." She picked at the coverlet. "Things are about to change, aren't they?"

Nodding, Essie thought the time for total honesty was now. In the past, she'd thought sheltering Gus was the best parenting method. But her daughter had earned respect and deserved a clear answer. "You're nearly grown. I've one last opportunity to show you something of the world, and then what you do with your life is your own choice."

Gus stretched. "I'm starving."

Pivoting, Essie leaned forward and brought together the shutters. While she draped the bar across the clasp, she had the sensation of shuttering out more than heat and dust, but closing a chapter in both her life and her daughter's. Turning, she walked over to Gus and sat on her bed's edge. "Me, too. What do you say we go get some breakfast?"

Slinging back the sheet, Gus smiled. "I'd say absolutely."

She patted her daughter's leg. "I sense we'll both be wanting a bath."

Gus jumped up and pulled her boots onto bare feet. "I'll fetch some water." She returned with two buckets and filled Essie's bowl before pouring the remainder in the tub.

Dipping a cloth into the cool water, Essie pressed it to her forehead and neck. As she took extra pains with her ablutions, she drizzled rivulets down her chest and along her arms. She wished she had something new to wear—something more attractive than her work clothes. While Gus soaked, Essie knelt by the chest and sighed.

Pulling back the protective layer of quilting, Essie stared at the white wool. She tugged the simple column sheath from its accompanying jacket and scratched a fingernail into the moth-pocked places. Laying a finger aside her cheek, she mused. "Could I?"

She snatched her sewing box, grabbed a spool of white thread, and rolled off a length. When it was long enough, she bit through it. *There's only one way to find out.* Hurriedly threading the end through a needle, she worked around the holes. She doused the dress with rosewater and slipped it over her head.

The feel of the fabric against her flesh took her back in time—the snow, the music, Augustus, and Victor Douglas, looking on with jealousy. Of course, she'd not known it then. *How could I have noticed anyone else in Augustus's presence?* Though small in stature, he was larger than life. Everyone knew it, even Victor. She recalled his confession the previous evening.

As Victor cupped her hands between his, he blushed. "I took one look at you and knew there would never be anyone comparable, although I searched the whole of America—including the territories—Mexico, Canada, and Spain. I scanned each audience in every city where I held a show only to be disappointed." He sighed.

Her palms warmed between his. "I stayed in Fort Laramie. I hoped Augustus would return someday, but…"

Victor pulled her to his chest and hugged her close. "As did I. Perhaps he can live again through Augusta and our shared memories of the rare soul that was her father." He caressed her cheek with his thumb.

With the recollection of the previous evening, Essie's pulse increased. She laid a palm to her cheek, reimagining his thumb when she'd ask the ultimate question. "When did you know you could fall for me at this time in our lives?"

He'd laughed and held her at arm's length. "The moment you marched through the post office doors and slung the saddlebags into the street. Although I was momentarily nonplussed, I lay awake that night and realized a woman still in love with the larger-than-life spirit of Augustus Baumgardner would never have done such a thing. I thought I had a chance, and then that crook got in the way." He sneered.

Essie felt her face heating with the memory of how she'd thrown herself at the man calling himself Pierre Lacroix. "And now?" she asked.

"Now, I keep thinking about the girl in the white dress in a small chapel during a snowstorm." He glanced beyond her shoulder.

She pulled the dress over her head and stared at it. Victor had looked past her as if seeing something in the distance. At the time, she wondered what he saw, but now she knew. They shared such a sweet moment in time with a man who was no longer with them. She rubbed the fabric with her thumb. *I've treated this dress like it was woven with the threads of my life and only the moths feasted upon it. Can I wear it again? Can I let go of the past?*

The door popped open, and Gus stomped through, dripping watery footprints across the floorboards. As she stared from her mother's face to the dress, she widened her eyes. She dropped the bath sheet and clapped her hands. "Turn around. Let me see you in it."

Essie snatched her black skirt and pressed it to her chest. "No, I don't think—" She caught herself making excuses, dropped the garment she used as a shield, and rocked back on her heels.

Gus grinned. "You look beautiful. I'd like to see you the way my father saw you, at least once."

Tears wet Essie's lashes as memories flooded her. "I haven't allowed myself to feel attractive in a very long time. I guess…well…having to be strong…to be both mother and father…" She gasped as she glanced at her daughter's crumpling face.

With a trembling lip, Gus whimpered. "It's because of me, ain't it? You've sacrificed your whole life because of me?"

Essie reached Gus in a single stride. With a forefinger, she lifted Gus's chin so that she could meet her stare. "Not sacrificed, my child, but rewarded. You are my life. I like to think we gave you all the best parts of ourselves, but I have worked very hard at burying my softer side."

Gus pulled back and raked a glance over her mother. "It certainly fits."

Essie tugged the fabric from her slightly-curvier-than-the-last-time-she-wore-it body. It clung to her hips and thighs. "It skimmed over my slight figure before."

Twirling a finger, Gus motioned to her mother. "Turn around again."

She slowly pivoted and felt Gus's fingertips working the buttons through the loops that fastened the back. "It's too snug. It won't work."

Gus flipped through the items in the trunk and grabbed a pink silk shawl patterned with red roses. She draped it around Essie's shoulders, stepped back, and winked. "Oh, it works, Mama. It really works. See for yourself." She gestured to the mirror.

Essie peered over her shoulder. The mirror's dark splotches bled across her reflection. Despite the tarnishing, she caught an image of someone she'd not allowed herself to be in a very long time. Shivering, she bit her lip. Her pulse quickened. "Maybe. What are you planning to wear?"

Gus grabbed the fabric brush and the blue dress she'd worn the previous day. "It was dark before Clyde arrived last night, so I thought I'd wear this one more time. You don't think anyone will mind, do you? Besides, the hem is soiled." She scrubbed at the dirt collected along the skirt's edge.

"Lula Mae isn't going to need it any time soon, that's for sure. It isn't part of the evidence, either—at least, I don't think it is. We'll give it to Sheriff Hanson tomorrow."

She harrumphed and scrubbed harder. "I want him to look at me the way he did the woman calling herself Francine. You know the expression—moon-faced and starry-eyed." Gus rolled her eyes. "I want him to realize I'm not really different on the outside, only where it matters"—she patted her chest—"in here."

Essie slipped her arms around Gus's shoulders. "The world is a great big place, full of people you might like better than Clyde. Don't get serious with the first boy who shows you some attention. Besides, he's…" She inhaled sharply and looked in the mirror. *I'm turning into my mother.* She pinched her cheek to make sure she wasn't dreaming. The radiating pain assured her she was the one spewing the all-too-familiar advice.

Gus blinked. "What's wrong, Mama? You look like you've seen a ghost."

Essie snapped her watery gaze onto Augusta's. "What? Ghost? You have no idea just how right you are."

Dropping the brush and the gown, Gus focused on her face. "Tell me then."

Tears sluiced paths down her cheeks. "Your mama

has been a stubborn, unforgiving woman."

Gus hugged Essie. "Not you—you're the nicest person in Wylder. You're even nice to nosey Nancy."

Pressing fingertips against her lids, Essie stemmed her tears. She turned and pulled her daughter tightly to her chest. "Everyone has a good side. Sometimes we have to look below the surface to find it, but it's there. Nancy showed that side yesterday."

Squirming, Gus pulled back. She frowned. "So, if you weren't talking about Nancy, who haven't you forgiven?"

Essie hung her head. She didn't want to see the disappointment in her daughter's face when she admitted her guilt. "Your grandmother, my mother. She didn't approve of me marrying Augustus—thought I was too young—that he was too irresponsible."

Gus tugged her mother's hand. "Was she right?"

Whether or not her mother's opinions had merit never occurred to Essie until now. She had reacted on her emotions and never looked back. Time and distance taught her she was not very different. When facing her daughter's interest in an immature young man, she'd had the same attitude. Essie clamped both hands onto her daughter's. "I didn't think so at the time, but now, I'm not so sure. She likely had my best interest at heart."

Wincing, Gus shuffled a foot. "Is it too late to tell her?"

Recollections of her wedding flashed through Essie's mind. As she recalled her anxious stares at the door with each hinge squeal and boot scrape, she was transported to the long-ago day in the prairie church and her silent pleading that her mother's face would appear when the snow flurries ceased dimming the view. Disappointment churned her stomach until she thought she'd be sick. She likely would have had Augustus not caressed her cheek. His voice wafted across the years. *"Why are you looking backward when you should be focused on our future?"*

Gus shook her arms. "Well—is it?"

Augustus' advice served her then, and it would likely serve her equally as well now. *Don't look back.* "Yes. But it isn't too late to avoid making the same mistakes. You're a smart young lady, Augusta. Whatever you decide to do and whoever you decide to do it with are your decisions. I'll support them."

Raising a brow, Augusta grinned. "Like Clyde?"

Essie threw up her hands and grimaced. "Like the Hartshorn boy and Victor's traveling show." She patted Gus's cheek. "I was wrong to think you needed to be more like your cousins. You are perfect just the way you are."

Gus radiated. "Let's get ready. I can't wait to tell Clyde."

What have I done? Essie forced a smile and sighed. "Right—can't wait."

Chapter 16

Sunday, July 21, 1878

The train sped into town with its usual steamy clouds painting the sky with fluffy shapes. All the buildings near the tracks shuddered from its mighty force. Accustomed to the weekly disruption, at the first tremor, Postmistress Estelle Baumgardner shoved the pen into its stand.

She spread her arms atop the last sheet of expensive stationery from the mercantile and tugged back the errant blotter bouncing toward the desk's edge. The post office walls rattled, but the recent arrest of the three-member Hanson gang had relieved her of the *Wanted* flyers.

Essie still had difficulty believing the intricacy of the crimes associated with the people the entire town had embraced. Trent, his young lover Lula Mae, and brother Jesse were clever—she'd give them that. Part of a traveling troupe, they'd overheard Victor's tales of the West and followed his path, planning to implicate him in the crimes. Sheriff Hanson had found costumes in their trunks linking them to a host of criminal activity.

They used their theatrical costumes and training to swindle good citizens across the West, including ordering items from places they claimed to know, such as the hat from the Paris Millinery. While she had no recent postings to swivel sideways against their nails, the single-pane windows vibrated until she feared one might plop from its frame and land against the sidewalk.

Chuff—chuff—chuff—chufff...chuff—chuff—chuff—chuff...

Wait it out.

The Union Pacific's steamy plume magnified the sound of its whistle. Another misty breath belched from the smokestack. The engineer blared the horn, and the brakemen engaged the brakes until they screeched with enough shrillness to set her teeth on edge.

A movement caught her eye as the ink vial scooted across the table. "Oh, no, you won't." Essie released the blotter.

But it was Nancy Finncannon who grabbed the escaping container. She raised a brow. "This is like an earthquake. Good heavens. Does it shake like this every Sunday?"

Essie smiled. "Pretty much, but you'll become accustomed to it, I promise." She held her breath until everything except the dust motes settled into place.

July's afternoon sun streamed through the windows and across the half-finished letter. Satisfied the danger of smudging the important note had passed, she lifted the pen and dipped it into the inkwell of watered-down, postal-provided Prussian-blue ink, allowing the excess to drip back into the vial until the last drop plopped from the nib. "I'll only be a moment." Angling her wrist against the page, she wrote:

Dear Blanche,

I fear for those who've had no chance for the

adventure awaiting Augusta and me. I'll write to you from France, my dearest cousin. The Wylder West Show isn't the biggest in the world, but it might be someday. If you long for your daughters to experience the majesty of wonder, send them to me, for there is nothing quite like the unexpected.

All my love,

Your cousin, Essie

She sealed the envelope with a nice dollop of wax, and a plop of the seal smashed into it. Laying three cents on the counter, she turned to Nancy. "You'll see this makes the coach, right?"

Nancy expanded her chest. "Of course. You can depend on me to take extra care with the post office. We both know it's yours again whenever you return."

Victor stood behind Essie with the real ambassador. The wildly successful western show he'd managed to pull off with dramatizations of kidnapping, Native American attacks, and buffalo herding, in addition to the usual trick riding, roping, and rodeoing, impressed the actual Pierre Lacroix, who had arrived in town for the Independence Day showing. Victor shoved a rolled parchment into his hands. "This is the arena plan. It details how much space we'll need for reenacting battles and herding calves." He unfurled a section and pointed. "These are the dimensions, and if you look over here—"

Pierre, a much older and less hardnosed Frenchman, patted his shoulder. "Yes, of course. I will make all the arguments for your inclusion in the next exposition in Paris. If I have any questions, I will write immediately. Do not fret, *Monsieur* Douglas. You will have the opportunity you desire." He stuffed the plans into his travel bag.

Victor offered a hand for a sturdy shake. "That's all I ask—a chance."

Tossing back his head, the man laughed. "You are not like other men, Victor Douglas. I will invest in your show myself."

Essie grinned. She heard excitement in Victor's tone, and Gus was so thrilled she feared she'd float out of her boots. "You'll not be sorry. Buffalo Vic has many fans, and his latest version of the Wylder West Show is nothing short of miraculous."

Ambassador Lacroix nodded. "*Mais bien sur.* My country will adore his bravado. Until then, my carriage is waiting." He pivoted.

Scrambling behind the ambassador, Victor lifted the bags he'd left by the entrance. "Let me help you."

"*Merci.*" He gestured to the waiting surrey and tipped his hat.

Essie waved. "I look forward to our next meeting, Ambassador Lacroix."

The Frenchman tilted forward in a slight bow. He lifted Essie's hand to his lips and brushed the back with a soft kiss. "As do I, *Madame* Postmistress. *Au revoir.*"

A crowd gathered just outside the door. Finn Wylder rushed in and grabbed Essie by the shoulder. With a crooked knuckle, he pushed his hat off his forehead. "Are you really leaving us, Miss Essie?"

She winked and held a finger to her lips. "Not for good—just for a visit." She sucked in a breath and turned watery eyes toward him. "I'm a little nervous. I've always wanted to travel, but this is my first chance."

Finn squeezed her fingertips. "I'm happy for you

and Gus...I mean...Miss Augusta."

Essie kneaded her skirt. "Thank you, Finn."

After depositing the ambassador's bags into the waiting surrey, Victor stomped across the porch. He placed his arm around Essie's shoulder. "Are you ready? Clyde's already delivered our luggage to the loader."

Essie glanced around the office with its cottonwood counter and the divided cubbies. She released a sigh and grappled with the strangeness of feeling excitement for a dream realized and homesickness for a home surrendered. Gathering courage, she nodded. "I'm ready."

Nancy marched to the desk and stood with a hand on its chair. "Essie?"

Turning, Essie noticed Nancy's twitching eyelid. "Yes?"

She rattled her cane. "I...you..." Nancy looked down and then back. "Well...Godspeed."

Clyde raced through the back door of the post office. "Gus said to hurry."

Dropping his arm, Victor snapped toward him. "You left her alone by the tracks?"

He shrugged. "Gus? Sure...I mean..."

Essie took Victor's elbow. "We'd better hurry. The train's about to leave."

Victor grunted. "Get back down there and make sure all the animals and trunks are loaded."

Clyde scratched his head. "Don't worry. I'll take care of things."

Essie stepped through the doors, onto the porch, and into the street. Every step put distance between her old life and her new one. As she looked around, her pulse raced.

The townspeople, including the Wylders, marched behind them. "When you return, you'll come to dinner," George Hawkins yelled.

Anastasia West waved a kerchief.

Phineas Atwater ran to her side. "Thank you for sending the letter. She's coming."

Essie raked a glance over his freshly scrubbed face and a clean shirt. "Risks are scary, but their rewards are rather wonderful."

He yanked his hat from his head and leaned close. "They are indeed, and my sister's teaching me to read a little. I can even write my name."

Tears pecked Essie's lids. "That's wonderful."

Essie neared the platform. She spied Augusta waiting by the train and took a deep breath.

Finn Wylder stopped and snatched her fingertips. "I'll be getting back, now. I just wanted to see you take off on your journey."

"Thank you, Finn." With Victor on one side and Finn on the other, she felt trapped between two places in time.

Victor led her to the first step.

Essie placed her foot on the rung.

"Miss Essie, wait."

She swiveled.

Clyde jogged through the crowd and ran toward her with a note grasped in his hand. He waved it back and forth. "Miss Essie, Mrs. Finncannon said to give you this."

Finn Wylder released his grip and shook his head. "I still can't believe you recommended Nosey Nancy to run the post office during your absence."

Essie's heart dropped. *Something must have happened. Maybe she's had second thoughts. This journey might never take place.* She peeled open the note, hurriedly reading across the carefully written page. She blinked back tears and then stuffed the message into the bodice pocket. "Everybody deserves a second chance."

Clyde nodded. "Yes, ma'am—me, too."

Knowing how difficult it must have been for Nancy to admit her mistakes—especially in a note addressed to the postmistress—made Nancy's success during her absence more important. Essie grabbed Finn's arm. "And you? Can I count on you to help Nancy while I'm gone?"

He winced. "Me? How would I help?"

She stepped upward, making herself eye-level with Finn. "You've much influence in this town. Heck, it bears your name. If you throw your support behind Nancy, the rest of the townspeople will fall into line, and if she misbehaves or abuses her authority in any way, you know what to do."

The train belched a head of steam, and the whistle sounded.

Victor eased her up to the platform.

Clyde rushed forward and openly hugged Augusta from behind. "They just got the last of the animals loaded."

Augusta called over her shoulder. "Lightning, too?"

Laughing, Clyde tossed back his head. "Yes, of course. How could we do a show in France without Lightning?"

She widened her eyes. "We? You're coming?"

Clyde shuffled his foot. "Ma will be fine until we return, but you'd be lost without me—in the show, I mean."

Gus wagged a finger. "I better not catch you staring at them French girls like you did Francine."

Shrugging, Essie shook Finn's hand. "Tell everyone good-bye for me."

Finn winked. "Write to us. Give Nancy something to find worthy of tearing through the mailbag."

She laughed. "I'll do just that—on a postcard, no less—so that she can read about my adventure without having to break an oath."

Finn guffawed and lifted his hat. "Safe travels." He shook Victor's hand.

Essie's gaze slipped to the horizon.

Two figures on horses broke the prairie's flatness. One lifted a lance and held it high.

The other—braids whipping over her shoulder—pulled her horse to a stop. She raised a hand.

Tarak and Meadowlark—oh, how I'll miss you. Tears dampened Essie's cheek, and she swiped at them with one hand while waving with fingers intertwined as Meadowlark had done. She'd always wondered what it would feel like to embark on a journey, and now that she was standing on the precipice, emotion threatened to overcome her. *Perhaps traveling away from people I love isn't all I've made it out to be. But if all goes well, maybe Tarak and Meadowlark will come next time.*

Victor tipped his hat and extended his arm. "Are you ready, Essie?"

She peered into his caring face. Courage welled from a spring that had slowly formed over time. *But then again, what about the new people I've yet to meet and those I'm just beginning to know?* Goose bumps pebbled her flesh. Her legs shook, but she lifted her chin and nodded. "I am," she replied with confidence and stepped through the opening leading to the train's compartments and into her long-awaited adventure.

A word about the author...

Renee Canter Johnson is a graduate of Gardner Webb University and a fellow at Noepe Center for Literary Arts on Martha's Vineyard, Massachusetts. Her essays have appeared in *Bonjour Paris*, *Study Abroad*, and *Storyhouse*.

To Ride a Wylder Horse is Johnson's sixth novel with The Wild Rose Press and highlights a few of her favorite things: storytelling, romance, sunsets, and horses.

She lives on a farm in North Carolina with her husband, Tony Johnson, a beloved Rocky Mountain horse, Choco, and a very spoiled German shepherd named Hansel.

Connect with Renee Johnson at:
reneejohnsonwrites.com
twitter.com/@writingfeemail
facebook.com/renee.johnson..549436.
amazon.com/author/johnsonrenee
https://instagram.com/reneejohnsonwrites

~*~

Other Titles by This Author
A Scoop of Romance
Acquisition
Behind the Mask
Herald Angels
Reminiscing Over Rainbow Gelato
The Haunting of William Gray